Gentl[...] [...]d our friends ex[...] [...]range and yellow [...] [...]e then treated us to a luau, where we gorged ourselves alongside three hundred other guests.

I escaped after the feast, wandering the grounds of the enormous beachside resort, ducked into a shirt shop, then returned along the edge of the unlit beach to avoid the crowds.

The flashing lights of an emergency unit distracted me. A uniformed man and woman lingered over a crumpled body sprawled on the beach, covered partially under a mass of stringy seaweed. Two police officers held back a crowd of onlookers, but I maneuvered behind the officer holding a flashlight, aiming its bright beam toward a body.

I presumed a drowning victim had washed ashore, but no, a hand twitched in the frothy, wet sand. A dripping orange scarf wound around the suffering man's neck—an odd piece of clothing for Hawaii. The gray face struggled to speak. He choked, foamy saltwater dribbling from his mouth. The purplish lips mumbled, "He's here…matej…sugar." His chin crashed to his chest.

An older man standing next to me elbowed me in the ribs. "What did he say? Somebody's here?"

I shrugged. "Maybe. I couldn't hear over those drums. Poor guy." Drumbeats. The show had started. "Excuse me." My detective brain disengaged, and I hurried back to the luau.

Praise for *Peculiar Activities*, Detective Henry Ike Pierce, Book 1

The author has woven a fascinating plot with realistic, interesting characters. Henry Ike Pierce is a great protagonist. The dialogue and setting are very genuine, and I was drawn into the story from the opening and engaged throughout. I love a good suspense/thriller, and this fits the bill. I look forward to the next in the series.

~*~

Well-written with a complex plot and intriguing storyline make this a "must-read." The characters, especially Henry Ike Pierce, are well developed. Secondary characters play a significant role … some can be trusted, some cannot. Can't wait to see what happens next in this detective's life.

~*~

The book is nicely paced, and the characters complex enough to keep you reading. The varied settings of the storyline add interest to the plot. Mr. Jones has the potential of becoming a highly regarded writer. Looking forward to the next book in the series.

~*~

I like Ike! The author has created some main characters that are people I'd like to know or feel as if I already know. I'm looking forward to book 2.

~*~

I was transported to Eastern Europe by interesting characters and an engaging story. Looking forward to what I hope will be more enjoyment as I follow future murder mysteries solved by Ike!

Shadowed Souls

by

Mark Edward Jones

A Henry Ike Pierce Novel, Book 2

This is a work of fiction. Names, characters, places, and incidents are either the product of the author's imagination or are used fictitiously, and any resemblance to actual persons living or dead, business establishments, events, or locales, is entirely coincidental.

Shadowed Souls

Cover Art by *Tina Lynn Stout*

The Wild Rose Press, Inc.
PO Box 708
Adams Basin, NY 14410-0708
Visit us at www.thewildrosepress.com

Publishing History
First Edition, 2022
Trade Paperback ISBN 978-1-5092-4406-5
Digital ISBN 978-1-5092-4407-2

A Henry Ike Pierce Novel, Book 2
Published in the United States of America

Dedication

To my family and friends for your encouragement, advice, reading drafts, and being a part of my life.

Acknowledgments

Ally Robertson has been an indispensable editor, advice giver, and guidance offeror. I look forward to working together in the future.

Robyn Conley has taken on editing early versions of my drafts and is a great resource.

Maria Veres, Carolyn Leonard, Judith Rycroft, and Nicki Rycroft – former writing classmates and instructor. I am thankful we met and consider you all good friends. Nicki offered her time as the first beta reader/editor of *Peculiar Activities*, and I would not have moved forward without her input.

Each substance of a grief has twenty shadows.
William Shakespeare, *Richard II*

Chapter One

Dawn in Hawaii—paradise, they say. I had imagined sitting on the lanai in the evening and listening to waves lapping along the black volcanic beach, but it wasn't to be, despite the internet ad. The inn's first-floor restaurant and bar had hosted streetside partiers who lingered well past midnight, keeping me awake and brooding. Each restless night had become an unexpected adversary. Months had passed since I had killed two men, but the memories returned, flooding my dreams. The crack of a thick branch against a man's skull was a noise I couldn't forget, nor the chokehold on another man. I knew I had acted in self-defense, but those sounds … and the vacant expressions afterward. Guilt casts a long shadow.

But today wasn't a day for introspection. My boss and mentor, Eddie Stone, chose Hawaii for a destination wedding, his second marriage. Eddie had insisted he didn't have a girlfriend until his surprise engagement to Doris Chen, our coworker in the forensics lab. Chen had never married, and Eddie's wife had died many years ago.

We gathered around the couple, gentle waves serenading us while watching our friends exchange

1

vows in the early evening's orange and yellow skies above Kā'anapali Beach. Eddie then treated us to a luau, where we gorged ourselves alongside three hundred other guests.

I escaped after the feast, wandering the grounds of the enormous beachside resort, ducked into a shirt shop, then returned along the edge of the unlit beach to avoid the crowds. An emergency unit's flashing lights distracted me.

A uniformed man and woman lingered over a crumpled body sprawled on the beach, covered partially under a mass of stringy seaweed. Two police officers held back a crowd of onlookers, but I maneuvered behind the officer holding a flashlight, aiming its bright beam toward a body.

I presumed a drowning victim had washed ashore, but no, a hand twitched in the frothy, wet sand. A dripping orange scarf wound around the suffering man's neck—an odd piece of clothing for Hawaii. The gray face struggled to speak. He choked, foamy saltwater dribbling from his mouth. The purplish lips mumbled, "He's here … matej … sugar." His chin crashed to his chest.

An older man standing next to me elbowed me in the ribs. "What did he say? Somebody's here?"

I shrugged. "Maybe. I couldn't hear well over those drums. Poor guy." Drumbeats. The show started. "Excuse me." My detective brain disengaged, and I hurried back to the luau.

Blinded when I stepped off the beach into the bright lights of the luau grounds, I couldn't locate our table.

"Ike … get over here."

I blinked twice, seeing Eddie Stone standing near our white plastic table, waving his dark arms as if guiding a plane to its terminal.

Doris Chen and our boss, Angie Marconi, gazed at the ocean, watching another beautiful sunset hued with streaks of light, matching the orchid leis strung around their necks. A man sitting next to them had turned toward the stage.

"You okay, Ike? You walked right by us," Eddie said.

"Sorry, folks." I pulled out a flimsy chair and placed it on the spongy grass. An aroma of roasted pig still flowed around us, mixed with the sweet smell of white plumeria nestled in a vase on our table. "My Hawaiian shirt didn't fit. I exchanged it for this one."

"It took long enough," my grandmother said, "and your new shirt will be too tight after you wash it, honey."

Angela Marconi showed her typical smirk. "I couldn't imagine you'd skip the hula dancers, Henry. You missed dessert, too."

"The other four courses of food will get me by," I replied.

Eddie and Doris Chen leaned their heads together.

"Hey, Eddie, I came across a body on the beach with police officers and EMTs scrambling around. Do you think they need a couple of real detectives to help?"

"All yours, Ike. I'm out."

My mother shook her head. "Henry, Ike, Ike, Henry. Angie, you and Eddie confuse me. Why can't you call him the same thing? His dad's name was Henry … my son is Ike."

Marconi sipped on another Mai Tai—I had lost

count. "But, Susan, *Henry* is the name he put on his employment records, and I'm used to calling him that. Eddie doesn't like the name for whatever reason."

Eddie frowned. "My high school principal was a Henry. Bad memories, which is all I'm going to say."

"Either is fine," I said as I scanned the man sitting at our table with his back to us. A bald patch on the crown of his head looked like a pink island surrounded by mottled gray and black hair shorn close, something like a military cut. Could it be? "Commander Hrubý?"

He turned toward me and smiled, an unusual expression on his typically grim face.

"This is a surprise," I said, then stood to shake his hand. "When did you arrive?"

"Please call me Stepan since we are not on a mission, *Henry Ike* Pierce." He winked, then dropped into the flimsy seat. "Weather delayed my plane in New York. I apologize again, Lieutenant and Mrs. Stone."

We had met Stepan Hrubý in early spring. He served as chief over several sections of the Czech police organization in Prague, including two specialty units—the Section One criminal division and the fittingly named Unit for Peculiar Activities. Hrubý used these units to monitor government corruption interwoven with Miomir Kurić's criminal organization, an enterprise emerging after the 1990s Balkan wars.

Doris Chen tilted a glass of champagne toward Hrubý. "If we can call you Stepan, you should call us Doris and Eddie. You're so kind to have made the long trek to Maui."

"Don't sit there with your mouth open, Henry," Marconi said. "I told you several weeks ago I had called Stepan. He did everything possible to get away from Prague for a few days."

My grandmother winked at my boss. "He's quite a looker, Angie. Can't blame you for calling."

Hrubý blushed and stirred his Mai Tai with its little blue umbrella.

Marconi's hazel-blue eyes shimmered, not matching her mouth's slight frown. "Rita Faye, I told you Stepan is excited to be a part of this—his choice."

My grandmother giggled. "Sure, Angie."

My mother raised her plastic champagne glass full of her favorite Riesling wine. "Eddie and Doris, we're thankful to be here for the ceremony, even if I still have sand all over me. The beach is such a lovely place to get married. I caught a piece of a rainbow in one of my pictures."

"Wonderful," Chen said. "I hope everyone will email me your pictures when you get home. We're grateful you came."

"I'll take the sand any time," my grandmother said. "Thank goodness I had my little stash of money so we could make the trip."

"A *little* stash?" my mother asked. Her mouth hung open. "Ike has been giving us money. I had no idea—"

"Hey, Mom, can you pass me what's left of your *Haupia*?" I asked. "I'd like to try a bite."

"My what?"

"Your cake … the cake. I want a bite."

"Sure, finish it for me. I hope the show starts soon. I'm a little anxious since I booked the wrong place so far south. We have to drive back to Kihei in the dark around those mountains."

"Then I'll drive my car, and you follow me," I said. "You said you have a pineapple for me at your condo?"

"Two, actually."

A few drops of rain sprinkled our table. My mother held up a hand, feeling the sprinkles. "This might be a quick show."

Eddie grinned and glanced at me. "The shorter the better, huh, Doris?"

Chen's face reddened, and she gave a slight punch to his arm. "Settle down, husband. Remember, you're sixty, not sixteen."

Eddie feigned a pain. "Ow. You punched my bullet wound."

Chen flashed a weak glare. "Sure, I did. It's your other arm, remember? Now be quiet."

My mother leaned toward my grandmother. "Momma, the girl dancers are *wahines*, and the boys are *kānes*."

"Don't be smart, Susan. I know you bought a Hawaiian dictionary."

Forty-five minutes passed while the performers displayed their traditional dances in stunning native costumes. A male dancer twirling a fire stick mesmerized my grandmother. The last act featured female dancers coaching audience members to try the hula. One pulled on Eddie's arm, but he refused, even after our prodding.

The sun had set, and the sprinkles returned. My mother and grandmother stood and said their goodbyes, then my mother leaned near my ear. "No worries, Ike. We can find our way back. Call me tomorrow. Granny and I want to try the road to Hana or go up to see the sunrise on Haleakalā."

"Big day, then," I said. "Call me when you get to your condo."

"Oh? Who's the parent here?" She patted me on my cheeks, my grandmother rubbed my arm, and off they went, looking for the parking garage.

Eddie wiped a raindrop from his forehead. "Hey, everybody, Doris and I are cutting out, too. Our condo is a mile up the road. Angie, call me tomorrow afternoon, and we can meet up for dinner. Ike, I hope you like the fishing boat we found—the cheapest one in the bay. *Aloha.*"

Chen nodded. "Good evening." They strolled away, holding hands and paying no attention to the sprinkles.

Marconi reseated herself in the seat between Hrubý and me. "God, I'm happy for him. I can't think of anyone who deserves this more than Eddie." She dug through her purse, found her nicotine gum, and pushed a piece into her mouth.

I leaned over and whispered, "I can think of one other person."

"Slow down."

Hrubý tilted his head. "Why are you whispering? Are you talking business again?"

"No," Marconi answered. "We were talking about Eddie and how happy we are for him."

"Of course."

"So, uh, Stepan," I asked, a little uncomfortable using his first name. "The news of Mr. Žicǎn's death shocked us."

"Yes, yes … a stunning loss," he said while scratching the growth of his several-day-old beard. "They repaired Mr. Žicǎn's wound after our March mission … or so we believed." He glanced down for a moment. "Sepsis afterward, as we have mentioned." He sighed. "But we must move on. Mr. Žăk continues his usual efficient ways of pursuing the Kurić organization. Mr. Kharkov returned to Kerch when his father became ill, but he has rejoined us. Lieutenant Talích continues to be … irritatingly competent." He grinned.

"Any more information concerning Miomir Kurić, the missing Royal Dukats—"

"Stop." Marconi threw a hand in front of each of our faces. "Let's talk at breakfast tomorrow. I'm staying at the Hokele Inn in Lahaina, as is Stepan." Angie Marconi had dithered over her hotel plans before we left, never mentioning where she had chosen to stay.

My right eyebrow arched into my forehead, which she followed with an eye roll.

"In different rooms."

"It's where I'm staying, too. I can be your chaperone. My room overlooks the old courthouse and the banyan tree park," I said.

"I'm on the other side, away from the street," Marconi replied.

Activities at the pool distracted me, and her words faded while she chattered about her suite.

"Ready?" she asked.

I stood, then stopped, knocking over my chair— Marconi bumped into me.

"What's wrong?"

I leaned back and spoke out of the side of my mouth. "Don't look to your left. Follow me to the hibiscus hedge by the exit." We drifted into the shadows of the bushes, away from the bright lights shining on the emptying tables.

"Okay, what's up?" she asked while dropping her new black purse into the damp grass.

Hrubý's stern face had returned. "This seems very mysterious."

"The party at the pool." I nodded toward the oval-shaped hot tub, spilling into the swimming pool a few steps off the beach. Hip-hop music thumped from the speakers while five men in the hot tub flirted with a woman, her dark hair pulled back in a ponytail.

"She's popular," Marconi said.

"Yes, she attracts attention," I replied. "There may be other guests here we know."

The woman stood and grabbed a towel.

"What do you mean? The young woman? I can't see her face," Marconi said.

"I recognize the backside," I said, trying to hide a grin.

"Henry, I'm thinking something I don't want to think. Is that Nika Campbell?"

"Yep."

"Nika Campbell?" Hrubý pursed his lips and rubbed his chin. "Is she—"

"An acquaintance of Henry … among other things," Marconi said, rolling her eyes. "She almost got him killed."

I rubbed the top of my previously stitched head. "It was a dark and gloomy cave. Nika's an associate of Chasna Kovačić and his bunch."

"Kovačić. The dead Serb connected to Kurić?" Hrubý asked. "That is a name I remember."

"Yes, the dead Serb," I said. A spasm hit my gut while thinking of the crack of the tree branch I had delivered against Kovačić's head.

"So, why the hell is Campbell here?" Marconi asked.

I shrugged. "Who knows? A coincidence?"

Marconi spit her gum in a trash barrel. "Nothing is a coincidence with the little—"

"It's possible," I replied. "Nika had told me her mother vacations here. Maybe she's just hanging out?"

Marconi shot a glare at the small woman, drying off in a teasing motion in front of her admirers. "Yeah, she's hanging out of her top."

"Come on," I said. "Let's get out of here. For all we know, Nika's seen us."

"I don't care if she's seen us or not," Marconi said, "but I want no intrigue screwing up Eddie's honeymoon. I'll contact the authorities, and we'll stick her little ass in jail for abetting an assault on you."

Hrubý touched Marconi on the shoulder and nodded toward the garage. "Tomorrow, Angela. I flew or sat at airports for twenty hours, and my body thinks it is noon in Prague."

"Okay. Let's the three of us meet at seven o'clock for breakfast," Marconi said. "We'll see Eddie and Doris tomorrow evening and check on the lovebirds."

They walked ahead of me, soon disappearing into the darkness to the right fork of the trail leading to a distant parking lot. Heading left into the garage, I turned up the steps to the third floor but hesitated. Should I stroll around the grounds of the hotel to make sure? No ... I knew better. Contact with Nika always brought me trouble.

I found my rented red Honda, opened the door, and then slid into the leather seat—much nicer than my old Toyota at home. The car splashed water on a passerby at the exit, and I joined a rush of traffic on the highway southeast to Lahaina.

Memories of Nika from last winter cluttered a great evening. The mysterious woman from the U.S. State Department befriended me at a bar during my first week as a detective in Alexandria. A nosy nuisance, our two awkward dates proved her insatiable only in her need for information. Now she's here.

Chapter Two

Again, that sound. I rolled over in the cheap cotton sheets, watching the ceiling fan's blades stir a breeze and nudge thin curtains against the shuttered windows. The pull chain jiggled with each lazy rotation, clacking against the teardrop-shaped globe. Another restless night over, I thought of the beach and the suffering man with the orange cloth draped around his neck. Were his disjointed mutterings simply the words of a dying man?

I groped for my glasses, then focused on the too-bright digital clock sitting on the dresser, insisting it was 6:30 a.m.—my watch concurred. Wanting coffee more than sleep, I pushed up from the bed, pulled the light chain, and stood in front of mirrors hung on the closet doors. The reflection too short, I had to bend over to see my face, a little scary this morning. My dark hair had plastered itself flat against the left side of my head, and seven months of detective work had not been kind to my once semi-athletic body.

I pulled on my new yellow and green floral Hawaiian shorts and shuffled to the kitchenette to make coffee. The cluttered sink needed a cleaning, but thoughts again of Nika Campbell distracted me, remembering her fake, ditzy female routine when we first met in Alexandria. Later, she led two friends to attack me inside a cave's dripping darkness. The coffee maker beeped, stirring me from the memories, and I poured the steaming liquid into a gold, pineapple-shaped mug.

My second-floor suite's lanai offered an ideal view of the sunrise blossoming over Haleakalā. Yesterday's sun had shone hot over Lahaina, and the early morning air warned of another scorcher. I leaned over the lanai's rail, watching a young boy push a long broom along the gutter toward a drain.

This hotel appeared old-school Maui, with thirty rooms built around a courtyard of hibiscus bushes, flowering in sunburst patterns of yellow blooms. The building's gray clapboard siding and emerald-green trim had seen better days. Still, the room seemed comfortable enough, and I preferred this location's charm over the massive resorts lining the beaches on the northwest part of the island.

Muffled thumps and bumps drifted from the bay, where a small navy of fishing boats, catamarans, and an assortment of yachts bobbed and rolled in the dark water. I had always wanted to try deep-sea fishing, so yesterday before the wedding, I had booked the *Miss Mio*, a well-worn, white and red charter boat. A fishing day in Maui—what could be better?

****

"You get sick easy, Mr. Pierce?" Danny Keaka asked. The *Miss Mio's* gray-haired captain stood five-and-a-half feet tall, with crepey brown skin probably damaged from years in the sun while hosting tourists on his fishing boat. He had left me a voice mail, insisting we go early to claim his best spot, as he declared. I begged off breakfast with my colleagues and boarded the *Miss Mio* a few minutes earlier than planned.

"Call me Henry. No, I rarely get motion sickness,

but I haven't fished in the ocean before. I brought a patch."

"Wear it. Slap it on now before it gets rough … just in case."

We plowed through small waves, weaving around and between other boats still anchored in the bay. In the distance, a score of trawlers headed to sea for another day of fishing. To our right, the island of Moloka'i reflected purple and blue in the sunrise, its mountain tops hidden by small clouds scudding from left to right. The island of Lana'i huddled to our left, growing brighter as the sun rose, barren except for scattered scrub brush.

Keaka pressed the engine harder as we headed into the 'Au'au Channel.

I pointed toward the bow. "Hey, Danny, I didn't realize this part of Hawaii is so dry."

"Yep. People forget that the leeward sides are drier, especially with Haleakalā and the West Maui Mountains sucking up the rain. Lana'i has little elevation, and not much rain falls."

I bounced more in my seat as the waves grew higher, then noticed he had shoved an unlit cigarette into his mouth. He left it dangling from his bottom lip.

"You're a smoker?" I asked. "My dad, too. He died before he turned sixty."

"Don't preach, braddah. I'm a reformed smoker … I never light them." He pointed to his face. "Gives my mouth something to do." He grinned, showing a space where an upper incisor should have been—an excellent spot to tuck the filter of his cigarette. "See straight ahead?"

"Is that Kaho … how do you say it?"

"Ka-ho-o-la-vey. It's red dirt and a few feral goats and pigs. The government used to use it for target practice."

"We're headed there?"

"Close, but if we go too far, we'll earn a visit from the Coast Guard. They protect part of this area from fishing, but I know my spots. I have an 'in' with a few people … the right people."

"Got it, and I agree. Let's not bother the Coast Guard."

"Right." He bellowed a great exhalation as we popped over a higher wave, salty ocean spray coating the deck and both of us. "Take a deep breath, Braddah Henry. The sea, the warming sun. I've been doing this for twenty-eight years, and I've never regretted a day of it."

"I could imagine that. It's a lot different from riding in a police car or investigating dead people."

His smile disappeared. "You're a cop?"

"I'm a detective in Alexandria, Virginia. Why? You have a problem with cops?"

Quiet for a moment, Keaka gazed toward the shore. He turned, and his eyes locked on mine. "No, I used to be one … in Honolulu. I got my criminal justice degree at UCLA in 1982, then I moved back home. Two weeks after graduation, I got a job offer over on O'ahu. The first four years were uneventful, then they transferred five of us to drug interdiction at the port. Man, things got too *lolo*, crazy for me. One of our guys got killed … he had three kids."

Bouncing through the waves, Keaka again grew silent. Kaho´olawe loomed closer, and the engines slowed. He pulled off his smudged white baseball cap and wiped his brow. "I couldn't keep doing that job. I returned to Maui in 1990, and I left only once for a bypass operation last year in Honolulu. Oh, new friend, it's a crowded place these days. Anyway, I took tourists out on whale-watching boats a few times a year, did security at the airport in Kahului, then said to hell with it. I bought my boat and started fishing, bringing along anybody paying me to fish with them." He smiled and killed the engines. "I'll drop anchor. We're right above a small mass of rocks forty feet down—the fish are teeming there. Be right back."

"Can I help?" I followed him to the side as he dropped anchor into the dark-blue water. "Hey, what kind of anchor is that?"

"You noticed, yeah?" His upper arms' loose tan skin tightened as he let the chain drop. He went around me again and opened a lid, serving double duty as a passenger bench seat.

"What's in there?"

"For you, braddah. Join me in my good luck breakfast beer, but you have to down it all, or we won't catch any fish." He handed me a cold Primo and finished it before I drank a third of mine. "Come on now … you're young. You can keep up."

I tried to catch my breath. "Give me a minute. Your anchor is unusual. What is it?"

"Right. It came from the bumper of a dead guy's Mercedes. The asshole driving was the one who killed my partner … then he floored it and came right for me. I took care of him. Shot him right above his left eye. It's the only time I ever killed someone—actually, the only time I ever had to point my gun. A buddy of mine owned the junkyard, and I paid him to pull the bumper and crunch it up into a block. After moving back to Maui, a friend over in Kahului dipped it in molten lead a few times until it got nice and heavy." He grabbed a red fiberglass fishing rod leaning against the boat's rail and handed it to me. "And what about you?"

"What about me?"

"You ever have to kill someone?" He snatched the end of my fishing pole, pulled me to the back, opened a white bucket, and slapped a piece of dead squid into my left hand. "For the kamanu. You catch 'em, I clean 'em."

"Sounds like a deal." I shoved the hook through the stinking squid's mantle, and Keaka watched as I pitched the weighted line over the boat's edge.

"Count to five and stop it. It won't take long with the weight on your line."

I counted. "Okay, I'm there."

"Good deal. Stick the pole in the bracket on the side, and you don't have to hold it." Back to the open lid of the passenger seat, he grabbed two more Primos. "Have another."

"It's not even seven thirty," I said, my comment bringing a grin to his face. "God, this bait stinks." I wiped my hand on a dirty-blue hand towel draped across the steering wheel.

"I'm waiting, braddah. Your turn." He slipped under the canopy, finding shade from the morning sun, and slid his butt into his captain's seat.

I glanced at a black petrel circling overhead, a wave of anxiety washing over me. My voice cracked. "I killed two people."

"On the job, yeah?" He gave me a pretend kick to my shin.

"Yeah. Count one as revenge, and another as an accident … three months ago."

"Revenge? Revenge stories are the best." He tossed his second empty can onto the slippery deck.

"It's weird."

"So? I'm weird. I like weird."

A tug on my line, then nothing. "Was that a bite?"

"Nah, they're teasing you. You'll know it when they take it."

"Anyway, a complex case, but a guy attacked me in a cave in Virginia. He and his friends left me for dead, and it took me weeks to recover. Later, working on a related case in Vienna, I booked an overnight bus trip to Prague, and the same guy who attacked me showed up as the bus driver. Gun for hire, I guess, but not coincidental, as I found out later. We stopped for a bathroom break, and he confronted me on a path. I used a branch for a club and then abandoned him like he had left me in the cave … leaning against a pile of rocks. Unfortunately for him, it grew much colder outside, and he froze to death before morning."

"Okay, now I'm confused. You're a detective from Virginia who killed a guy in Europe?"

"Two … I killed two men. Here's the condensed version. Five ethnic murders happened in Alexandria in the nineties. A Serb patriarch in the community printed counterfeit euros and sent them to Prague. The local bartender was a Croatian killer who worked in a protection force for an international organization, hoarding fake euros and stealing old Yugoslav gold coins. A Bosnian bakery owner posed as an Austrian government agent in Vienna. And a guy jumped from a TV tower in Prague after I tried to talk him down."

Keaka recrossed his legs and locked his hands around a knee. "Look, braddah, no need to be shitting me. I'm an honest guy, which is what I expect from you."

"I know how it sounds, Danny, but it's the truth. A man shot my assistant director, the lieutenant in the department, while we were there. Eddie's the guy who came with me yesterday when we rented the boat. It served as his wake-up call, so he proposed to his girlfriend. It's why we're here. They married yesterday, late afternoon, near Kā'anapali. Last night, we went to a luau, and I escaped from friends and family this morning."

He rubbed his temples. "Yeah, Eddie's a nice guy. I'll have to think over the rest. And the second man?"

"The other man who died was old but dangerous. I restrained him, and he had a heart attack, I guess."

"Accidents happen. By the way, your pole looks like an upside-down U. One of them took it."

"What? Oh, crap." I pulled the pole from the support and started reeling in the line, my left foot flat against the side of the boat for more leverage.

He stood and grinned. "Five fathoms to go. *Wikiwiki* … faster." A fish broke the surface and again submerged. "Holy smokes, new friend, you got a big damn fish."

It took all my strength to finish. Keaka disappeared behind me, then jabbed a net into the water to my left. "Pull, braddah. We don't want this to be only a fish tale."

Keaka's lean muscles did their best while he fought to haul in the net. I dropped my fishing line and grabbed onto the end of the pole to help. "Come on, braddah. One, two, three, pull!" The net burst over the side, dumping a massive silver-bellied fish with dark-blue streaks running down its spine, highlighted by yellow stripes on its sides. "Got him." He opened the bench toward the front of the boat, revealing a water storage area two feet deep. We watched the fish thrash in the water until it settled.

"A kamanu?" I asked while wiping my brow with the dirty towel.

"Yep, several varieties, but this one is the largest—two-and-a-half feet and close to thirty pounds, I'd say."

"The biggest thing I've caught is an eight-pound crappie in a Virginia reservoir."

"I told you the Primo is magic juice, braddah." He kissed two fingers twice, then pointed to the sky. "So … time for another."

Between us, four more Primos brought two more kamanu and an odd-looking sea bass Keaka threw back. "Too bony," he said.

My head spun from the rougher sea and all the beer. "Can we pull anchor? We're bobbing more, and it's doing a number on me."

"Don't you want the initiation of throwing up over the side? I think the fish expect it."

"Not today."

"I know another spot toward Kihei, or we can head in, yeah?" He grabbed the manual winch and reeled the anchor. In a moment, we were on our way.

The sea breeze flowed over my face, and I huddled in the shade under the canopy, trying to cool off.

"Your color looks better, expert fisherman. After I clean those, you'll have about twenty-five pounds of fish filets to eat. Got any place to store it?"

"No, or to cook it. You take it, Danny."

"Tell you what, the restaurant on the first floor of the Hokele Inn?"

"I've walked by it."

"They take my catch. We'll put the cooler in the freezer, and I'll clean them later. Bring your friends, and all of you can eat a meal you caught. How would you like that?"

"It couldn't be any better."

He ran a hand through his wind-blown, mostly gray hair. "I believe you, man."

"Believe what?"

"Your Europe story. My partners and I got involved in weird stuff in Honolulu over three decades ago. I think we found more intrigue than drugs."

"Oh?" My head throbbed, and I leaned back against the stained canvas canopy.

He nodded, then flipped the unlit cigarette onto the deck. "Twice, we busted open this big-ass drug case. The second time we found over a ton of cocaine hidden in a container unit … I mean, literally boxcar size. We had those guys cold as ice. A week later, someone bailed them, and the evidence disappeared … not only the cocaine but the whole damn boxcar." He pursed his lips and stared toward the docks a mile away, his smile long gone. "You want to fish anymore?"

"Nah, I'm good. This has been the greatest, something I always wanted to do."

Keaka showed half a grin. "Funny, I hear the same every trip." He slowed the engine to a putter.

I spotted tiny figures of people milling on the boardwalk next to the dock, then pulled up my seat to find one lonely beer floating in the icy water. "Why did you name your boat the *Miss Mio*?" I handed him the can, and he popped the top.

He cast me a sheepish smile. "The name of an old girlfriend—younger than me, hot as the sun, and a foreigner ... Slovenian, she told me. She started school in Honolulu but quit, then followed me here to Maui. I thought she had to be the one, but nope. She hooked up with another guy, and they traveled everywhere before she went back to Europe for good. I tried to contact her several times but never got a response. She just vanished. I think they call it ghosting now, yeah?"

"Something like that. Slovenian ... interesting." My phone vibrated, and I had to pull it from my left shorts pocket with my stinking, fishy hands. "Hey, boss. I'm coming back from my fishing trip."

"Tell me later," Marconi said. "Stepan and I are here at the Hokele bar with Eddie."

"All right. Save a spot for me, but I need to wash up."

"Be quick. Henry ... Doris left. Eddie drove her to the airport this morning."

Chapter Three

Keaka and I each grabbed a cooler filled with iced-down fish, then plodded across the street from the dock to the hotel. He nodded and smiled at the boy sweeping the sidewalk, who opened the restaurant's service entrance, facing the park with the enormous banyan tree. "Sup, Kana?"

The boy dropped his broom, skipped to us, then grabbed Keaka around the waist. "Uncle D, take me fishing again."

"You threw up last time."

"Come on, Uncle D."

"All right, all right. Let's try next week."

"Yea. Thanks." The boy gave me a sideways glance, then thumbed toward me. "Who's the *haole*?"

Keaka frowned. "See now, Kana. Don't be a little *Okole*. This is my new friend. Open the door for us."

The boy pouted his way to the door, grabbed the handle, and pulled it open. "I'll be ready Saturday."

"Tell your momma to give you a motion patch. I'm not cleaning your mess again."

Turning sideways with the cooler, I eased through the entrance into the kitchen. I winked at him. "*Mahalo*, Kana."

Keaka grinned and nodded. "My brother's son. We're almost there, braddah."

We eased past the cooks cleaning up from

breakfast and another boy mopping the floors. The smell of bacon, fruit, and fish floated around us.

"It's back here."

We rested the coolers next to a thick-slatted wooden door, looking like it belonged on an old sailing ship. Keaka slid the shiny chrome handle straight up, then pulled the door out to give us access to the freezer. "Shove it to the back. I'll tell Iulio you and your friends are having dinner here tonight." Frigid air swept my face as I shoved the cooler past the racks of pork and beef into the far-right corner. The door thumped—freezing darkness enveloped me.

"Danny?" I felt my way along the shelves and found the door handle upright. Fighting panic, I kicked the door open to find Keaka bent over, washing his hands. "What the hell?"

He grabbed a dishtowel and scowled. "What the hell, what?"

"You closed the door on me."

"Huh? Relax, man. The thing won't stay open. We rigged it, so we won't have any accidental thawing."

"Oh. Well … I've got six more days here. Can we fish again?"

"You're hooked, yeah? Hit me up a day ahead of time, and we'll plan it. Now wash over here in the cooks' sinks and go find your friends. Sounds like a little trouble in paradise?"

"I hope not. See ya."

"*Aloha.*" He slapped me on the back and hurried out the service door. A cook pulled off his apron and pointed at a sink. Almost as round as tall, I guessed him near Keaka's age.

"Right over there, Danny's friend. Use the soap up

and down your arms." He smiled. "It smells like you've been to a fishery *and* a brewery, but Danny always smells that way."

"Thanks."

"What time you eating dinner? And I'm Malo." He offered his hand until he noticed the unrinsed soap covering my arms.

"Good to meet you. I'm Henry Pierce, and I'll ask my friends about dinner." I scrubbed my arms, filling the sink with bubbles.

"You tell them six o'clock. It's less busy. What did you catch?"

"It's all kamanu."

"Hmm—not my favorite, but I will make it yours." He grinned again, his enormous smile showing a missing tooth in the same spot as Keaka. He leaned toward me as if to tell me a secret. "I'm a better cook than Iulio, but Danny likes him better."

"Oh?"

"For today, anyway. I pissed Danny off playing poker. I won all his money."

"You do it much?"

"Play poker? Yessir. Twice a week at his place. Our mother comes over and cooks us dinner, then we play cards. She's usually the one who wins." He winked.

"Your mother? You mean you and Danny are brothers?"

"Yep. I'm a Keaka. Iulio's our youngest brother."

"Is Danny his proper name?" I asked.

"Nah, he liked the Danno guy on *Hawaii Five-O*. His actual name is Dado."

"Danny fits him."

"Yeah, my mother is the only one who calls him Dado. The three of us bought the restaurant fifteen years ago and the hotel shortly after. Our cousins manage the hotel part. Danny is the majority owner, but mainly he's our chief fisherman." His smile vanished. "And he has another job sometimes."

"Oh? He never mentioned it while we fished."

"Nah, he's a little sensitive about the Honolulu stuff. He bought this place with the settlement money from the feds," he said.

"Settlement?"

"Wrongful dismissal from Honolulu P.D. many years ago. The feds put all kinds of pressure on the police to push Danny out. Crooked judge, Danny said. They hung up his lawsuit in court for thirteen years."

"I'd like to hear more, Malo, but I need to get out to my friends. At six o'clock tonight, I'll make sure we're all here."

"Sounds good, man. Let me know when you get seated tonight. Tell the server your friend Malo said to give you the best seats."

"I will."

****

Eddie Stone, Stepan Hrubý, and Angie Marconi perched high on bamboo bar stools near the far-right end of the mahogany bar, a semicircle surrounding the bartender, with scores of liquor and beer bottles on display behind him. Sitting with their backs to the banyan park, they gazed at the goings-on in the bay. Each had a large glass of red liquid with a celery stick—a Bloody Mary, I presumed. Eddie sat in the middle, his head down toward his lap. Marconi had swung to the left, her knees touching Eddie's hip while she rubbed his shoulder. Hrubý fanned himself with a blue ball cap. They hadn't noticed me.

"Good morning. Eddie, you making it?"

"Oh, hey, Ike," he mumbled, then yanked the celery stick out of the glass, giving it a crunchy bite.

"What's going on?"

He blew out his cheeks. "Doris went home."

"Went home?"

Marconi rotated toward me, her back to the bar. "Not Alexandria. Taiwan."

Eddie glanced up and wiped his brow. "Her mother died, Ike. She found out in the middle of the night. It happened over a week ago. She and her brother aren't on the best terms, and he didn't call her … a cousin did. She only had forty-eight hours to get to Taipei for the family gathering. It's like a graveside service, I guess. Doris's mother was ten when they fled the Chinese mainland. Funny, though. Doris had never said much about her mother. There … that's the story."

"Will she be back in time for—"

"Nope. Her trip is open-ended until she knows what's going on with the estate. She'll book a flight to Alexandria later."

I placed both hands on his shoulders. "I'm sorry, Eddie. It must be disappointing."

He raised his right hand and gave me a pat on the face. "Thank you, buddy. We'll be fine. I feel for Doris, though. I guess her brother would have buried their mother without ever calling."

"We hate it for you," Marconi said. "I'll give Linda Alvarez a call later. She can take over the lab for now." Her straw made a slurping sound at the bottom of the glass. "Wow, who drank my Bloody Mary?"

The bartender gave me a wink. "Mr. Pierce, your and your friends' drinks are on the house. Mr. Keaka said so." My three colleagues glanced at the bartender, then at me.

"What did you expect?" I pretended to preen in front of the mirror hanging in the center of the bar.

The bartender held his hand up for a high five and snorted.

"Henry Pierce," I said.

"You can't pronounce my name, so call me Stoney. Everyone else does."

"What the hell?" Marconi asked. "And what's that smell?"

Hrubý stopped fanning himself and used his cap to stir the air surrounding me. "Detective Sergeant Pierce, you remind me of my time in the Czech army—days and days with no hygiene."

"Yeah, it's me—beer, sweat, and fish. Sorry, but you'll thank me later. We had great luck fishing this morning. The owner of the boat will clean my catch for our meal tonight. Be here at six o'clock sharp, though. Malo said so."

"Malo?" Marconi asked.

"One of the cooks—a brother of the owner," I said.

The bartender winked. "And they are my cousins."

"Nice," Eddie said. His mood seemed to brighten. "Ike, I want to do it. I've always wanted to fish in the ocean since I was a kid. I've got free time now. Hey, what about you two?"

"I'm not a water person," Hrubý said. "Prague is a nice, landlocked city. I enjoy the beauty of this bay but feel better with my feet on the ground."

"I'm out, Eddie," Marconi said. "Stepan and I are

driving to the ʻĪao Valley this afternoon. You should come with us. The pictures I've seen are gorgeous."

"Nah, thanks for the offer, though. You two enjoy it. I think I'll hang with Ike if he's up to it."

"It'll be great," I said, realizing my alone time appeared to be finished. "Eddie and I will find trouble."

Marconi exaggerated an eye roll. "God, watch out, Maui. But remember, Lieutenant Stone, you're not a bachelor anymore."

"Should we warn law enforcement?" Hrubý asked, giving us a harsh glare.

"We'll be good." Eddie shoved his empty glass toward the bartender. "Ike, get yourself washed, and let's find the red-and-white fishing boat. I want to make reservations as soon as possible."

"Okay, give me twenty minutes." I nodded toward Hrubý. "And I'll see you two later. Six o'clock. Right here for dinner."

****

"Nice guy." Eddie slid his phone into his left pocket after taking pictures of the banyan tree. "Danny Keaka. Cool name too. Ke—ak—aaaa. I always liked that name."

"You know the name?"

Eddie took a deep breath and closed his eyes. "This is great, huh?"

"You appear to have snapped out of your funk."

"I'm okay, man, but I miss Doris."

I leaned against a banyan tree tendril that had grown into a supporting root several feet away from the main trunk. "Wait'll you hear Danny's story. He said he used to be a Honolulu cop. I'll bet he has as many stories as you."

"Right. You know, I had several explosive training trips in Las Vegas after I started as a cop in Jacksonville … forty years ago … can't be." He looked away and smiled. "Anyway, I can't wait for tomorrow morning. Oh, man, take a whiff, Ike. Those same white flowers are right outside our door at the hotel."

"I have a great idea, Eddie."

"What?"

"Check out of your hotel this afternoon. Tell them Doris's story, and I bet they'll let you out of your reservation. I've got the fold-out couch in the living area, and there are two bathrooms. It's a cool atmosphere. Old school and *vibrant* at night. A lanai is a great place for coffee and donuts in the morning."

"Donuts?" He nearly shouted.

"Yep. A block up Front Street on the right. I got a half dozen yesterday morning. Danny's boat left early, so I didn't get any today."

"I'm in. Want to go with me to the hotel?" he asked.

"No, I'll straighten up and have the room ready to go, then take a nap."

"Okay, sleeping beauty. I'll check out Lahaina when I get back. I'll buzz you about four o'clock, get settled in, and head to dinner."

****

Eddie propped his feet high on the lanai's rail, a palm frond licking the soles of his sandals. He had turned on his Motown music list, listening to *Distant Lover* by Marvin Gaye. He shut his eyes and burped. "Excuse me." He had found a twelve-pack of a local craft beer while touring old town Lahaina and shoved it into the refrigerator after unpacking his things. "Hey,

Ike, you let me know if they charge you for a second person in this room."

"No worries. I'll let you know, but our new friends have been a good bunch." I had already dressed for supper and noticed a line of sand, trailing from the entrance onto the kitchen floor.

"What are you doing in there, Ike? Come out here with me and have a beer. Watching those boats float around and listening to the ocean will put me to sleep. Hey, see if you can find a local Motown station. My phone's about out of juice."

"I'm playing maid and cleaning the kitchen because somebody brought in sand, but I'll be right there." I did my best, placed the whisk broom into its spot in the side pantry, grabbed a beer, headed outside, and scooted the bar-high chair up to the round cocktail table on the lanai. "The radio doesn't work except for the clock. So, what do you think, Eddie? I've never been an ocean guy, but I could get lost here on purpose. I'm not sure what I would do, but it might be nice to find out."

"Me, too. I snuck down to the beach a lot when I was growing up. I liked to watch the waves, but I didn't need the tan." He shoved his dark arm in my face.

"Relaxing, huh?"

"Yep. I wonder if Doris would move. Taiwan is a lot closer to here than Virginia."

"It would be an easier trip, but is there anybody left there she cares to see?" I asked. "You said most of her family has died except a brother."

"True, but she said she has several nieces, nephews, and cousins. Anyway … there's something I wanted to mention to you without Angie around." He crushed an empty beer can and dropped it on the lanai's concrete deck.

"Oh? Is this work stuff?"

"Afraid so. Look, I don't want to spook you, but …"

"But?"

His jaws clenched, and he gave me a side glance. "I think I spotted your Nika woman today when I checked out of my room." He watched me for a reaction as I tilted my can of beer. "But maybe I'm wrong. Angie showed me her picture after they attacked you in the caverns. Maybe someone else?"

I wiped beer foam from my lips. "It's possible, Eddie. I'm sure she was by the pool last night at the luau. Angie saw her, too, but I left it to her to decide what to do. She didn't want to disturb your honeymoon by flying off to Honolulu."

"It's a moot point now, huh?"

"Guess so. Should we pursue it?" I asked.

"Hell, yes. I want Ms. Campbell in jail for assisting in a murder attempt. Yours!"

"We can talk to Angie tonight."

"Something else too, Ike. You know, many people don't think I'm the smartest cop in the business."

"Who? I never—"

"It's fine. I don't care what they say. But this isn't an accident."

"Huh?"

"When we got back from Prague … and I introduced Doris as my fiancé?"

"Right, the guy who said he didn't have a girlfriend." I got up from my chair, grabbed our empty cans, and headed to the kitchen.

"Ha-ha, yep, that guy," he yelled.

I returned with two more beers. "Sorry, this will finish half your twelve pack."

He responded by staring at the can for a moment. "I need to tell you something, Ike."

"Go ahead."

"I haven't been upfront with everyone."

"You? Eddie, you don't have a dishonest molecule in your body."

"No, I'm not dishonest." He nodded and gave me another sideways glance. "Look, it's thrilled Doris to come to Hawaii for the wedding and honeymoon, and I always wanted to visit. But back in March, your Czech friends discussed Nika Campbell the evening before your mission with those guys. They said she drops out of sight ... maybe to Hawaii sometimes. And after the attack on you, she disappeared again."

"She told me once she comes here with her mother."

"That's what I mean. I heard you mention it ... and I put it all together and decided Maui might allow you and Angie to do a little research on Ms. Campbell and her mother while we were here for my wedding." He stared at me like a child in trouble.

"What a sly fox you are, Lieutenant Stone," I said, then held my beer up for a fake toast. "It offers the opportunity, doesn't it?"

He didn't return the toast. "With Doris gone, I hoped I could help, too, and then damn if I didn't see Ms. Campbell in the lobby of my hotel. You know, there's not much research to do if it's really her. And you never can tell what the local authorities already know."

"Maybe it's our minds playing tricks, Eddie."

"It seems too easy, doesn't it? Anyway, I got that off my chest."

"I won't say a thing," I said, now wishing I had left this beer in the refrigerator. I wiped the moisture off the can and rubbed my face. "Man, I need something to eat. I've had five beers today."

"Okay. Let's put these cans back and get downstairs for dinner. We'll mention Nika Campbell and ask Angie what she wants to do. Hrubý might show interest, too, seeing how we think Campbell is a component of the Kurić organization."

I slid the lanai door shut and locked it. "Is this more of your hokey-pokey?" We shoved the unfinished beer in the refrigerator and headed downstairs.

"Yep, more damn hokey-pokey. For now, let's go eat your fish."

****

The four of us sat next to the side street, where traffic ran lighter than on the avenue running parallel to the dock. Tourists strode past us, many sniffing the air and stopping to consider the menu placed at the dining area's entrance. Malo's skill as a cook wasn't only a bragging point. He had deboned the fish, lightly breaded it, then grilled it. They served a nice Caesar salad with pineapple chunks, along with broccoli and garlic potatoes. Malo came from the kitchen to introduce himself. He delivered macadamia nut ice cream topped with chocolate sauce—all washed down with the restaurant's own guava wine.

"Oh my." Eddie rubbed his protruding belly and shut his eyes. "The best."

"I can't argue." Marconi shoved her empty ice

cream dish aside and swished the wine in her glass. "Stepan? You've been awfully quiet."

Hrubý moaned and wiped his mouth with his maroon cloth napkin. "I cannot think of the correct English word for the goodness of everything I have eaten. This has been better than any food I ate on my last trip to Paris."

Malo appeared again, an elderly woman following along beside the other man from the kitchen that morning. They stopped next to our table.

"Malo, you're in time to hear all the good things about your cooking," I said.

"*Mahalo*, Henry Pierce and friends. Henry caught the fish in today's catch. This is my little brother, Iulio, and he is the best cook, no matter what I said earlier."

Marconi nodded to Iulio. "Good to meet you. I'm Angie, and this is Stepan on my right and Eddie to my left."

"I'm glad all of you are here, and I would like you to meet my favorite person in the world, my mother, Kehaulani Keaka."

She smiled and bowed her head.

"Kehaulani means 'dew from the sky,' " Iulio said.

"Welcome to our restaurant," Kehaulani said. "My sons and nephews have made this corner of Lahaina a favorite of tourists and many locals."

"It's perfect," Marconi said. "I'm sure you're proud of your sons and the rest of the family."

"*Mahalo*, and yes, very proud. They have done well, considering their father left us shortly after Iulio joined our family."

Iulio placed his right arm around her shoulders. "Let's not go there." He motioned her toward the entrance. "Good evening, everyone. I hope to see you tomorrow."

"Good evening," we all said.

"Thanks for the fish, Ike," Eddie said. "We'll have more tomorrow after our fishing trip."

"You sound confident," Marconi said.

"Neither one of you looks too sunburned after today," I mentioned. Angie Marconi had told me her fair skin stayed sunburned most every summer.

"No problem for either of us today." She dug in her purse, then pulled out another piece of nicotine gum. "The clouds thickened down in the valley, and we got a heavy mist most of the day. Thankfully, the Jeep helped on those wet roads. It's much different on that part of the island."

"A beautiful part of the island." Hrubý shut his eyes. "I would miss Prague, but not for long if I lived here. So, Henry Pierce, how have your mother and grandmother gotten along today?" His eyes opened wider and showed the piercing blue stare I had grown used to in Prague.

My face flushed with an immediate pang of guilt. "I don't know." I glanced at my watch. "Last time I tried calling was three o'clock … it's seven thirty already. Let me call again." I excused myself and walked across the street to the banyan park, a din of bird noises drifting around me as I tried my mother's number. She answered on the first ring. "Mom? What's going on? You two have a big day? I hadn't heard from you."

"It's fine. We wore ourselves out. We changed our minds and went to Hana instead of the volcano after waking up too late for the sunrise. It took us over ten hours there and back ... and the road, my goodness. Granny is asleep already, and I'm exhausted. Did you have a good day?"

"It's been great. I caught several fish today, and the boat's captain also owns the restaurant on the ground floor of my hotel. They prepared my catch for us. Eddie and I are going out again tomorrow. Oh ... Doris's mom passed. She got on a plane in the middle of the night for Taiwan."

"How unfortunate."

"Mom?"

"Hang on, honey." More background noises. A squeaky hinge creaked, and a screen door slammed. A voice in the distance, my mother responded, then silence.

"Mom?"

"Sorry. I'm out on the sidewalk next to our condo. Our neighbors walked by."

"Okay, tell me what's up."

"Ike, I said nothing to Granny today, but I got the feeling someone followed us."

"What?"

"Oh, it's probably my anxiety, but I felt ... something on the way back. We stopped at a fruit stand for mangoes. I wanted a fresh one—they were delicious, Ike. I should have saved you one. Your granny—"

"Mom."

"Oh, yes. While we waited, a big SUV slowed down ... black with darkened windows. It stopped in the road for a few seconds until a car behind it honked. I thought I had seen it earlier driving to Hana when we stopped at a huge botanical garden. It's lovely in case you want to go."

"Did you catch the license plate?" I didn't like the sound of this. Black SUVs seemed to be the standard vehicle used by the perps in our last investigation.

"Yes."

"Well?"

"I'm not …" Her voice shook. "I don't remember, but it had to be a government car."

"Government tags?" This threw me. Our bad guys in Alexandria had private tags, a few from Virginia and more from the district.

"Yes. White background, blue lettering, and a seal on the left at the top said, 'U.S. Government,' and the bottom said, 'For Official Use Only.'"

"No doubt, then," I said. "But the government owns a lot of property on the islands, and many vehicles will have those kinds of tags. Anything else?"

Silence again.

A horn honked to my right. A bicyclist gave a middle finger to a dark-blue Ford, forcing its way into a tight parallel space on the street, a few feet away from where we had been sitting for dinner. Marconi and Hrubý had vanished. Eddie stood in the distance, leaning over a wooden rail and watching the waves lap against a beach of black volcanic rocks.

"And another time. Our condo is across the road from the beach and next to a few stores. Another government vehicle parked in the lot of a shopping strip."

Two men in khaki shorts and Hawaiian shirts had gotten out of the Ford and strolled toward the red souvenir kiosk behind me. "I'll grab Eddie, and we'll come down—"

"Detective Sergeant Henry Pierce?" a voice asked from behind. I turned to find the two men from the blue car standing close.

"Hey, Mom, I need to hang up. I'll call you back." Staring at the man's extended right arm, his hand held a *U.S. Marshal* badge. "I'm Henry Pierce. What can I do for you?"

"I'm Marshal James Allerton, and this is Marshal Dayap Olan. We need to talk, Detective Pierce." His partner stood two inches taller than me and stepped closer.

"You know I'm a detective? Again, what is this about?" To my right, Eddie had seen us and hurried toward the park.

"The U.S. Marshal's office here on Maui would like to talk to you. Our office is in Kahului, near the airport. We would appreciate your cooperation."

"And I'll ask again … concerning what?"

The man called Olan nodded toward his car. "Let's make this easy."

"For whom?" I asked.

Eddie stopped at the curb. "Ike?"

"This doesn't concern you, Lieutenant Stone … at least not yet," Olan said.

"If it concerns Ike Pierce, then it concerns me." Eddie stepped closer, his jaws clenched.

I glanced at the two men. "I'll fill you in later, Eddie. We're supposedly going to the U.S. Marshals office in Kahului. Do me a favor, though." The three of us walked to their car, trailed by Eddie. "Go to the Charley Young Beach condos in Kihei. My folks are in Room 357. Take a change of clothes and stay tonight. My mother thinks someone followed them today."

I slid into the back seat.

"Followed?" Eddie asked while rubbing his neck. "I'll go check—"

Marshal Olan slammed the door.

Chapter Four

The thirty-minute ride had been quiet—neither of the two marshals had turned toward me from the front seat. I tried twice to get them to tell me more, but they offered nothing, assuring me further discussions would come. I wasn't suspicious of them during our brief trip until we slowed near a road leading to the edge of the West Maui Mountains. Marshal Allerton pointed and mumbled something about a new golf course, bringing a corresponding grunt from Marshal Olan. We didn't linger, then sped along the busy four-lane highway into Kahului. This didn't feel like a kidnapping, but it certainly seemed an odd bit of intrigue.

The road changed into a boulevard, and we at once turned right into a parking lot, passing a granite sign with the U.S. Marshals emblem. We stopped near the entrance of a white V-shaped building serving as the marshals' home in Maui. Its two wings, connected by a circular lobby, appeared new, with several ubiquitous palms lining the long sidewalk. Two other trees leaned toward one another on either side of the entrance, red blooms splashed among their crowns.

Marshal Olan opened my car door, then nodded toward the front of the building. "Please proceed to Conference Room A-3, second floor, then to the right at the end of the hall."

"Our escort duties have ended, Detective Pierce,"

Allerton said. "Someone will take you back to your hotel a little later."

I struggled to get out of the back seat. "What? You're dumping me off?"

Olan said nothing else, sliding back into the front passenger seat.

"Consider this an opportunity, Detective Pierce," Marshal Allerton said. "My understanding is an investigation you became a part of several months ago … continues."

"In Prague? We resolved our piece—"

He held up a hand. "Please. I wasn't told the details. Continue to the conference room. Most everyone has gone for the day. Good evening." Allerton returned to his car, slammed his door without looking up, then turned the Ford toward the street.

After eight p.m. now, the parking lot was empty except for another dark-blue Ford sedan and an orange Jeep. I walked into the lobby, noticed an elevator to the left, and nodded to the security officer leaning on his desk near the entrance.

He pointed at me. "If your name is Henry Pierce, take the elevator. If it's not, you're trespassing."

"I'm Pierce."

"I guessed it by the description they gave me. Head on up, kid. Don't keep them waiting."

"Them?"

He smiled, then hurried to the front entrance. I strolled into the elevator as he pulled his keys off his belt, locked the door, and turned down the lights.

"Have a good evening," I offered. The elevator doors closed and then a bumpy stop.

The doors opened to another lobby with a small

sitting area encircled by four picture windows. I stepped behind the leather couch sitting on the tan carpet, a smell of newness drifting around me. Looking toward the Maui high country, as they called it here, the fading twilight showed thousands of acres of pineapples stretching up the slope of Haleakalā. I wandered down the hallway, stopping next to an emergency exit with fake palmettos on either side of a closed door labeled A-3. I breathed deeply and grabbed the knob, wondering if I would ever become an ordinary detective.

A smell of new leather greeted me as I stopped next to a rectangular conference table with plush leather chairs in the middle of the wood-paneled room—a new office with mid-century styling. A window opened to the parking lot, where LED security lights flickered to life on top of their poles. Five of the eight chairs were empty, but three held Danny Keaka, Stepan Hrubý, and Angie Marconi.

Keaka had shaved and changed from his old t-shirt into a white polo, and Hrubý leaned back in his chair, yawning and looking to the ceiling with his arms crossed.

Marconi chewed away on her gum. She tilted her head and offered a weak smile. "Hi, Henry. It seems it's sucked us in again."

"Detective Sergeant Pierce," Hrubý said. "Please join us."

I placed my hands on the back of a chair and stared at my boss. "What the hell, Angie?"

"Sit. These two have a story for us, and they think we can help."

I sat at the end of the table opposite Hrubý, then

exaggerated scanning the room. "I think I'll need a drink."

"Later." Keaka smiled at me as he had on the boat.

"The orange Jeep in the lot looked familiar," I said.

Marconi glared at Hrubý. "Stepan pulled me out of the restaurant when you left to call your mother. We got here five minutes before you did. Stepan, or should I call you Commander Hrubý again, explained a few things to me on the way."

Keaka ignored her and said, "Henry, please assume nothing, yeah? I did not deceive you. It truly was only a fishing trip for me this morning … and a good one. Everything I told you is true, but I didn't feel the need to mention I'm still an adjunct to the U.S. Marshals. It's part of the settlement Malo said he mentioned to you. I got the money, but I'm used sometimes for consulting on other matters."

"So, why are we here?" My folks were my primary concern, and I pictured my remaining vacation days circling the drain.

"Miomir Kurić," Hrubý said, "or Kurić's organization. What else?"

"Angie?" I asked.

"Yes?"

"Please tell me you knew nothing of this."

Marconi shook her head. "Hell no. I never again wanted to hear of Kurić."

"And Eddie?"

"What about him? Where is he, by the way?" she asked.

"He's going to Kihei to hang with my folks. My mother said someone followed her all day."

"Yes, U.S. Marshals followed them," Keaka said.

"I learned we had background chatter from our informers concerning Kurić's people. I ordered a follow of two women, not knowing who they might be, but our guys got careless, and one woman noticed them. Stepan told me this afternoon an associate of the Kurić organization, Nika Campbell, has been spotted at a resort near Kā'anapali.

Only twelve hours earlier, I had drunk beer and fished with this guy. "Not good, Danny," I said. "It worried my mother to death."

"I've taken care of it. The two men who brought you here will relieve the men in Kihei. I've ordered them to make themselves visible to your family and, it seems, Eddie Stone. I think it will be best if your mother and grandmother stay protected for the time being. They can still be tourists, but the marshals will be nearby. Tomorrow morning, two female U.S. Marshals will take their place. I hope it will help."

Marconi clasped her hands together, using them as a hammock to hold her chin. "Sorry, Henry. I told you once before this crap is like a black hole."

I bowed my head, staring at the tabletop, tears filling the corner of my eyes. My voice cracked. "This is the first time … they've gotten away from the farm since my dad died. Now I'm finding out their lives are at risk."

Marconi fidgeted with her hands. "We can send them home—"

"Absolutely not." Marconi and I had come to figurative blows several times on our Prague trip, to the point of me submitting my resignation. She had told Eddie and me ninety percent of the truth. The other ten percent she had kept to herself, almost getting us killed more than once. "They've been nowhere since my dad died, so they're both staying. Did you know of Eddie's intention for coming here?"

Marconi leaned forward. "What? You mean getting married?"

"That's most of it ... but Nika Campbell, too," I said.

"Nika Campbell, Nika Campbell," Hrubý said. "What powers she seems to have."

I ignored him. "Eddie heard our Czech friends talking of her while we were in Prague, and me, too, about her telling me she vacationed in Hawaii with her mother. Eddie chose Maui for the ceremony to give us a chance to do research while he honeymooned. Then we stumbled across the little ... shit at the 'Ino luau."

"Hotel 'Ino?" Keaka asked.

"Right."

Keaka clasped his hands and stared at this lap. "We found a man on the beach there last night. He died before the medical folks could do much. It seemed a simple drowning at first, but the coroner believes it a murder. There were marks around his neck, and he had several ribs broken."

"I came across him last night on my way back to our table at the luau," I said. "He died on the beach after trying to talk, and it was an orange scarf that left the marks on his neck. A coincidence it occurred in the same hotel where we spotted Nika?"

Marconi slapped her hands down on the conference table. "Nothing is a damn coincidence with these folks. I mentioned to Stepan last night I considered flying over to Honolulu to talk to the F.B.I. And you, Stepan, is all this just a convenience for you, too? Another way to investigate this?"

Hrubý stared straight ahead. "Angela, I am not two-faced—"

Marconi frowned. "A liar—"

"No."

"But?" she asked.

"Yes," Hrubý added. "We have known of the organization's operations in the Hawaiian Islands, but I wasn't aware Ms. Campbell lurked so near."

Keaka exhaled a loud moan. "Tell them the rest, Stepan."

"You know each other?" I asked.

Hrubý scowled. "Danny Keaka and I have never met, Detective Sergeant Pierce. Our Unit of Peculiar Activities—"

"Peculiar activities?" Keaka asked.

Hrubý sighed. "Yes … *Jednotka pro Zvláštní Činnosti*. Peculiar Activities is the best translation I can offer." He seemed out of his element, something unaccustomed, I guessed. "Our unit has contacts all over the world. We've communicated with someone named Keaka several times. I assumed it to be a code name."

I shook my head. "All these conspiracies and oopses … but wait a minute. Danny, how did this thing work with me booking our fishing trip? Did you plan this?"

"Me?" Keaka flashed anger I hadn't seen from him. "Hey, I didn't come to you, braddah. Fate, karma, whatever you want to call it—it's your doing, not mine. But I got curious about your convoluted Europe story."

Marconi pointed at me. "Henry. Did you blab everything again?"

Before last Thanksgiving, I had learned the hard way not to tell more than I should in public, but I didn't appreciate her tone. "What would I blab? I said nothing to reveal information concerning an ongoing investigation. We went on a fishing trip, and I tried to relax. I assumed our little secret forays into investigating old crimes were long over."

"Wait, wait, shh." Keaka put a finger to his lips, stood, and stretched. He turned and leaned his back against the marble windowsill. "Let's not go crazy, yeah? The story of Henry's European adventure interested me, as I said. After dumping the fish in the freezer, I called my contact in Europe. They routed me to a man named Hrubý, and the person I spoke to in Prague seemed to know more of me than I know of them. I soon talked to a guy named Hrubý, staying in my hotel only thirty yards across the street from my boat. My Honolulu contact confirmed it's legit and for me to make plans to protect our mainland visitors. I asked Commander Hrubý to join me this evening and bring you two, if possible, not realizing it would turn into such a cluster … I mean, I wanted information and your thoughts on this. Again, I intended no subterfuge. Stay if you wish or go home sooner, I don't care, but I insist the U.S. Marshals accompany you until you leave Maui. The Kurić organization takes no prisoners."

Keaka pushed back a side door into an office, his office, I presumed, with windows opening to a view of the bay. He unlocked a desk drawer, pulled out two bottles, set an expensive-looking brandy in front of us, then retrieved four shot glasses with a yellow *Aloha* stamped on the side. He settled in his chair and passed a glass to each of us.

"Now, we'll have a couple of shots and loosen up a bit. You three are tighter than … something."

I sniffed the sweet-smelling liquor, and we each knocked back a slug.

I wandered over to the door into his office, staring out his office windows at the darkening bay. "So, Marshal Keaka, early this morning, I guessed you as a washed-up cop living the rest of his days in a fishing boat, something a lot of guys dream of. Now here we are in your corner office looking out on Kahului Bay. I understood you won a big lawsuit against the government, and that's how you bought the hotel and restaurant."

Keaka shrugged. "All true. Should I call you Detective Sergeant Pierce since we seem to be so formal, or will Henry still work?"

Marconi and Hrubý remained silent.

"Henry it will stay then, but on the *Miss Mio* tomorrow with Eddie Stone, I'll call you braddah. A habit." He winked. "So, yeah, I won the lawsuit after a decade and a half fighting the Department of Justice. Someone didn't appreciate our shutting down a drug gang. A crooked judge helped the bad guys bail out of jail and then they disappeared … along with the evidence. I got a little pushy with the judge, and soon I needed to find another job. I sued and headed back to Maui. After all those years in the courts, I got an offer to settle out of the blue with one condition: I would be an advisor on special projects. They offered it after all that time of fighting me … new management, I guess." He refilled our shot glasses. "But it's worked out. I can fish and run my business, and now and then, I have to wear a collared shirt." The gap in his teeth showed again with his big smile.

Marconi knocked back her second shot of brandy. "So, Danny, you've been here your whole life. What do you know of Miomir Kurić and Nika Campbell?"

Keaka hesitated a moment, pushed his chair back facing the door, and placed his feet on the conference table. He supported the back of his head with his interlocked fingers and gazed at the ceiling. "We're familiar with an organization controlled by a person named Miomir Kurić. It's been mostly a European concern since the nineties, but its sewage seeped into the D.C. area, as you all are aware."

Hrubý shuffled his and Marconi's empty shot glasses around like chess pieces. He glanced up at Keaka. "And Angela and her colleagues destroyed the organization's cell in Alexandria except for a few stray elements."

"Oh?" Marconi snatched her shot glass from him. "When were you going to tell me about the stray elements?" She adjusted her bangs and leaned forward.

Hrubý matched her movements, his elbows on the table. "You told me you wanted the intrigue to be over when you left Prague."

"Yes, but now it looks like I'm involved again, huh?"

"It seems so. As I mentioned to you earlier today, Marshal Keaka, the Alexandria detectives helped us severely damage the Kurić organization in Prague. We have a few components left at home, more than in Washington, D.C., but we have placed a … crimp … is that the correct word?"

Europe didn't concern me. "Danny, you said it's been mostly a European worry. What else do you know?" I asked.

Keaka spun a black pen on the table, first clockwise, then counterclockwise. "And here's a thing you may not know … we believe there are elements of Kurić's organization in China. Many of the significant white-collar crimes here have involved government officials. Plus, we believe elements in the Chinese government are quick to halt any investigations there, something we, apparently, have all experienced. There are similarities in operations, but it's uncertain if this relates to Kurić."

"Anything else?" Hrubý squinted at Keaka.

Keaka hesitated, then said, "We think a few Chinese government officials may support Kurić, at least covertly."

"What?" Marconi slammed her left palm on the table and grabbed the near-empty decanter of brandy, looking as if she would take a swallow from the bottle.

"Look, folks, I'm as hamstrung as you guys have been with your investigations. And I'm not even a full-time employee," Keaka said.

"The Chinese are supporting Kurić in what way?" Hrubý asked.

"A degree of financial support exists—call it a payoff if you will."

"And what do the Chinese get in return?" I asked.

"Noninterference in their country. Of course, that organization's trustworthiness isn't a part of its mission statement. They may have already placed cells in China, no matter the agreement."

"And disruptions in other countries would advantage China," Hrubý said. "As an example, the release of those hundreds of millions of counterfeit euros we intercepted in the spring would have devastated the European Union."

"So, how does this interest you, Danny?" Marconi asked.

"My interest here in Hawaii is direct—Miomir Kurić. Counterfeit currency has not been a concern, and the gold Yugoslav dukats are simply a distraction to us. I'm more worried about drug and human trafficking. Kurić's arrest, her neutralization, would destroy the organization and all its operations. But if she frequents these islands, she must do it under an assumed name."

"Do you have a picture? Wait," Marconi said. She picked up her purse and plowed through the contents. We watched as she pulled out her purple wallet. "Hang on, it's in here somewhere."

"What are you looking for?" Hrubý asked.

"The copy of the picture you gave me."

"We never identified who—"

"There." Marconi slapped the postage-stamp-sized picture of a woman on the table, then slid it over to Keaka. "A man in the organization's so-called 'Protection Force' had been a colleague of my late husband, Jack Marconi, but in a jealous rage, Manny killed Jack. The Czech authorities found this picture in his possession."

Keaka glanced at the faded image of the dark-haired woman, dropped it on the table, and leaned back in his chair. "Hmm." His face flushed. We waited, and he offered nothing else.

I had been mulling something all day. "Danny, tell me again … the name of the woman you named your boat after?"

"Mio, obviously. The *Miss Mio*."

"Mio what?"

"Mio Kulp," Keaka answered.

"An Americanized name?" Marconi asked.

"Short for Miomir?" I asked.

Marconi held up both arms and waved. "Wait, wait, wait. You knew a woman named Miomir?"

Keaka stared over our heads, his brows furrowed. He opened his mouth to speak, closed it, then glanced at Hrubý. "I've never heard the name Miomir before. You're saying Mio Kulp could have been Miomir Kurić?"

"Doubtful. It seems too coincidental," Hrubý said, "and that picture isn't the best. Remember, though, this would have been before the Yugoslav breakup and the mayhem that followed."

"Yes … right. But how in the hell …?" Keaka picked up the woman's picture again, then passed it back to Marconi. "Yeah, it could be, but I don't know. You guys are trying to tell me my Mio became a Balkans war criminal? It doesn't sound plausible."

Hrubý shook his head. "I do not believe that is her."

"Why?" Marconi asked, raising an eyebrow.

Hrubý pursed his lips, looking away from her. "That person does not match … the descriptions I remember."

"Oh? That leads me to the next surprise," she said.

I guessed what was coming. "Nika—"

"Who is Miomir Kurić's daughter?" Marconi asked.

"Danny?" I asked. His face had lost all expression. "Nika told me more than once that her father abandoned them but left a lot of money."

Keaka chuckled, then held up his hands. "It's not me. I couldn't rub two pennies together when I knew my Mio. I assumed that's why she ran off with the other guy. But Ms. Campbell would have to be near twenty-eight if she were my daughter. Does it work out?"

"She's five years younger than me, so … twenty-five, twenty-six," I answered.

Marconi fidgeted in her chair. "Danny, when in Prague, Stepan's men seemed convinced that my husband, Jack Marconi, had an affair with Miomir Kurić while he investigated her organization. They told me he fathered a child."

"Angela, it is heavy speculation," Hrubý said. "We believe Kurić had a daughter, and I believe Nika Campbell is likely that girl. Despite our speculation, that story is what, a stretch, as you say. Jack Marconi died in early 1996, correct?"

Marconi sighed. "Yeah."

"The child would be near the same age … but not exact."

Marconi blew out her cheeks. "Any of those dates could fit through a tight window."

Keaka shook his head. "Angie, I wouldn't go too far down that road. As I told Henry today, the Mio I had a relationship with ran off with a guy who sounded like a jet setter, or whatever the term might be today. Lots of money and lots of travel. Surely, he would be Nika Campbell's father."

"Did you ever get the name of the guy?" Marconi asked.

"Nope."

This guessing game had grown old. "And who gives a damn? Nika, like her mother, if it is her mother, is part of a criminal organization, no matter her DNA. And what if she is Jack Marconi's biological daughter, Angie? Are you going to make friends with her?"

"Seriously? I want them all in jail."

"And you, Danny?" I asked. "Do you want a big reunion with the woman named Campbell?"

"Hell, no. I'd rather my boat sink with me in it."

"So, let's move on. I want to get out of here and check on my folks."

"Henry's right," Marconi said. She stood and stretched her back. "What do you need from us, Danny? And you, Stepan? Cat got your tongue?"

"Why would a cat—"

"Never mind. You've told me there's been little headway finding the half-billion euros of gold dukats." She scanned through the books shelved on the case next to the exit. The two men glanced at each other and then at Marconi.

"Gold coins aren't my thing, so I'll defer to Stepan on that one." Keaka appeared to hold back a smile. He leaned on an elbow, his hand covering his mouth.

Hrubý rubbed his forehead with both hands and shut his eyes for a moment. "We think a large cache of the dukats has arrived here in Kahului, hidden in a container ship docked at the port. It is an Austrian-owned ship with a German flag."

"Seriously?" Marconi stopped next to me at the door to Keaka's office. "Another reason you came here? I don't want to keep chasing this MacGuffin of yours, Stepan. I chased my own, my husband's killer, for twenty-five years, and it almost killed me."

"The information about the ship came to me after I had made plans to come here for the wedding, Angela.

And your participation is optional," Hrubý said. He looked down and twirled a shot glass.

Marconi turned away, hands on her hips while staring out the window.

Keaka sighed and shoved away from the table. "You two will need to work it out. Anyway, a German-flagged ship, yeah? Interesting. I can round up twenty marshals in an hour if we need to hit something. Tell me which ship, and we'll take it apart."

"I appreciate the offer, Marshal Keaka, but I need to wait on my assets," Hrubý said.

"Assets?" Keaka asked.

"Yes, three of my men from Prague have landed in Honolulu this evening, and they will be here at the Kahului airport at ten o'clock tonight."

"Which men?" I asked.

"The three you worked with, Henry Pierce—Lieutenant Talích and Mr. Žák, along with Vitaly Kharkov."

"Kharkov, too?" I asked. "His father is better?"

Hrubý shrugged. "Apparently, coming to Hawaii overrode any family concerns."

"Hang on, hang on. I insist you and your men meet with this office before pursuing any independent operations," Keaka said. "We can make it much easier … or more difficult."

"I understand. I would do the same. Much planning needs to occur, and your resources will benefit us. When should we meet?"

Keaka eyed me and smiled. "Two o'clock tomorrow afternoon. I promised a fishing trip with a couple of friends in the morning."

"Eddie and I will be there at seven-thirty," I said.

Keaka shook his head. "Nope. Make it at nine o'clock. I'm going to file papers to change the name of my boat."

Chapter Five

Well past midnight, I had collapsed into bed after accompanying Hrubý to the airport to pick up his men, people I considered my friends after our business in Prague. Mr. Žăk had been considered the leader, and the blond crewcut, military-trained head of this team, was the man Hrubý trusted without question. Lieutenant Talích, a paramilitary officer with black, caterpillar-like eyebrows, served as chief of Prague's Section One criminal division. He seemed a pedant and often an irritant to Hrubý, but his efficiency made up for his abrasiveness, and Vitaly Kharkov, a tall, skinny man who served as the technological wiz of the group. Luckily, he didn't hold a grudge after a rough start with Eddie Stone and me in Prague, which included a fight and us drugging him, then locking him in a closet. I would catch up with them at Keaka's office.

A phone call woke me early.

"Hey, Eddie."

"Good morning, Ike. I'm ready for our fishing trip."

"How are my mom and granny?"

"Your folks are fine after your phone call last night eased their minds. The trip to Hana exhausted them, and they're still sleeping."

"Keaka said he would assign women as today's marshals on duty."

"Yep, figured that one out. I'm out on the lanai drinking coffee, and close to an hour ago, I noticed a dark-blue U.S. Marshals' sedan replace the black SUV. I'll pay them a visit after I hang up and push for one of them to stay inside the condo."

"Good idea," I said, "but don't scare them."

"The marshals?"

"No … my folks."

"Oh, we talked last night. I told them Keaka is only taking a precaution—the marshals shouldn't have followed them without letting us know, etcetera."

"Thank you. Well?"

"Well, what?"

"You called me."

"Oh, right. Want to have breakfast … and not only donuts? I spotted a bakery across the street, and I'll buy a bag full of pastries for your momma and granny."

"They'll appreciate it, I'm sure. After that, why don't you come up here and we'll have a big meal? It may seem counterintuitive on a rough sea, but a big meal may set better on your stomach instead of something sweet."

"Sounds good. But remember, I spent the summers of my teenage years near the coast of St. Pete's working the docks. I've had lots of little boat trips."

"Right, but I'm bringing patches … just in case."

"I'm okay, I promise. Let's get there at seven-thirty—we can eat then wait for Danny."

"Right. You two acted like old friends yesterday when we reserved his boat."

He didn't respond.

"Eddie?

"I'm here, I'm here, and right, Keaka's a good guy.

I'll park near the banyan park and meet you downstairs. And my treat this morning."

"Oh? Hawaii brings out the best in Eddie Stone."

****

We waited for Danny Keaka on the deck of the *Miss Mio*. He finally showed a half-hour late.

"Sorry, guys—bureaucrats—they talk story while we stand in line." He held up a piece of paper. "But I have an official document here to finish for the boat's name change. I'll name it after my mom, but I'm not sure she'll like it." He grinned. "She thinks the boat is ugly." He stuffed the wrinkled paper under the cushion of his captain's seat.

Eddie lifted his plastic sack onto the passenger bench and pulled out what remained of another twelve-pack of Primo. "Ike says you like this stuff. I had a few last night, and it wasn't bad. I'm a Heineken guy myself."

"*Mahalo*, sir." He winked and pointed. "Lift the bench seat and shove it into the ice. I came by before seven and iced mine already, and you'll find more in the white Styrofoam cooler."

"Where are we headed today?" I asked.

"North," Keaka said after a glance at Eddie. "Near the Nakalele Blowhole. It will take nearly forty-five minutes to get there."

"Outstanding," Eddie said. "Riding in a boat will be as much fun as fishing."

Keaka dug his phone from his pocket, lost in his thoughts. We eased away from the dock and headed north, dodging fishing boats and other vessels. He ran a hand through his thick hair. "I should let you know we'll meet others there."

"Oh? Buddies of yours?" I asked.

He looked away. "More business than pleasure, guys. I agreed to meet our Prague friends and your boss off the coast a mile or so from Nakalele." He revved the engine, and we bounced through the waves headed north in a much heavier sea today. Keaka inhaled the breeze.

"Why would we do that? Don't we already have it scheduled at your office?" I asked.

Eddie crossed his legs. "Let the man explain." He shifted on the vinyl seat and closed his eyes in a spray of ocean water.

"Marshals Allerton and Olan are bringing them on one of our boats to meet us." Keaka plopped hard on the captain's seat, staring at his beer can but not taking a drink. "Pretty sure we have a leaker in my office, guys."

Eddie and I exchanged glances.

"I guess it's nothing new if you get mixed up with Kurić," Eddie said. "Commander Hrubý has had to fight it in Prague, and we have firsthand experience. Right, Ike?"

I nodded.

"We're in good company then," Keaka said. "Anyway, we'll have our scheduled meeting, and then we fish for a while. Tonight is another poker night with my mother and brothers, though. I don't want to miss it."

****

We found the marshals' patrol boat waiting for us off the coast. The gray steel ship appeared at least five times larger than the *Miss Mio* and floated much steadier in the water. Despite Eddie's bragging, he should have worn a patch. He surrendered after a few minutes and attached one behind his ear, poured out his beer, and leaned back against the canvas covering.

Keaka slowed the engine, easing closer to the *Lanakila*. I noticed Marconi waving and Hrubý standing next to her. Three men rested with their faces to the sun, and another man stood leaning over the side, extending the *Lanakila's* ladder. We drifted nearer. The man by the ladder appeared to be Marshal Olan, one of the men who picked me up at the banyan tree park.

Keaka tossed a rope to Olan, dropped anchor, and offered a weak salute. "Ahoy, Marshal Olan. Tie the rope tight for towing. Permission to come aboard."

Olan didn't return his smile. "Good morning, sir. I have news."

We boarded, then Keaka and Olan ducked into the control room and shut the door.

Eddie and I headed to the stern, where Marconi, Hrubý, and his three colleagues rested in the sun. We took turns shaking hands except for Mr. Žăk, who had been practicing his fist bump. While on duty, Mr. Žăk wore an all-black uniform with a red beret. Today, he dressed similarly, wearing black shorts and a red tank top. Lieutenant Talích wore only red shorts, and Vitaly Kharkov sported jean shorts and a sea-green Maui t-shirt with a white dolphin imprinted on the front.

"Welcome aboard, Henry," Marconi said.

"Thanks, boss. Good morning, gentlemen," I said. "Are y'all going to fish?"

Talích pulled his cap off his face, ruffling his black, caterpillar-like eyebrows. "Must it require effort on my part?" He covered his face again and folded his hands over his chest.

Hrubý gave Talích a slight kick to his feet. "Not too comfortable, Talích. We meet in half an hour, and I would appreciate you wearing a shirt."

Talích again lifted his cap. "Did you remember today is my birthday, Commander Hrubý? Do I not receive any special dispensations?"

"You are in Hawaii—that is your dispensation. And now you are the oldest of our unit for a few days. Mr. Žák will become thirty-two next week as well."

"You're both older than me." I grinned and winked. "I'm thirty."

"Kudos to you, Henry Pierce," Talích mumbled.

"Don't forget me," Kharkov said. "I am only twenty-seven."

"Oh, stop it," Marconi said. "I can't even remember forty."

Hrubý crossed his arms. "No comment."

"Well, it's thirty times two for me," Eddie said. He found his way to a sliver of shade near the control room. "Man, I'm ready to get this show on the road." He stuck his face against the tinted glass. "Where'd they go?"

The door opened, and Marshal Olan stepped on deck.

Keaka ignored us, then disappeared through another door.

"Please follow me," Olan said. "Marshal Keaka would like to get started."

"No fishing?" Kharkov asked. Olan didn't answer.

Mr. Žák stroked his blond crewcut hair, closed an eye, and showed a frown. "Lieutenant Talích, please put on a shirt. I do not want to view your hairy nipples while making our plans."

Talích mumbled something again and grabbed his tank top.

This boat seemed larger inside than it appeared on the outside. We trailed one another down a circular steel ladder, finding Keaka sitting at a conference table hosting seven yellow-and-black plaid cloth chairs. Marconi sat to his left, Eddie chose a chair near the ladder, and I leaned against the ladder's chrome rail, gazing at another conference room best described as mid-century modern. The wood-paneled walls held several Hawaii maps, and a medium-sized TV screen occupied the wall above a door leading into the bathroom.

Olan followed us in, leaned over for a word with Keaka, then disappeared up the steps.

Keaka opened his arms. "*Mahalo*, everyone, for being here. I must admit I wouldn't have guessed a few days ago I'd lead such a disparate group of people in a discussion."

Eddie shifted in his chair and placed his hands on the table.

"So, unless anyone has objections?" Keaka glanced to his right at Hrubý, who remained silent. "Good. Our original reason for getting together has ... evolved. The *Müller*, the German container ship with Austrian ownership, departed Kahului Bay this morning and will dock in Honolulu about dusk."

Hrubý leaned back and shut his eyes. "We have missed our chance for the coins."

"Nope. This boat will get us to Honolulu two hours before the cargo ship. I have contacts at the port, and we can move forward with inspection of the *Müller*."

The engines hummed, and I sensed movement.

"We're on the way now, but I have more important news."

"What's more important?" Marconi asked while glancing at Hrubý.

Keaka inhaled and dropped his pencil on his pad. "I've been told the body found close to your luau the other night is an informer of ours who washed ashore. Someone tried to strangle him, then dumped him in the water. He had scheduled a meeting with a person of interest in a secluded area south of Lahaina."

"Who would be the person of interest?" Hrubý asked.

Keaka glanced around the room. "Someone we believe is part of the Kurić organization."

Marconi blew out a groan. "Apparently, the meeting didn't go well."

"Sugar," I said.

Tilting his head, Keaka scratched an eyebrow, then pursed his lips. "Sugar? That's pretty random, braddah."

"No, your guy who died on the beach. I walked by during the luau and found the EMT folks working on him. They had him propped up, and he said something like 'he's here' and then said the word 'sugar.' "

"Who is here?" Hrubý asked.

"That's what I wondered. The man died right after saying it."

Keaka tapped his fingers on the desk. "Sugar? I have no idea … I'll think it over, though. I wish the first responders had passed the info along. Anyway, James Allerton, Marshal Olan's partner, did not show for work this morning." He stood, then opened an oversized cabinet door, revealing sandwiches, chips, containers of fruit, and a score of water bottles.

"You suspect foul play?" Marconi asked.

"Allerton is an exemplary marshal. He wouldn't skip an assignment without notice."

"Where was he last seen?" Hrubý asked.

Keaka pointed at the shelves. "Please grab a sandwich and whatever else you like."

I thought I had smelled bread earlier, but I let the others go first. I grabbed a wrapped sandwich and stood by the stairs, munching on salami, while Eddie injected his pastrami with several packets of spicy mustard.

Keaka wiped his mouth. "Allerton showed up at Haleakalā. His younger brother works at the ranger station at the park's entrance, and someone told the brother they saw Allerton earlier in the morning. Allerton waited in his car outside the ranger station for a few minutes without talking to anyone, then headed to the summit. No one has seen him since."

"It doesn't sound good." Marconi jotted something on her yellow notepad, shoved a potato chip into her mouth, then muttered, "And his brother?"

"Late getting to work, apparently, but he later met our search group at the summit. They'll walk it today—it's misty, tough to see. We can't get a helicopter in there."

"What can we do to help?" I asked.

"Glad you offered," Keaka said, "and the answer is nothing … on Maui at least. But we have our own plans to make. Marshal Olan will keep us updated concerning the Allerton search. Commander Hrubý, and I'll call you that in front of your men, please tell us about this container ship."

"I will defer to Lieutenant Talích."

Talích grinned. In Prague, he seemed to enjoy the attention while presenting in front of other people. As usual, his head tilted to the left when speaking. "The German registry shows the *Müller* to be a standard cargo ship, a tramp tanker of twenty-five thousand deadweight tons. Its owner leases it to private parties who need to move something. Usually legitimate, but we know the tramp tanker business can be used for hiding cargo that these private parties do not want to be discovered."

"What's the owner's name? Individual, a company?" Eddie asked.

"A Doctor Emmerich Müller, who lives in Vienna," Talích answered.

"The neurologist?" I asked.

Kharkov smiled. "Yes, Sergeant Pierce. The office where we first met, and you ran away from me."

"What are you talking about?" Marconi asked.

I sighed. "You remember … the name of the neurologist in Vienna where you insisted I have a secret meeting with Rijad Kastrati."

"No way? The neurologist is a part of this?" she asked.

"Apparently, someone is using the doctor's name, legitimately or not," Kharkov answered. "We discovered an Emmerich Müller who received his neurologist license and set up a practice in Vienna … in 1972, and he passed away in 2016."

Marconi squinted as if looking into the sun. "So, who the hell is running the office?"

Keaka waved his hands and smiled. "Let's not get too bogged down in the weeds, or the barnacles, but tell me, how do you know this name?"

Kharkov grabbed another water bottle. "One man killed in Prague last spring was Rijad Kastrati, a Bosnian immigrant who owned two bakeries in Alexandria, Virginia. Several years ago, he had attached himself to the Austrian security service, supposedly to inform the authorities of immigrant issues in southeast Europe. Professionally, I served as his so-called partner, mainly to monitor him. He arranged for our three Alexandria colleagues to travel to Vienna, then Prague. He and I had planned to meet Detective Pierce in the neurologist's office, the doctor named Müller, at a pretend appointment to relay information to the Americans. I remember a receptionist but never met a doctor."

Marconi rolled her eyes. "I can't believe I fell for it."

Hrubý smiled. "Desperation, Angela. The truth had become so close—"

"Truth? It came with a kick in the butt. My desperation blinded me and almost got my friends and me killed."

"But we got him, didn't we, Angie?" Eddie asked.

"You got him?" Keaka asked.

"Yep. I shot him twice in the leg, then Angie nailed him in the jugular. Bled out in the mud," Eddie answered.

Marconi nodded. "And another man named Manfred Jurić, Danny, the man who killed my husband. Kastrati killed Jurić."

Talích again tilted his head. "Jurić had his own history of dismembering bodies proficiently as a part of the Kurić organization's Protection Force."

Keaka tapped his pencil. "Dang, I'm lost again.

Anyway, it sounds like the good guys won that round, but to summarize … the name of Dr. Müller is of interest connecting this ship to Kurić. Let's leave it there for now and move on." He picked up his phone. "Still nothing on Allerton. Commander, I assume you have, or had, a plan to board and search the ship. If so, please tell us your arrangements."

Hrubý nodded. "Very well. Mr. Kharkov manufactured IDs for us. Our original plans were to board the ship tonight as part of the crew. We intended to search the ship for the missing Royal Dukats reportedly on board."

Keaka's eyebrows arched into his forehead. "Reportedly? Are you uncertain?"

Hrubý nodded toward Mr. Žăk, who straightened in his chair. "Mr. Žăk?"

"Yes, sir. Our source aboard the ship has told us of Chinese agents and a Macedonian man, and this source has learned of gold coins, but he didn't call them dukats. Unfortunately, he cannot identify the coins' location."

"Chinese agents?" Marconi asked, then frowned. "And where does the *Müller* go after Honolulu?"

Talích's caterpillar-like eyebrows jiggled. "Shanghai, Dubai, then back to Bremerhaven, Germany, from where it departed."

"Interesting route," Eddie said.

"It's a twenty-five-thousand-ton ship," Keaka said, "which gives them all kinds of nooks and crannies to hide coins."

"My source is impeccable," Žăk said. "I believe a significant number of dukats are aboard the ship. For Marshal Keaka's information, the Yugoslav Royal

Dukats are in individual blue pewter containers, each holding two hundred coins. Our recent analysis concluded each container is worth two million American dollars. Based on the coins we collected in Prague, if this ship holds half of all the dukats, this haul might be worth a half-billion dollars."

"Unbelievable," Marconi said.

"So, if you find the dukats," Keaka asked, "then what? A quick guess would be over fifty thousand coins, yeah? And how much would it weigh? I'm guessing almost a ton of gold, not counting the pewter boxes."

"We need a conveyance," Žăk said. "Maybe a small handtruck, plus the four of us to move it."

"And you planned to just slip away and go back to Prague with a ton of gold?" Keaka asked. "That's a lot of suitcases. I'm having a problem with this, Stepan. I don't care for outside groups taking the law into their hands."

Hrubý's face reddened. "We intended to go to the Honolulu authorities."

"Which might be good or bad," Keaka said. "The import/export folks … well, I've had issues with them in a past life. They might have grabbed the coins and thrown you in jail. And what's the goal? You don't want the Kurić organization to have them, or the Chinese, and understandably so, but what would the Czech government do with them? Shouldn't they belong to the Serbian government? Belgrade would have served as home to the royals, correct?"

Hrubý glanced at Žăk. "Belgrade is the original home, but we believe the Serbians sold the Royal Dukats to Kurić to start the transaction. We will not give them back to those officials. We are working with the European Union to determine proper ownership."

Keaka leaned back in his chair and smiled. "Ahh, so maybe Kurić is the go-between on a sale of these coins from Serbia to China. Interesting. If we intercept the coins, I'm sure the Chinese would want a refund, correct?"

Eddie grinned. "The Chinese would decide who to get it from—the Serbs or Kurić."

Keaka nodded. "Right. Now … since we're all partners, it's my responsibility to involve more than the European Union. We're on American soil, so I presume our authorities will work with the European agencies to return the coins to a proper location."

"But what the hell?" Eddie asked. "What would the Chinese want with European gold dukats?" Eddie asked. "Those are a tiny drop in the world gold trade."

Keaka scratched an ear lobe. "Stepan?"

"I will defer again to Lieutenant Talích."

Talích beamed a smile. "Thank you, Commander Hrubý. This has become less a Chinese governmental transaction than one related to its military. A lieutenant general named Shai of the People's Liberation Army in Shanghai commands the PLA Unit 61398, the country's main computer hacking unit. The hacking part is irrelevant for our purposes, but it seems Shai is a collector of old baubles—coins in this case."

Intrigued, I asked, "A personal collector?"

"Apparently."

Keaka scratched his unshaven neck. "If your information is correct, then he managed the payment to the Kurić organization of half a billion dollars for all these coins? Where would he get that kind of money?"

A sly smile flipped from the semi-permanent frown on Hrubý's face. "His compensation methods might interest the Chinese government."

Keaka nodded. "And it will interest our authorities, too. I may need our Honolulu command to contact the Treasury agents at the port."

"A logical strategy, but I would be extremely cautious," Hrubý said.

Keaka smiled. "Sure, and we will see, but I can't allow you to confiscate a ton of coins and somehow transport them back to Prague without a review by our government. It's not an option."

I changed the subject. "You mentioned a Macedonian. I encountered a Macedonian in Prague who I, uh, choked."

Keaka winked at me. "So, this is one of the two men you disposed of?"

Hrubý grimaced, then said, "The Tasevs have a long history in Europe—I have had firsthand experiences with them. People called them *nezničitelný,* indestructible, until Henry Pierce took care of the older man."

"Tasevs?" I asked. "As in plural … more than one?"

Žăk tapped a pen on the table and smiled. "Yes, the old Macedonian died in your chokehold. The other is Karanos Tasev … *Junior*. He, too, is an assassin for the organization and is filling the role too well. We know him to be a particularly vengeful person. You should be aware … for the rest of his life."

My throat tightened.

Eddie scooted his chair back, then stood next to me. "Danny, I've worked with these guys before, and they can make it happen. Everything else is up to you. I was suspicious of our involvement in Prague, you know it, too, Angie, and I'm not too keen on this stuff either."

"*Mahalo*, Eddie. You haven't changed," Keaka said.

Marconi rested her chin in her right hand. "Okay, enough of this, Eddie. You and Danny have been whirling around like you're square dancing. How do you know each other?"

Keaka grinned. "Go ahead."

Eddie groaned as he sat again, his elbows propped on the table. "We met at an explosives training session in Arizona in 1983, and we stayed connected. I hadn't seen him since he came to my late wife's funeral a few years ago."

"You've mentioned no one from Hawaii," Marconi said.

Eddie smiled. "He stood right behind you at the gravesite, Angie."

"So, you recognize me, Danny?" Marconi asked.

Keaka winked. "Unsure. Eddie had other things on his mind besides introductions."

"But there's more," Eddie said. "This makes me sound like an asshole schemer, but there's a reason I picked Maui to get married. And I've told a little of this to Ike since Doris left."

"He mentioned something," she said.

Eddie glanced at me, frowning. "Anyway, Doris liked the idea of a destination wedding in Hawaii. And I remembered our little friend, Nika Campbell, and her mother like to visit Maui … and Danny lived here, too. I didn't realize he had become a 'special projects' guy with the marshals, but I assumed he still had contacts, even after retirement. I researched, narrowed down which boat was Danny's, and suggested it to Ike the other day."

"Busy, busy, busy." Keaka shook his head and pointed toward me. "And again, braddah, I did not understand who you were at first on our fishing trip, yeah? I recognized Eddie right away when you rented the boat, of course … even without his hair." He grabbed his vibrating phone.

Eddie gazed at his lap. "Angie, please, believe me, okay? I had no negative intentions of traveling here for my wedding and wouldn't take anything away from Doris's happiness. I hoped it might be an opportunity for you and Ike to investigate a little more while Doris and I honeymooned."

Marconi rubbed her eyes, looking tired again as she had in Prague. "I get it, Eddie. You're always the detective." She flashed a grin at Hrubý, then Keaka. "Well … here we all are together by deception, accident, unbelievable coincidence, or a million other things, and with similar goals. We need to get in sync and decide what we'll do."

"Let's discuss later." Keaka glanced toward the stairs where Dayap Olan waited on the bottom step. "Honolulu will be late this afternoon. I'll be in contact with my connections before we arrive, but I must make a phone call. They found Marshal Allerton in the crater … dead."

Chapter Six

Towing the *Miss Mio* slowed us more than Keaka had guessed. After the meeting and three hours away from Malala Bay and Honolulu, our Prague colleagues shifted to the *Lanakila's* stern for more sun. Keaka and Olan sealed themselves in the control room—I presumed to communicate with the search party that found James Allerton's body. Marconi, Eddie, and I made our way up top to the boat's forward. I welcomed separation from the others.

Marconi chewed her nicotine gum, made herself comfortable on a cushioned bench, and stretched her legs in the sun. She ran her fingers through her blonde-gray hair and adjusted her sunglasses. "The clouds are moving in." She glanced at her watch. "It's almost eight o'clock at home. I need to call Commissioner Bates— I'll make sure Alexandria's not drowning in a crime wave since he's down three people. We leave—"

"Monday morning, and then we get home at midnight," Eddie said. "Our original itinerary, at least."

A fine spray splashed me as I leaned against the rail, watching the *Lanakila's* bow slice through the dark-blue water. A school of dolphins raced with us, leaping through the air and frolicking in the waves. I inhaled the sea air and turned toward Eddie. "I should call my folks."

"Good idea, Ike. Put them on speaker. Make sure

those marshals are still with them, too."

Marconi gulped her water. "Yes, put them on speaker," Marconi said, pushing up to a sit. "I haven't talked to Susan and Rita Faye in two days."

Two rings and my mother answered. "Hey, Ike. What's going on? Did you and Eddie get back from your fishing trip?"

"We're not finished. The captain is taking us on an adventure." I winked at Eddie.

"Oh? Well, your granny and I have had quite a time today."

"Did the new marshals come, Mom?"

"Yes, yes. Trish and Kai got here at ten this morning, and Kai is here in the condo right now. Say hello, Kai."

"Um, hello, everyone." Dishes rattled in the background.

"After the trip and stress of yesterday, our big adventure was to a local grocer this morning, and we've been helping Kai prepare a few of her recipes. What is it again, Kai?"

"It's pineapple muffins sprinkled with cinnamon and sugar."

My grandmother laughed. "Kai is great, Ike. She's supposed to switch with Trish in a few minutes to babysit us. Ha-ha."

Marconi stepped closer to me and leaned toward the phone. "Hey, it's Angie. Sounds like today is going much better?"

"Angie? You went fishing, too?"

Marconi blew out a sigh. "Right. Stepan is here, and others. I'm sure your son can fill you in later."

"Hi, Angie. It's Rita Faye. I love Kihei. I woke up

first this morning, walked across the street to the bakery, took a cinnamon roll and my coffee down to the beach, then found a place to sit and watch the waves."

"Wake me tomorrow, Momma," my mother said. "I want to go with you."

"It would be advisable if Trish or I went, too," Kai said.

"Oh, I suppose," my mother responded. "I hate for y'all to have to follow us. How's Eddie?"

"Hey, Susan. Doing good … but missing Doris."

"Have you heard from her?"

Eddie clenched his jaws while pulling out his phone. "No, not since late last night. Today is the gravesite service. It's early tomorrow morning there."

"You try her later, Eddie," my grandmother said. "She's under a lot of stress. Don't forget."

"I won't."

"Mom, we need to go," I said. "I'll call you later to catch up. Our fishing plans got a little complicated. It may be tomorrow before we see you."

"Take care then. We're having a big dinner tonight with Trish and Kai. Have a great time." She ended the call.

Marconi stood and patted me on the shoulder. "Sounds like they're in expert hands, Henry. Listen, if anyone is looking for me, I'll be downstairs, calling the commissioner."

Eddie laughed, then wiped his forehead of sweat. "Send him hugs from his favorite detectives."

****

Danny Keaka's face showed lines I hadn't noticed before now. He had grabbed a sandwich, then joined Eddie and me on deck, disassembling his snack without speaking. He threw the bread in the air toward several brown petrels keeping pace with us. The tomato and lettuce fell into the water, then he nibbled the leftover ham.

"What can you tell us, Danny?" Eddie asked.

Keaka smiled and put his hand on Eddie's shoulder. "Eddie, damn good to see you. That's the first thing I can tell you."

"You too, man."

Keaka glanced at me, the gap in his teeth showing with his smile. "Eddie and I lived thousands of miles apart, but he's always been like a best friend. How many conventions did we go to over the years?"

"I think seven before you retired," Eddie answered. "Ike, he's a good man for advice and always had an ear for me, even if he always called at weird hours."

"I couldn't help it if you're six hours ahead. Eddie, I still think of your late wife … such a gracious lady. She loved Las Vegas, didn't she?"

"Oh, yes. Once we moved to Alexandria, she made it to Atlantic City now and then, usually after a visit with Edward." Eddie shot me a glance. He had never told me the story I had heard, partially from Marconi, concerning his son in a New Jersey prison. "Well, Ike, you might as well know—"

"You don't have to say anything," I said.

Eddie unclenched his jaws, then said, "Drunk driving. He got fifteen years for manslaughter after a young couple died in the other car. It …" He shook his head. "My wife. She didn't come up for air for a year … then she got cancer. They wouldn't even let Edward out for her funeral." Eddie closed his eyes. "The world I had known for forty years … collapsed."

I wasn't sure how to respond. Eddie had seemed such a private man. "You're one of the best men I've ever met," I said. "I hope Doris knows how lucky she is."

He wiped his face and gave a slight smile. "Yeah … she's damn lucky."

We all three leaned over the rail, watching the waves. Eddie changed the subject. "What's going on, Danny? What happened to your man Allerton?"

"Strangled … like our informer on the beach. Ligature markings, almost exact. It sounded like someone used a strip of cloth again. It's like pea soup up in the crater this morning. Someone could've murdered him twenty feet away from the tourist center, and no one would've seen it."

"Why there?" I asked.

"Not sure … yet. Allerton should have joined Marshal Olan and sailed with us today."

"You said his brother works up there?" Eddie asked.

"And that's another story. James Allerton got his little brother, Matty, a job a year ago. Their mother and dad died in a car wreck before Matty started high school, and James and his wife finished raising him. The kid had a knack for finding trouble, embarrassing his family several times. Stupid stuff, too. He stole a car from a friend and wrecked it—he got caught with weed twice in the high school parking lot. I helped get him out of jail three times, but they finally got him graduated and an entry job at the ranger's desk. James would check on Matty now and then, knowing we were going to Honolulu today. Matty said he usually gets a visit from him before his Friday shift. He didn't know

79

why he would have come on a Wednesday. Allerton leaves a wife and a three-year-old son."

"A three-year-old, huh?" Eddie rubbed his bald head, his jaws clenched once more.

Marconi and Hrubý appeared behind us. As I turned, I noticed their hands release from one another.

Hrubý nodded at Eddie and me, then turned to Keaka. "My men and I offer our condolences on your officer. It leaves … an emptiness."

"I appreciate it, Stepan. How are the guys?"

"Mr. Kharkov wanted to fish, but we are moving too fast. The other two have been relaxing in the sun, but now we have clouds, and they are complaining."

Marconi shrugged. "Your men are paler than me and turning pink. I'm especially anxious about Mr. Kharkov." Marconi glimpsed at the sky. "The clouds are tricky. Those guys can get burned without realizing it."

"I will check on them later," Hrubý said.

"How's the commissioner, Angie?" Eddie asked.

"Pretty well. Nothing major going on other than a couple of human resource issues."

"Did you tell him we're headed to Honolulu?" I asked.

"Yes, he knows. He blew up at first but understands what the stakes are. Stepan, he passed his greetings to you. Danny, he said he hopes you find your man's killer, and he wants us to help before we leave next Monday."

"Very kind. I appreciate the support," Keaka said.

"How should we proceed, Marshal Keaka?" Hrubý couldn't seem to let go of the formality when talking business. "The four of us, plus our contact on board the cargo ship, are available. We have our Alexandria colleagues and your men in Honolulu."

Keaka motioned to sit on the benches fastened along the railing in front of the command area. Olan watched over us while steering. "I'm not going in with a big bang. My contacts at the port have dwindled, and I don't want to make a big announcement to the U.S. Marshals' office there. The section chief is a friend of mine, though, and he knows what's up. He'll have two other men at the dock for us. They can keep their mouths shut. We'll board the ship when it docks, investigate and search, and if they offer resistance, we'll go from there. My friends reviewed the ship's manifest, and it listed no American citizens as passengers."

"As was our conclusion," Hrubý replied.

"We found no Macedonians registered either. You mentioned one earlier, yeah?"

"Mr. Žák researched it for us. Such a man wasn't on the manifest."

"And no Chinese?" Keaka asked.

"Correct, not on the records. Mr. Žák received the information through his onboard source, one that went quiet two days ago."

"Excellent," Keaka said, "and this allows us to claim we're investigating deficiencies in the manifest. I can keep them busy while others search for the dukats. It doesn't show the coins on the manifest, so it will be an easy smuggling charge, too."

"Do you think we can connect the Chinese nationals to the lieutenant-general?" I asked.

"Unknown," Hrubý answered. The corners of his mouth curved upward. "We must talk to them directly to find out."

Olan tapped on the glass separating us from the control room. He pointed at Keaka and motioned upward with his chin. A chopping sound in the distance—a familiar noise, but I couldn't identify it.

"Excuse me." Keaka hurried inside, then returned at once. "We may have an issue. Look up. Two o'clock." A black speck flew under low clouds, hugging the mountains of far western Moloka'i. "A helicopter."

"And?" Eddie asked.

"Unidentified and moving toward us near seventy knots, but slowing. I'd guess three minutes away." Keaka grabbed my arm. "Come with me, braddah. Let's untie my boat. I'll drop anchor, and we can circle back to it in a minute."

Marconi followed us, Hrubý and Eddie trailing behind her. "Why?" she asked.

Keaka jumped to the lower deck and shouted. "Maneuverability."

I followed close behind, then bumped into Keaka when he spun toward our colleagues. "Angie, Eddie, please go below into the conference room. Stepan, get your men downstairs, too. Open the cabinet next to where we had the sandwiches. You'll find rifles and ammunition. Be ready to come back on deck if you hear from me."

I stood in my spot, confused.

Keaka grabbed the rope linking us to the *Miss Mio* and started pulling. "Come on, braddah. Give an old man some help."

I joined him, and we pulled his boat flush against us.

The chopping sound grew louder.

"Hang tight," he said. Keaka rushed to the stern and shouted to me. "The water is very deep here, so the anchor may not help." Popping sounds filled the air, and something buzzed my ear. Keaka pointed at me. "Henry, get out of here."

"What?"

He stumbled over onto the *Miss Mio's* bow, crawled back closer, then unleashed his end of the rope.

Olan throttled the engines, and I shouted over the noise. "Danny? Get on board."

"Those are real bullets, braddah." He waved and ran back to his captain's chair.

The *Miss Mio's* engine started, and Keaka drifted away. Olan rammed us forward into the waves, slamming me against the rail. The helicopter pulled hard left. Hrubý and his men burst onto the deck, each holding a rifle, crouching behind whatever cover they found. I climbed the shiny chrome stairs to the upper deck and noticed Marconi grab Eddie's arm and hurry into the ship's control room with Olan. Keaka and the *Miss Mio* floated a half-mile away.

The helicopter slowed as it approached, hovering in a tight circle but still out of range of our rifles. Matte black paint and reflective tinted windows made it look like a flying bug. A cargo door slid open on the right side—figures in black masks crouched near the edge.

Eddie threw open the control room door. "Ike, get in here."

"I need a rifle."

Žák pointed toward us. "I found only four. Get your friends downstairs."

Two steps toward Eddie, and I again heard

splintering and cracking glass. A window burst into the control room, and a line of divots sprouted across the deck, passing near Kharkov. Hrubý and his men returned a spray of bullets toward our assailants. The helicopter pulled away as the *Lanakila* slowed and lurched to port. Behind us, the aircraft veered toward Keaka and the *Miss Mio*.

The *Lanakila* wandered counter-clockwise. The control room hatch burst open, and Eddie staggered toward me, grabbing me by both shoulders. Blood covered the front of his yellow and blue Hawaiian shirt. "Ike. Help us get this thing moving in a straight line."

Marconi appeared, blood spatter across her face. "Henry … what happened?"

Hrubý grabbed her and slammed her face against his chest. "Are you hurt?"

"They killed Olan. The bullets … his head … exploded."

I glanced at the control room. Olan's body had fallen from the seat onto the gray steel floor.

Eddie pointed at Hrubý. "Stepan. Can any of your men drive a boat?"

"Mr. Kharkov?"

"Yes, sir?"

"Figure this out and get us moving. Now. We must help Danny Keaka."

Kharkov shoved his rifle into my hands. He hurried to the wheel, glanced at Olan's body, then found the throttle. The two powerful engines revved, and we tilted hard to our left, pulling out of our clockwise drift. Talích landed on his back, his rifle flying across the upper deck and over the side.

Hrubý grabbed the rail, pulled himself to his feet,

and pointed. "Get us to that fishing boat."

"Danny's a sitting duck out there," Eddie said. He used a sleeve of his shirt to wipe the blood from Marconi's face.

"Where is it?" Kharkov called to us.

Žăk tossed his rifle to me, then slid down the ladder to the lower deck. I grabbed his gun, and he propped himself against the stern's rail, shading his eyes. "Henry Pierce, tell Vitaly the location of Marshal Keaka is six o'clock. Due south. Approximately two kilometers."

I yelled toward the control room. Kharkov steadied us, and we charged ahead through the waves. Hrubý and Talích joined me at the ladder, watching the helicopter's silhouette grow larger.

I waved at Eddie. "You and Angie get below." He wrapped his arm around her shoulders, and they disappeared into the hold. Brief bursts of gunfire erupted again, but we were too far away to see Keaka.

Hrubý grabbed Talích's right arm. "Lieutenant, station yourself below us and behind the ladder for a steady shot. Go. Mr. Žăk, your sniper training is now useful. No matter the circumstances, I want you aiming at the door gunners first and then the cockpit."

Žăk nodded. "I will do my best, but these are not long-range rifles."

"Yes … do your best."

The helicopter approached Keaka and began its now-familiar slow circle. We drew close enough to the *Miss Mio* to see a small figure move to the stern.

Keaka pointed his pistol and shot toward the aircraft. The helicopter returned fire with another burst of gunshots. He fell to the deck.

Kharkov slowed the engines a hundred feet away from the *Miss Mio*. Žăk let loose a torrent of fire on his target. More bullets sprayed toward Keaka, and smoke erupted from the *Miss Mio's* bow. The helicopter hovered in place for a moment. Talích fired. A crouched masked gunman tumbled against the cargo opening and then steadied himself. Talích found his target again, and the man collapsed and fell forward, plunging into the ocean.

A flash of light erupted on the *Miss Mio*. Fire covered the deck. I continued shooting at the cargo bay, but the other gunman could not be seen. Žăk resumed a barrage on the cockpit.

Kharkov pushed us closer, but Hrubý called out. "Hold your position. The boat may blow."

The helicopter pulled away, listing left, turned hard right, then headed higher, its nose pointed up before veering back hard left. Žăk darted to starboard, and I jumped again to the lower deck. The copter gave up its fight, plunging downward, its body gyrating opposite the propellers' rotating circle. It smashed into the water, its blades chopping the waves in a stubborn last gasp before disappearing.

"Mr. Žăk, you got the pilot." I winked.

He nodded.

Kharkov maneuvered us around the *Miss Mio*, fire now blanketing the deck. The name of the boat burned away, its hull disintegrating. She would sink in seconds. "Cut the engines," Hrubý yelled. All grew quiet except for crackling flames.

Eddie and Marconi met Hrubý near the ladder. "Where's Danny?" Eddie called.

I shrugged. "Don't know. I haven't seen him on

deck since the fire started."

"Damn." Eddie shuffled down the ladder and stood next to me. "Hey, Stepan, tell Kharkov to circle one more time. Let's make sure."

We could do nothing else. The *Miss Mio* disappeared, her flames consumed as she vanished under the waves.

Eddie pounded his fist on the rail. "Dammit, dammit."

Marconi leaned her head against Hrubý.

Talích dashed from the command room. "Commander? To your left—one hundred meters." A square white object bobbed in the waves with a man holding on, his arms wrapped around it, and his chin resting on top.

Kharkov eased us toward the figure.

We drew close, and I shoved a pole into the water. Keaka grabbed it with one hand, holding himself against the Styrofoam chest with his other arm.

Hrubý helped me pull him in, grabbing his shirt and yanking him on deck.

Eddie kneeled next to him. "Danny? You look like hell."

Keaka rolled onto his back. "Thanks, old friend. You, too. Now be a good sport and grab the chest. I saved the beer."

****

Hrubý and Talích took care of Olan's body, wrapping him in towels and carrying him out of sight into the boat's storage room. Žák swept the control room's shattered glass, found a sponge, and mopped away as much blood as possible.

Keaka reviewed the *Lanakila's* controls with

Kharkov, and we were on our way. Despite his levity when we pulled him from the water, Keaka excused himself into one of the two lower deck sleeping quarters and closed the door. Eddie seated himself at the conference table, waiting for his old buddy, who had lost two of his friends on the same day.

I rejoined the others, all packed into the control room. Our route had taken us into the dark skies rolling toward us from the west. At first, light showers grew fierce, and the wind drove moisture through the control room's broken window.

Kharkov wiped his face and grimaced. "Commander, we may have hours of this. Marshal Keaka programmed the route. But can someone find the weather? Surely, we have a radar on a boat with this sophistication. Could we get current conditions to Honolulu?"

We all shuffled about in the tight space. Marconi raised her arms and shoved her way to the door. "Hey … hey, guys. I'll join Eddie downstairs. We tried to keep it quiet down there, but I'm getting claustrophobic. Henry? Want to join me?"

"I'm good. I'll see what I can do to help," I said.

Hrubý bumped me. "I'll join you, Angela. You need comforting."

Kharkov chuckled, bringing a shoulder grab by Žăk. "Pay attention, Mr. Kharkov. They have programmed the route, but you need to keep yourself engaged."

"Yes, sir. So … has anyone found the radar?"

Žăk pointed to a green screen on Kharkov's right. "It is right here."

"I see. I should have noticed."

"What do you make of it, Mr. Kharkov?" Talích asked. "We appear to be moving toward the dark green streak."

"Yes … directly. It is between O'ahu and us. A rough ride is coming, and I can do nothing to avoid it other than turn back and try to outrun it."

Žăk stepped outside and squinted in the rain. "I must inform Commander Hrubý. Mr. Kharkov, please do your best, but do not change course unless you hear from us."

Kharkov leaned toward me. "Review the map and tell me how far we are from Honolulu."

The complicated instruments confused me, so I guessed. "We passed the west side of Moloka'i five minutes ago. We have an open sea for thirty nautical miles before reaching the coast of O'ahu. From there, another seven miles to Honolulu's port." I touched Kharkov's arm. "You don't look so good, Vitaly."

Kharkov wiped his face. "On a calm day, we would reach Honolulu in less than two hours. I will have to slow us through the storm, though. The squall line is not wide, but the sea will be heavy, and I cannot risk pushing us too fast. Lieutenant Talích?"

Talích had rolled the tail of his tank top into a ball, trying to squeeze out the water. "Yes?"

"Please advise everyone downstairs of our situation. I would suggest Marshal Keaka take the helm, as I do not wish to guide a large boat through heavy seas, especially considering I am a virgin steering such a craft."

I laughed. "You're losing that today. Let me try to talk to them. Hang on for a minute." I slipped through the doorway.

Despite my better instincts, I grabbed the rail and pulled my way forward to the *Lanakila's* bow. The swells crested near ten feet or two-thirds up the gray hull and would likely worsen as we traveled through the squall. I pivoted and lost my grip on the slick metal rail. We tossed to the starboard side, causing me to lose my footing, sliding toward the water as if skating on an ice rink. I slammed against the outside wall of the control room, grasping for anything to stop me from going overboard. A hand appeared and grabbed my arm.

Talích held on to the hatch's door frame with one arm and to Žăk with the other. Žăk stretched to pull me in, then slipped onto his rear but never let go. He pulled while I flopped myself like a fish toward them. His muscled arm dragged me near Talích. We both got to our feet, and Talích pulled us back into the control room.

Talích shouted. "What in hell were you doing, Henry Pierce?"

I wiped my face with my drenched sleeve. "I wanted to report on the ocean conditions but see first for myself." A massive wave smashed across the bow.

"You could have been shark food." Žăk crossed his arms and shot me a glare. "I suggest you follow through and report to our superiors. No more stunts."

I backed out of the control room and then grabbed the hatch leading down to the conference room. Hanging on while I circled down the ladder, I heard Keaka and Hrubý bickering with raised voices. Five steps from the bottom, I stuck my head under the bulkhead. Marconi noticed me. "Hey, Henry, how's it going? You're a little wet there."

"I noticed. Danny? How are you doing?"

"I'm making it."

"I almost went overboard trying to get down here, and Kharkov is close to another anxiety attack steering this thing. We're moving into a storm line, according to the radar. I think we need an experienced captain to do this."

Keaka ran his hands through his hair. "It'll pass quickly."

I grabbed the back of Keaka's chair.

"Not so easy, Danny. You need to come topside and give us directions, at least."

"Come on, Ike. Give the man his space," Eddie said.

"I don't think y'all are grasping our situation," I said. "Danny, I know it's tough, but we need you topside right now."

Keaka slammed his fist on the black Formica. "It's only a damn squall."

"Tell Kharkov to turn off the engines, and we'll ride it out," Eddie said.

Keaka leaned his head back and closed his eyes, ignoring us for a moment. "It's okay, Eddie." He groaned while pushing his chair against me, stood, then slapped my shoulder. "Come on, braddah. It's time for me to save lives ... again." The ship shifted thirty degrees hard to starboard—the cabinet doors popped open, plastic water bottles flying from the shelves.

Eddie grabbed onto the table. "Hurry, Danny."

Keaka smiled. "Stepan, I'll send your men down except Kharkov. Braddah Henry, you're with me. Eddie, if you feel queasy, come up top. Hang near the hatch so you can at least view the horizon. If that doesn't work ... get a barf bag, which goes for all of you. This won't take long, but it'll be rough."

Keaka and I found our footing and stepped into the control room. He shoved Kharkov away from the wheel. We had to shout over the noise of the thunder and heavy seas. "You're shredding it, Vitaly, doing good. I'll take over now, but please stand behind me."

"Vitaly?" I asked. "The anxiety meds are working?"

"Yes, yes, I will not faint. Marshal Keaka, note the rainwater is seeping into everything. I would like to have plastic or something over this broken window."

"You can try. There are trash bags down below, but you will have to get creative to attach them. The rain has drenched everything."

"Yes, as I already said." Kharkov disappeared through the hatch.

Keaka scanned the radar, then glanced over his shoulder and smiled. "Hang loose, braddah. I'm changing course. I've got an idea."

"Where?"

"We're six miles west of Moloka'i. I know a nice bay back there where we can anchor for a bit. The squall line will move south of there, and we can get situated … figure out what's broken. The radio is on the fritz—bullet holes if you'll look there. I'll try to message my friends in Honolulu and update them."

"And the *Müller*? Won't she dock before us? What if the people we're looking for disembark before we get there?"

Keaka pushed us hard to port, causing me to slip and grab onto his seat. He grinned, showing the space in his teeth. "Quit worrying for now. The *Müller* can plow her way through this storm, but it will slow her down, too. If I can get through to my buddies, they can drag their feet on ship inspections. There's usually a line to dock, so the *Müller* will have to wait its turn."

"You're a sly fox, Danny."

"A fox? Nah. But maybe an old dog with a few tricks left."

Keaka was prescient as usual. Twenty minutes northeast, we drifted into a cove surrounded by Moloka'i's cliffs. The sun shone, and the stormy skies charged to the southeast.

Kharkov's plastic bag fix had not been helpful and was now not needed. He brooded for a minute until the sunshine brought out a brilliant smile, his face showing his slight sunburn. "Finally."

Everyone else emerged, squinting into the afternoon sun.

"Wonderful job, Danny," Eddie shouted. "Any other time, I'd say, let's leave the *Müller* to someone else and hang out in this bay for the rest of the day."

Hrubý reciprocated with one of his icy stares.

Marconi had pulled a cushion up from the lower deck and stretched across it. "Eddie, I know you're joking, but look at my t-shirt. It has blood on it still. And Marshal Olan's body …"

Eddie groaned. "I know, I know. It's been a helluva three-hour cruise."

Chapter Seven

We sailed by Pearl Harbor as the sun set, then maneuvered past three cruise ships harbored near Waikiki Beach. Keaka verified the container ship *Müller* had docked, and he confirmed his plans to question the crew over its manifest.

A hearse met us at the dock to pick up Olan's body. Keaka went ashore, and two uniformed U.S. Marshals met him on the pier. He glanced at us, gave us an okay sign before a U.S. Marshal opened the back of their SUV, handed Keaka a change of clothes, and pulled a shotgun and three rifles from the back seat. Keaka slumped into the middle to change, stuffed his dirty clothes in a bag, and grabbed a gun.

Keaka waved us down to the dock. "Welcome to Honolulu," he said after we came ashore. He shoved the butt of a shotgun into my chest—Hrubý and his men carried rifles from the *Lanakila*. He handed Marconi a fresh white t-shirt and winked at Eddie, giving him a purple O'ahu t-shirt. "I hope it's big enough, and you're too old for this, friend. I wish for you to stay here and monitor our communications." He nodded to another of the marshals who raised the trunk of his sedan, showing a load of electronics. "Seriously, Eddie, I've assigned everyone else to the ship. I need someone here to listen to our comms. And if it sounds like things are not going well, call 9-1-1."

Marconi elbowed Eddie. "Is he serious?"

Eddie stifled a grin. "Sure."

Keaka smiled. "Angie, if you like, join the marshals in questioning the crew. You might hear something of interest, yeah?"

"I will. Thanks, Danny."

Keaka kissed two fingers, then pointed. "You two take care. Everyone else, follow me."

I hesitated but asked, "What's more important, Danny, looking for people or gold coins?"

Keaka whispered, "People for us. Not sure what Hrubý prefers."

A three-minute walk brought us to a flurry of activity near the gangplank of a massive yellow and red container ship. Keaka's friends maneuvered bright klieg-type lights along the dock, highlighting streaks of rust stretching vertically every few feet from the deck to the waterline. Six U.S. Marshals circled a group of nine detained men.

Keaka and I, and Hrubý and his men hustled up the sloping entrance into a murky cargo hold. Kharkov and I teamed together, turned to our left, and hurried down a passageway.

Kharkov halted, causing us to collide. He leaned his rifle against the wall and glanced at his phone. "Mr. Žăk says they are proceeding into the main hold." He dropped his phone back into his shirt pocket. "I wish we had our regular communication headsets. Otherwise, it is hard to connect with certainty."

The ship's internal lighting either didn't function or was nonexistent in this area. We pointed our flashlights ahead and pressed into the darkness.

"You called him *Mr.* Žăk? Shouldn't I be Mr. Žích,

as you called me in Prague?" I asked.

"This is not a sanctioned mission, we are not in Prague, and you do not get to use that name."

"Fine. But seriously, I know we need to recover the dukats, but it's secondary. The people not listed on the manifest … shouldn't they be our focus? Has Commander Hrubý lost sight of that?"

He paused again. "Your words are not a correct characterization of Commander Hrubý's thinking. Crippling the organization's finances is one way to hurt it, and you understood the discussion of east Asian involvement. A successful alliance between Kurić and elements of the Chinese government would be horrific, considering Kurić has already functioned as an intermediary between the Serbian government and the Chinese—"

"General Shai, you mean," I said. "I wonder how many of his superiors know?"

"Wait." Kharkov's arm slammed against my chest. He pressed a finger to his lips.

I leaned toward him and whispered. "What?"

"Footsteps." We pointed our flashlights toward the same spot down the passageway.

I nodded. "Nothing." We stepped forward.

"Stop." I spun toward him, hearing metal scraping metal. "Are we imagining things?" I asked.

"Then we both imagined it, like something opened or closed."

"I noticed two hatches twenty yards back."

Kharkov groaned. "We should go look … I guess." He turned and shuffled back down the passageway, me following closely.

"So … your anxiety meds, Vitaly?"

"Yes."

"Can I have one?"

"No."

"Look … there on the left," I said.

Kharkov slapped the wall. "No. It is a steel plate, not a hatch." He crashed to the floor, falling on top of his rifle and his flashlight rolling down the passage.

Two eyes glared at me through my flashlight beam. I swatted at them, but a violent blow smashed me against the bulkhead. A body shoved past me, and hurried footsteps echoed in the dark.

"Vitaly?"

He held his head while grabbing his flashlight, then stood and swayed as if dizzy. "I am okay. The safety on my rifle is off. I am glad it did not discharge."

"My shotgun buried itself in my back when someone pushed me." I pointed down the hall. "The footsteps went aft."

Kharkov nodded. "And that sound?"

"I heard it, too. Metal scraping on something again."

He threw me a sideways glance. "A rusty hatch opening or closing."

We marched back down the passageway as fast as we dared—no sign of our attacker. A solid bulkhead reared ahead of us. "Dead end," I said. "A ghost knocked us down?"

Kharkov pointed his flashlight above us, tilting its beam up and down the wall. "Russian ghost stories are worse. So, this man had to go somewhere. Look up. There are two ladders—one on each side here. We will divide and conquer. Message me when you can."

"I will. Eyes wide open."

****

I stepped onto the steel-mesh ladder's top step—a humming sound grew louder. I followed the noise into another dim passageway. One light bulb hugged the ceiling encased in a lattice-like cover, and the remnants of a second one hung in the dark a few feet away. The area smelled of mold until something dripped on my shoulder with the heavy odor of diesel fuel. To my right, another steel hatch, this one with a wheeled device to open and shut it, its chrome finish gleaming from years of use. Seven lime-green lockers lined the wall on my left, all closed and padlocked. I pulled my vibrating phone from my pocket. *All clear so far,* Kharkov messaged, and I responded likewise.

The wheel wouldn't turn with one hand. I shoved my phone back into my pants pocket, hugged my gun, and placed my flashlight on the floor. A slight turn of the wheel surprised me with a loud squeal—I wouldn't surprise anyone now. Two more tries and it rotated enough to release the door from the bulkhead. Pulling harder, I caused another screech of metal on hinges as the hatch opened into blackness. My flashlight offered only a narrow beam into the void. Stepping over the threshold, I pointed the light straight ahead while lugging my shotgun under my right armpit.

Turning in a slow circle in the square room, I noticed a ceiling of ten or so feet. Broken wood slats occupied a corner, likely old storage crates. Someone had dropped a man's raincoat in the opposite corner—a pair of alligator shoes rested next to the mound, draped by cuffed khaki pants. Was there movement? I adjusted my light upward and noticed a belt holding up the pants. A hand filled the left front pocket, the other jerked upward, and a pair of fluorescent lights blinked. The man yanked a pistol from his front pocket and pointed it at me.

"Put the gun on the floor, then kick toward me. And make no moves. I am proficient with this pistol."

I did as told.

"American?" he asked.

"Yes. And you are?"

He ignored my question. "You walked through the passageway with a Russian, it sounded. Interesting pair." He spoke with a heavy accent—a familiar one. "What are you doing here? What's your business with this ship?" He looked about fifty years old, a brooding face with a slightly graying, unkempt beard and light-brown hair topped with a … fedora.

I had no reason to be coy. "I'm working with the U.S. Marshals Office. We've boarded the ship to investigate a falsified manifest. My colleagues are searching the ship for contraband. Once we complete our investigation, the ship can be on its way. You should aim your gun elsewhere."

"And you should be more concerned about yourself. Your friends are irrelevant, and why would it bother me? My employer has long tentacles … more than you can imagine."

"My friends are familiar with your organization."

He tilted his head and gazed at my face.

"See something you like?"

He sneered. "Hardly. Your face … seems familiar."

"We haven't met."

"I did not say we have met. I have seen a picture. Tell me your name." He raised his hand, and a shot exploded toward the ceiling, the bullet ricocheting twice. He stepped closer and pointed the pistol at my head. "Tell me, or I will splatter your brains."

"Henry Pierce."

"Pierce? I was correct then," he said.

"How do you know me?" His face didn't remind me of anyone, but his voice offered something I couldn't quite remember.

He breathed heavily through his mouth. "I am Karanos Tasev … Junior. You killed my father."

I shuddered. The accent and the fedora should have been obvious. "The Macedonian?"

"Yes … we are Macedonian."

"Northern or Southern?"

"Do not be stupid. We are not Greek."

"Northern then. Your old man died a natural death. A heart attack," I said.

Even through the dim fluorescent light, his face seemed to redden. "Because of your efforts to bind him. My sources tell me you attacked my father at an apartment—"

"Your sources are wrong. The old man and his friends kidnapped one of my colleagues. I wanted information."

He shoved his pistol to my temple. "I hope it is worth your life."

"Why are you here?" I asked.

He hesitated at my question and pulled the gun back.

"And I will ask you the same. Does your Virginia police department not have enough for you to do? Vienna, Prague … now Hawaii?"

"You know all that? I'm here for a—"

"Don't bother lying. It is Czech law enforcement again, is it not? I heard your words with the Russian. They make themselves pests, buzzing around, causing trouble. The commander … his name?"

I didn't respond.

"No matter. It is Hrubý. It is always Hrubý. Did he tell you of his father's acquaintance with my father?"

"Can't say he has," I said, wondering what had happened to Kharkov or anyone else.

"Stepan is like his father—always getting in the way."

"I know nothing of his father."

"Professor Valentýn Hrubý. An underground agent in Prague in the late 1960s, he abused his position as a physics professor at *Univerzita Karlova*. He and others shoveled secrets to the west and took part in the so-called Prague Spring. The Soviets pressured President Husák, who ordered the Czech State Security to end it. The government contracted my father to … assist."

"An assassin," I said.

"A harsh word, but correct, I suppose. My father had an exceptionally lengthy career, which included the elimination of Professor Hrubý and many others. The Czech underground succumbed, and with it, the remnants of the Prague Spring. President Husák grew appreciative, of course. My father's abilities were legendary, and after the fall of the communists, he returned to another organization."

"Kurić."

"Yes, yes, excellent for you, *Detective* Pierce. He helped found the organization, you know, and functioned as a coordinator of its operations. As he grew older, my father redirected his efforts to …

facilitate other projects." He smiled. "Yes, yes, facilitate projects for the Kurić organization … until you ended it." He waved the pistol's barrel in front of my nose. "You see, Hrubý and I are not that different. We both want retribution for our fathers' deaths. The commander can pretend he is chasing gold coins, but this, ultimately, is about revenge."

"I think you misjudge him to your disadvantage," I said.

Tasev chuckled. "But you will never know. You will be dead." He cocked the gun's trigger, pulled an orange scarf from his back pocket, and smiled. "You have made this too easy. I will disable you, then strangle you like the others … number thirty … a nice round number."

"It was you that strangled the men on the beach and in the crater?"

"Of course. Like father, like son. And those men were getting in my way. I do not like informants, and the U.S. Marshal followed us from …. Oh no, Detective Pierce, I almost volunteered more than I should have."

A screech. The wheel turned, catching Tasev's attention. I dove for his legs, and we both fell to the floor, wrestling for his weapon. A shot ricocheted again. I grabbed his gun and tossed it toward the moving door.

He seized my throat with both hands. "My revenge," he shouted, "for my father."

I choked. "He deserved it."

The hatch swung inward, and Vitaly Kharkov stepped through, pointing his rifle at Tasev. "*Zapre*. I will shoot."

Tasev hesitated, then released his grip. Kharkov

kicked the pistol into a corner.

"Just in time, Vitaly," I said.

"Luck follows me today," he said. "I found nothing on my search, so I came your way. I started back down the ladder when a gunshot echoed, and voices followed." He kicked at our prisoner's feet. "This man's accent—Karanos Tasev, I presume?"

Tasev glared.

"I want you to stand, your back to us, and march straight ahead until your face is against the wall. Do not turn your head."

I helped Tasev to his feet and gave him a shove to the wall. "He figured out my name. He wants to avenge his father or some such."

Kharkov grinned. "Well, Tasev, it seems the revenge is mine. Your father and his associates took me into an apartment and left me—"

Tasev yelled and dove for the pistol. I grabbed my gun as he rolled over and aimed.

A shot erupted from Kharkov's rifle. Tasev screamed. His left pant leg burst into red, a bloodstain expanding along his shin.

"Nice shot," I said.

Kharkov dropped his hands to his side. "I have never had to do that."

I touched his shoulder. "You saved us both."

He nodded. "I must tell Commander Hrubý."

Tasev moaned, then shouted. "*Majka ti bea kurvi.*"

"What did he say?" I asked.

"He questions our mothers' marital status when we were born, and he is threatening us."

"Tasev, I wouldn't try anything, or my friend will shoot your other leg," I said. "In the meantime, Vitaly,

I'll check those lockers in the hall. Keep watch."

"You think the coins are in there?"

"Tasev lurked here for a reason." I stepped past the doorway, aimed Tasev's small-caliber Czech pistol at the first locker, and fired. The padlock burst, but this locker held nothing. Three more shots, then the jackpot. The fourth locker harbored twenty rectangular, blue-gray pewter containers, the same as those we seized in Prague. Each had the Yugoslav royal family crest carved into the otherwise smooth lids. I slid the tops back on each container, and it appeared the 1930s gold coins filled their pewter homes.

Multiple steps plodded and echoed from the stairwell. I shut the locker, leaving the other containers, and rejoined Kharkov. "Someone's coming," I said. We pushed ourselves against the bulkhead next to the hatch, guns ready. The hinges squealed, and a foot in a brown loafer stepped over the threshold.

"Henry Pierce? Where are you?" Keaka asked. I peered around the door and found Hrubý standing behind him. "Well, braddah, you and Mr. Kharkov have taken care of another one of our problems."

Hrubý hurried over to our prisoner, kicked Tasev's wounded shin, gave a sideways glance to Keaka, then stopped himself from delivering a second blow to the leg. Keaka searched Tasev, finding something in his left pants pocket. "Airline ticket booked for tomorrow—Honolulu, Shanghai, then to Dubai, and finally, Skopje."

"Quite the tourist," Keaka said.

I handed him a pewter box. "There are nineteen more of these in the middle locker out there."

"Twenty boxes?" Hrubý asked. "Only a small

portion of what we thought, then."

Keaka slid back the lid and blew a whistle. "Nice and shiny. Good deal, braddah. Our next step is to figure out ownership. My contact said the State Department is eager to get involved."

I replied with a wink. "I'm sure they're our best and brightest."

Keaka rolled his eyes. "No doubt."

"Did you find the Chinese men we believed on board?" Kharkov asked.

Keaka nodded. "Yeah, we searched the ship. The crew acted clueless the whole time, but we found two men hiding in a women's restroom. Lieutenant Talích is holding them."

"Did they have anything to say?" I asked.

"They whipped out their passports and claimed diplomatic immunity. They didn't impress me as diplomats, but we'll hold them overnight in our facility on the northwest side of O'ahu. Tomorrow, we'll turn them over to the Chinese legation's office near Diamond Head."

"Maybe they will offer something before then?" Kharkov asked.

Keaka nodded. "Could be, but we don't want to cause an incident. And speaking of the women's restroom, it sat across the passageway from an area where we believed we heard a woman crying. We found a section of the ship with twenty Hispanic underage women closed together in a tiny room. Human trafficking. One of the women told us they had been kidnapped, then loaded on board in Panama."

"Harboring fugitives, smuggling, and trafficking in humans. It sounds like this ship will stay here for a while," I said.

Keaka nodded. "Yep. The *Müller* is now the property of the U.S. Marshals. Stepan, I can arrange for you and your men to return to Maui tonight. We have access to a five-passenger Beechcraft that can get you there before midnight. I'll let Angie decide if she will return with you. Eddie already told me he is staying an extra day."

"We will welcome the opportunity," Hrubý said.

"What happened to your informant?" I asked.

"Unknown," Hrubý answered. "He is not on board, and shipmates offered no information."

Tasev mocked us through his pain. "He does not swim well."

Keaka hesitated, then placed a hand on Hrubý's shoulder. "Could I borrow your men … Mr. Žák, at least? I have McNelly's help for another day, but the other marshals must go back to their regular assignments."

"Of course," Hrubý said. "And Tasev? I would like to … talk with him."

Keaka closed an eye. "Well … he needs medical attention, but he is a foreign national who threatened American law enforcement. After we fix his leg, I'm taking him up to the Coconut Castle."

Hrubý scowled. "A castle?"

Keaka winked. "No moats, but a special place for O'ahu law enforcement. After you leave the ship, ask for Marshal McNelly. He'll take you directly to an airstrip eight miles northwest of here. I'll arrange for Angie and the others."

"Thank you." He and Kharkov hurried down the stairs, pounding each step as they descended.

Tasev groaned. "Listen to me, Henry Pierce. You have taken someone away from me. I will do the same for you."

Keaka laughed. "Whatever, man. A lame guy sitting in a jail cell isn't a threat, yeah? Braddah Henry, come with me tonight. I'll see what Eddie wants to do—he might join us."

"For what?" I asked.

"A trip up the mountains to our lair, to a place on the slopes of Kaála."

"Your party place?"

He winked. "Sometimes. Tonight, we'll have Chinese food."

Chapter Eight

I leaned hard against the Jeep's heavy canvas passenger door. "How much farther?"

Keaka grinned. "You need to pee?"

"No … well, yeah, but you know the way, right?" We came out of the tight curve directly into another. "I'm getting a little queasy. Good thing Eddie didn't come."

"You hold, braddah. Eddie wanted a little downtime to talk to his new bride. McNelly told me Eddie found a cheap hotel a half-mile from Waikiki. Anyway, we're nearby … I think."

"You think?"

"Dude, it's dark. I'm following the van's taillights in front of us. McNelly knows the way, but it's my first time at night. Take it easy and look to your right. You can see the lights from the towns down in the valleys."

My eyes darted right, then straight ahead. "Yeah, it's great. So, how high are we going?"

"The summit of Kaála is near four thousand feet and houses an FAA facility. Our castle is on a slope at thirty-eight hundred feet. The best thing is the nice, cool nights."

"I bet." I grabbed the dash as we rounded another curve. "So … you have a castle?" We slowed, and the van in front of us turned right, bouncing onto a gravel road.

"You'll see," Keaka said. Our jeep followed and rocked along on the pebbly lane, the route near black except for our vehicles' headlights piercing the night. The leading van slowed, then took a hard-right turn onto a crumbling cement driveway, its lights finding a building a hundred feet ahead. The van suddenly stopped, so Keaka pulled us to the left and killed the engine. "Here we are, Henry Ike Pierce. Coconut Castle."

"This? It looks like an old machine gun nest from the war." The square-shaped facility showed a structure of cinderblocks and cement with dark green paint peeling and flaking onto the overgrown jungle floor. An emplacement on the roof must have been where a weapon had nestled during the war.

Keaka grinned and slid out of his seat, then turned toward me. He made a sucking sound through the space in his teeth and smiled. "Good guess. It had an anti-aircraft gun on the roof and an underground bunker for the governor and other big wigs. They built it after the Pearl Harbor attack. Come on, the inside is nicer. I'll show you around after we unload our prisoners."

McNelly and Žăk stepped to the back of the first van, opened the doors, and pulled out the three prisoners, their hands still handcuffed behind their backs. Both vehicles' headlights lit our way, and each man guided their guests past the left side of the structure.

Keaka stopped, unlocked a metal box on the wall, and threw a switch. Floodlights burst bright around us, the glow of the lights offering a look behind the building. A well-maintained garden surrounded a rectangular, dented tin door lying flat on the ground—I assumed it protected an underground entrance. An enormous, rust-colored padlock connected the door handle to a steel notch embedded in a concrete block lying half-buried in the dirt.

Tasev threw an elbow and squirmed away from McNelly. Žăk kicked Tasev in the butt, smashing his face into a light post before McNelly grabbed Tasev's shoulders. "Thank you, Mr. Žăk."

Tasev spat blood on the ground. "What are you doing with us? I am a foreign national. You cannot treat me this way."

One of the Chinese men backed away from Žăk, but the skinny prisoner had no chance. "My government will not appreciate this treatment."

"I'm not concerned with your government," Keaka said. He patted the man on his back. "Maybe the U.S. Marshals should go public, showing you two have something to do with smuggling and human trafficking. What would your government think?"

The prisoner glanced at his partner. "We had nothing to do with trafficking."

"So only the smuggling?"

The prisoner glared, then gazed at his feet.

McNelly motioned toward me with his head. "Detective Pierce? Take this key off my belt. Please turn off the headlights on our vehicles. On the way back, lock the circuit box, too, then open the big padlock for us."

"Should I lock up your cars?" I asked.

"Yes, great," Keaka said.

I did so and hurried back. The padlock looked the size of my fist, but it slid open with only a slight twist. "Hang on to the key, Pierce," McNelly said. "When we get situated, we'll use the padlock to lock us in for the night. Now, you pull the door up and loop the rope over the pole to your left. Tie a good knot."

The door wasn't as heavy as it looked. I hauled it up, tied the rope in a loop over the oxidizing pole, and stepped aside as everyone else descended the concrete stairs into the bunker. The inside lights were already on, and Keaka stopped on the third step and thumbed behind him. "Hey, braddah, pull the door behind us. I smell the nightly rain coming. See the iron half-circle coming out of the wall by the top step?"

"Yes."

"Lock us in." He leaned closer to me and whispered. "Your bedroom will be the third one to the right. There's a nail jabbed into the wall under the bathroom sink. Hang the key there. Out of sight, out of mind, right?"

"Sure. Why the secrecy, Danny?"

"If one of those goobers tries anything, we're all locked in together."

Four steps down, and I had to duck under a concrete buttress. The living area opened before me. Chrome and vinyl furniture seemed the decoration of choice, as in their other facilities. Two projection-style televisions rested next to one another, one with a carved wooden U.S. Marshals insignia perched on it and the other with a basket of assorted fake Hawaiian fruit. A ping-pong table squatted against a wall next to a lime-green fabric couch. Their dining room table featured four yellow-vinyl chairs arranged around it, one blocking the opening into the kitchenette. All the walls showed a faded army-green tint, so worn and stained it must have been the original paint.

I noticed two closed doors to the left—bedrooms, I guessed, and three doors on the right. Keaka shoved aside the vinyl chair and headed to the kitchenette, where he groaned, bending over while opening and closing cabinet doors. McNelly pulled Tasev into a bedroom, and Žăk followed, directing his two prisoners. McNelly raised his voice, followed by the prisoners' angrier responses. Žăk smiled at me as he exited. McNelly pulled a barred metal door closed behind him.

Tasev limped toward us and glared through the bars. "I will watch you, Pierce."

"Enjoy yourself."

McNelly grabbed the oak door's knob. "You might as well make yourself at home, Tasev. If you or your friends cause any trouble, we'll handcuff each of you to your beds. In the meantime, relax … take a nap, even. The bathroom is to the right of the closet. We'll feed and interview you shortly."

"Where is my fedora?"

"This is Hawaii. Try a cap," Keaka said.

McNelly slammed the door in Tasev's face.

Keaka pulled and pushed several pots thrown in a drawer under the stove. "Dammit. Never the right size. These three will have to do." He brought the pile to the sink and waited for the water to get hot. "Hey, Mr. Žăk, look at the top of the pantry. You'll find several bottles of my guava wine. I brought it here from my restaurant. Open two bottles for us since our beer stash has disappeared. McNelly?"

McNelly grinned and plopped himself on the couch. "I plead guilty."

Žăk, still dressed in his black tank top and red shorts, placed two bottles of wine on the counter. "I picked these, Marshal Keaka."

"Please call me Danny. Do I have to call you, *Mister* Žăk?" He winked. "Seems too formal down here." Keaka pulled a pineapple from the refrigerator, found a long knife, and cut away the husk.

I laughed. "It's an assigned name for work. An undercover name, if you will. He let me drop the *Mister* when we aren't working, right, Žăk?"

Žăk glanced at me with half a smile. "Yes, *Mister* Žích."

Keaka rolled his eyes. "Mr. Žích? Yeah, braddah, whatever. Žăk, the middle bedroom on your right … you can sleep there. Dig through the dresser. The bathroom has a shower. You'll find white t-shirts with our logo and several pairs of khaki shorts. Maybe something will fit you."

Žăk smiled. "Thank you. I welcome a shower. This day has been endless."

Keaka winked. "Make house, guys. Get comfortable."

****

Keaka's cooking rivaled his brothers' skills. He fed our group of five a mahi-mahi salad, the fish pulled from frozen packages stuffed in an upright freezer shoved in the corner of the first bedroom. We had all showered and eaten, but our day continued. Keaka took another turn at the stove and prepared several Chinese dishes for two of our guests. McNelly guided them to the table.

"Have a seat, Mr. Liang, Mr. Tseung. Sit to my right," Keaka said.

They acted famished, offering no comments. Žăk leaned back from the table, munching on macadamia nuts while the two prisoners and Keaka devoured their meals. Since we had not handcuffed the two while they ate, McNelly and I stood nearby, making a visible show of our pistols. The meal finished, Žăk cleared the table.

Keaka pulled a cigarette and stuck it in the gap between his teeth. "So, gentlemen, apparently the food is tolerable. We have no leftovers."

Tseung showed a slight smile. "Excellent. Your skills are commendable."

Liang glared at his comrade.

"Let's get started," Keaka said. "You both have sufficient knowledge of English, yeah?"

Neither man commented.

"But to make myself clear, *Wô huí shè nî de pìgu.* If you behave, I'll leave you uncuffed for the time being. Do we have an understanding?"

They both nodded.

"What did you say?" I asked.

He turned and smiled. "I said I would shoot their asses."

Liang leaned back and crossed his arms. "We did not know you spoke Chinese."

Keaka grinned. "I've understood most everything you've said since we detained you."

Liang frowned. "Why did you bring us to this facility? I do not believe we are in Honolulu, as the night air is much cooler than it would be near a beach."

"Very observant, Mr. Liang. We are on the slope of a mountain. Lucky for you, we're only forty-five minutes away from your government's consulate in Honolulu. However, your quick release depends on your ability to offer me the information I need."

Liang leaned forward and sneered. "Hawaii will be

ours someday."

Tseung frowned at his associate. "At the moment, however, we are prisoners, Liang. I would suggest no further ugliness. But may I ask something?"

Keaka nodded.

"What do you think you are doing bringing us here? What will your state department think of you pulling two Chinese citizens from a ship and then detaining us in an unknown facility? Is this your extraordinary—"

"No, it's not extraordinary rendition." Keaka flicked salt granules off the table. He glanced up. "I've been in touch with my contacts at the Department of State. They are aware of your status and that you're in our custody, and they are interested in knowing why you were aboard the ship since neither of you showed on its manifest. They have also communicated with the Honduran embassy concerning the women we found locked away on the *Müller*. And then the matter of the stolen gold coins on board—"

Liang slammed a fist on the table. "It is the Macedonian's responsibility."

McNelly pulled his gun and stepped closer. Žăk rose from his seat.

"Careful, Mr. Liang. Marshal McNelly is excitable." Keaka pulled the unlit cigarette from his mouth and dropped it into the ashtray. "So, again, it sounds like you knew of the coins?"

Liang and Tseung leaned back again in their chairs.

Keaka grinned. "So, let's move forward. How do you know the Macedonian?" They offered nothing. "Either of you?"

More silence.

"Here's what I believe—you're appended to a Chinese government apparatus. You report to a General Shai, head of the People's Liberation Army Unit 61398."

Liang's face flushed, then he swallowed hard. "I have never heard of him or this PLA unit."

Tseung interlocked his fingers and stared at Liang.

"We must disagree," Keaka said. "An efficient unit, we are told, and General Shai may appear later in our conversations."

"Later?" Tseung asked. "Earlier, you led us to believe our release to our consulate would be at 8:00 a.m. tomorrow morning."

"I'm aware, Mr. Tseung," Keaka answered. He picked up the unlit cigarette. "Marshal McNelly? Can you check the fax machine in my room and find out if our information has come in?"

"Sure, boss." McNelly holstered his gun and left the table.

Žăk stepped closer behind our guests.

"You still fax things, Danny?" I asked.

"No choice. Internet service … email is intermittent up here." Keaka placed his palms on the table and fanned his fingers. "My law enforcement ties are fewer than they used to be, but I still have several friends in the Honolulu branch of the FBI."

McNelly returned from a bedroom, holding several sheets of paper. He leaned near Keaka's ear and whispered for several seconds. Nodding, Keaka took the faxed pages, yanked his reading glasses off his collar, and spread the four pages apart.

Tseung strained his eyes, trying for a quick glimpse of the information.

"Interesting." Keaka held faxed photos of our two Chinese guests sitting at an outside tabletop. "Recognize these two faces?"

They glanced at one another. Liang smirked. "Very handsome gentlemen. Would you like more poses?"

"So, you confirm it's you and Mr. Tseung?" Keaka asked.

Silence.

"Good to know. These photos are from a Viennese coffee shop."

"We have been to Vienna," Liang said. "Is this a grand discovery on your part? We could have told you. We have visited other European capitals."

"Detective Pierce? Can you tell our guests what the coffee shop sits next to?" Keaka asked.

I glanced over Tseung's shoulder. "It looks familiar. Wait … I've been there … in March. That's where I met Vitaly Kharkov for the first time at Dr. Müller's … wait, the same Müller …"

"*Mahalo*, braddah." Keaka cradled his unlit cigarette between two fingers. "Gentlemen, don't you think it's ironic you drank coffee and enjoyed yourselves next to a Dr. Müller's office, then three months later, you're sailing on a cargo ship named the *Müller* registered to the same man? Anything you want to offer?"

Liang smiled. "Our export business requires our travel to many places."

"Of course." Keaka dropped his cigarette into the ashtray again and picked up another faxed page. "Our information shows you two traveled from Shanghai to Belgrade, then Vienna and Prague in April. You made your way to Bremerhaven, Germany, and boarded the

Müller on May fifteenth. After a stop in the Azores, for who knows what? Then you arrived in Kahului on June first." He peered over his reading glasses to catch any reaction from the two. "And now, here you are with us." Keaka smiled.

Liang rested his chin on a hand. "We are very busy … as I said."

"Oh, it's good to stay busy. But here's my idea. We've learned of a transaction by the Serbian government that sold old gold coins worth tens of millions of euros. According to my sources, someone sold the coins almost two years ago to a multinational syndicate controlled by the Serb war criminal, Miomir Kurić. Her criminal organization sought to destroy the Euro with a counterfeiting scheme, which, it seems, would have inflated the dukats' value—then they would sell the coins to the highest bidder. Your General Shai is a dilettante buyer of old monetary artifacts, and he sought to be a player in the international market for these coins." Keaka dropped his readers on the table, picked up the fax pages, and handed them to McNelly. "Does any of this sound familiar?"

Liang's cheeks reddened. "A nice, what do you say … fairy tale?"

Tseung stirred, then stared again at his lap.

Keaka stood and stretched his back. "Mr. Tseung? You have a comment?"

Tseung shook his head.

"I see. So, our other friend joining us this evening, Mr. Tasev, had airline tickets in his pants pocket." Keaka cut his eyes toward me. "Correct, Detective Pierce?"

I circled my right index finger along the edge of

my wineglass. "Yes. We found those after Mr. Kharkov shot him."

Keaka nodded. "And tell us his destinations."

"Tasev intended to stay in Honolulu until Friday, then on to Shanghai before other destinations."

Keaka smiled. He stood, stepped toward a TV, and grabbed a fake pineapple off it, tossing it several times. "Amazing how Shanghai keeps coming into this. A popular spot, Mr. Tseung?"

Tseung didn't respond.

"The People's Liberation Army Unit 61398, and your General Shai, are housed at Shanghai's main naval base. Another coincidence?"

Tseung sighed. "How do you know this?"

"And a black helicopter," I said. "Anyone you know fly copters?"

Liang ran his hands through his black hair. "I prefer SU-35s."

A buzzing sounded from one of McNelly's khaki pockets. He pulled out his phone, mumbled something, and pressed the screen. He nodded toward Keaka. "They're pulling in the drive."

Keaka returned his nod. "*Mahalo*, gentlemen. Thank you for visiting with us, and I hope you enjoyed your stay, but I don't have a survey form for you to complete." He stepped away to the kitchen and gestured at me.

Liang and Tseung appeared confused, as were Žăk and I. Moving around Keaka, I stood by the sink while he filled it with soap and water. "What's going on, Danny? You cut them off."

He cleared his throat and leaned closer toward me. "Yeah. Our guy in FBI-Honolulu was, what's the best word, admonished by people from the immigration service. The Chinese officials went straight to the U.S. State Department and demanded our new acquaintances' release."

I pulled open several drawers, looking for a dishtowel. "Convenient. There's always someone, somewhere, bailing out these types of guys."

Žăk chose a barstool across from us. "Information, please?"

"Right," Keaka said, leaning closer over the bar. "Twenty minutes ago, a U.S. government stooge ordered us to release these two to the immigration folks. Braddah Henry, unlock us, and we'll escort them to a maroon van waiting in the driveway. The people in it can stay there because I don't need the immigration folks to see these facilities. Marshal McNelly?"

"Yes, sir."

"I would like for you to follow our immigration friends back to Honolulu and make sure their destination is the Chinese consulate … to put my mind at ease." He winked. "Apparently, their authorities can't wait the eleven hours until tomorrow morning's scheduled release, which our government has bent over to help them … as always. And this after I went through the trouble to cook them dinner. Oh, and ask Eddie Stone if he wants to join us … and bring back a six-pack of Primo, yeah?"

McNelly winked. "Will do, sir."

I unlocked the door. Žăk pulled the Chinese men to their feet and motioned them to the stairs.

Keaka leaned farther over the bar and brushed off crumbs. He glared at our two prisoners as they approached the steps. "Another thing, gentlemen. Pass our greetings to whomever you work for and let them know … uh, we have twenty containers of their gold coins. No refunds."

Chapter Nine

I padlocked the door after McNelly left, then bumped my head again on the concrete buttress above the stairs' last step. Žăk had pulled the ping-pong table from the wall and searched through an oak chest for the paddles and balls. Keaka watched after pouring us another round of guava wine. "Hey, guys, feel free to play, but not too long. We still have the Macedonian jackass to talk to, and it's getting late."

Žăk motioned for me to join him.

I splashed my hands in the tepid water to wash off the sticky wine spilled when Keaka had poured. Slipping by Žăk, I took a position, paddle in hand. "So, what do you think of our first two guests, Danny?"

"I don't know. Let me ask you guys first."

Žăk spewed a Czech curse when he hit the table net for the third time in a row.

I sipped the wine and readied for Žăk's serve. "Someone is helping the Kurić organization in our government."

"I guessed that, too, braddah, and it's likely many someones. This round, the immigration boys jumped first."

Žăk cursed again, dropped his paddle, then flopped on the couch.

"Mr. Žăk, are you giving up?" I asked.

He shook his head. "I should not have even tried.

Petar was the best ping-pong player. I could never keep up." He flushed a bright shade of red.

I pounced at his blunder. "Petar? Mr. Žicǎn? His proper name was Petar?"

Žǎk rubbed his forehead. "No, no, no. Please do not tell Commander Hrubý. He would be furious."

Keaka snorted. "We won't … so tell us your name, and it will be even."

Žǎk hid his mouth, trying to hide a smile. "Živko," he said.

"Živko?" I asked.

He nodded. "It's an old family name."

"Wait a minute. Is this how you came up with naming people in your unit with a name starting with Z?"

He nodded again, and his eyes teared. "I should tell you the rest." Žǎk sighed. "Petar and I are … were … brothers." He wiped his face.

I patted his shoulder and smiled. "Not a surprise. I noticed a resemblance, but I figured the uniforms caused it."

Žǎk blew out a breath. "Please do not tell the commander of my mistake."

I drummed my fingers on the bar's yellowed countertops. "And I suppose you have a last name?"

"No." Žǎk scowled. "Revealing our last name may put our family in danger. Do not repeat my given name—I cannot tell you more."

Keaka rubbed his closed eyelids. "Understood, Mr. Žǎk. We'll leave it at that."

Tasev pounded on the door to our left and shouted.

"Ah, I guess our boy is hungry. Unfortunately, I don't know any Macedonian dishes."

"A loaf of bread?" I asked. "He'll bring the bologna."

"Agreed. Let's bring him out, but be vigilant, my friends. He gives me the chicken skin."

****

I chose a seat across from Tasev, and he volunteered much more than asked while he ate leftovers, especially stories about his father. He assumed we were interested, and the older Tasev had had quite a life. The Nazis had killed his parents, and he grew up in an orphanage after the war. He then found his way into criminal organizations operating in Greece and became infamous in southeast Europe for his assassinations. His killing M.O. included the capture and eventual strangulation of his victims with an orange scarf—and, as the younger Tasev had said, like father, like son. After the fall of the Iron Curtain, the Kurić organization used 'the Macedonian' for other activities. The organization employed him less for his aging skills as a killer than for his contact list running deep into many countries. Toward the end, the old man functioned as a mule, carrying euros for payoffs to associates of Kurić, a function he fulfilled when he met me … and my too powerful headlock.

Tasev, still breathing through his mouth, tried to wipe his lips with a napkin but dropped it onto his near-empty plate. McNelly loosened his handcuffs but left them fastened. He struggled to raise his fork. "Why could you not release my hands to eat?"

McNelly smirked. "Because."

I supported my chin with a hand and glanced at Tasev. "Somewhere in one of your long monologues, you've mentioned a cousin … female. What happened to her?"

"More Tasevs?" Keaka asked. "What are you guys … Skywalkers?"

Tasev glared. "Nothing happened to her. She is, oh, here and there. I'm the muscle, and she's the brains of the family. And there are others, too." He smiled. "So … am I officially charged with something?"

"Should we charge you with something?" I asked.

Tasev sneered. "I asked first."

Keaka snatched the near-empty plate, bumping it against Tasev's forehead. "Excuse, please." He lowered the plate into the sink and turned on the water for a moment. "Another dish to wash." Keaka came back around the bar, jerked a chair backward, and sat, staring at our guest. "So, you wonder if we'll charge you? Let's see … we found a man strangled on the beach with an orange cloth, we found a U.S. Marshal strangled in the Haleakalā crater, and someone attacked a U.S. Marshals' seacraft from a helicopter, which killed another one of my men, and then they sank my damn fishing boat. And the funny thing is, little orange scarves were everywhere, like the one we found on you."

Tasev grinned, a dreamy look in his eyes. "Orange is my favorite color, just like my father's. It brings good luck. Before working for the Greek syndicates, my father's family built a glass company after the First World War. His favorite things to produce were square glass paperweights … trendy items … trinkets, really. The orange ones were special, though—they glowed if the right person held them correctly." He smiled. "Each had names implanted in it. Stunning, but they had a limited production … regrettably." His eyes drifted back to the table.

"Glassmaker? And then an assassin?" I asked

Tasev seemed to float back into reality, then nodded. "And I do not know how to fly helicopters."

Keaka rested his chin on the back of the plastic chair. "It's a good thing. We shot back." He motioned with his head.

Žăk heaved Tasev to a stand, unlocked the handcuffs, pulled his hands behind his back, then relocked the cuffs. He pushed on Tasev's shoulders, forcing him to sit.

Tasev grimaced with the push, trying to get comfortable in his chair. "You can prove nothing."

I laughed and stepped behind him. "You admitted to me you killed those people."

The corners of his mouth turned upward. "No, you must be mistaken."

I grabbed his collar and bent over toward his right ear. "You showed me the orange scarf you strangled them with."

Keaka yanked on my sleeve and motioned for me to sit. "So, Tasev, like the captain of the *Müller* and a few of his men, your guilt is unquestionable, and I would guess you will spend many years in the United States … but, hopefully, not Hawaii."

"I have many friends, gentlemen. As I said, the organization has more like me … not only my cousins. All around Europe, we have a network my father passed to me. He raised his son well."

I crossed my arms. "He doesn't get it, Danny. He's sitting here in cuffs to be charged with multiple murders, and he thinks he'll walk away a free man … or should I say *limp* away?"

Keaka pointed to a big-screen television. "Mr. Žăk, please turn on the TV to the left. Someone busted the remote, but you'll find a button on the lower right of the unit."

Žăk did so, and the screen came alive—a black-and-white picture of a bedroom.

"Thank you. Tasev, I believe it's your bedtime. But don't get crazy … bad dreams and that type of thing." Keaka held up a thumb like a hitchhiker and pointed to the television. "You get your own bedroom, and as you can see, we'll be watching. Your lights will dim but not turn off completely. Mr. Žăk, please take our guest to his room and uncuff him. Pull the bars shut and then the wooden door after it. If he offers resistance, beat him like a rented mule."

Žăk grinned, pulled him up, and led him to his chamber. Tasev limped, offering us nothing else. Žăk slammed the door, and we lounged near the TV, watching our prisoner.

"Well, braddah, he's a damn boring dude. More wine, my friends?" Keaka asked.

Žăk shook his head.

"No, thanks," I said. "I could use a beer, though. When will McNelly return?"

Keaka glanced at his watch. "It's almost eleven o'clock. It won't be long … depending on what Eddie decided."

****

Heavy footsteps plodded down the stairs. Eddie Stone grinned as he peered around McNelly. "Hey, men, nice to see you again."

Near midnight, I had dozed off several times on the couch. Tasev had fallen asleep in his clothes on top of

127

the bed's covers, and Žăk had gone to bed.

Keaka rubbed his eyes. "Any trouble, McNelly?"

McNelly slid a six-pack into the refrigerator. "Not really. I followed the immigration van to their office. Does the middle finger mean the same in Chinese? If so, I returned their salute."

Keaka gave him a real salute. "Good job, sir. Eddie, I hope you didn't cause any trouble?"

"No more than usual," Eddie replied. "My little hotel turned out to be seedier inside than it looked from the outside." He stood with his hands on his hips and glanced around the room. "This is your Coconut Castle, huh? It looks more like a frat house basement … and smells like it, too."

I walked past McNelly and opened the refrigerator. Busting open the six-pack, I handed each man a beer. "A nightcap. Bottoms up." All grew quiet except for the slurping. I burped and said, "So, Eddie, you say it's like a frat house?"

"Crazy, huh?" Eddie gulped again, then tossed his can in the blue recycle bin. "So, Danny, McNelly told me someone gave you a gut punch on the Chinese guys. Their people got all hot and bothered?"

Keaka wiped his eyes. "Yeah. And it tells me those men aren't random smugglers. Someone in their government got a little anxious, and a contact in our immigration office is happy to help—another reason you're here, old friend."

Eddie nudged me aside and opened the refrigerator. "What's to eat? And what do you mean?"

Keaka bent over and shoved his head next to Eddie, looking over the food. "We've got vegetable fried rice, pineapple, and Cantonese chicken soup."

Eddie backed away. "Hmm. Maybe the rice and pineapple. Not much, though, or I'll be up all night."

I rolled my eyes. "Eddie means I'll hear his bodily noises all night."

Keaka handed him the containers and a plate. "Microwave is over there—plastic ware is in the drawer right below. And to answer your second question, I wanted to make sure you stayed safe. I didn't trust an old man by himself in Honolulu."

Eddie grinned and pulled the lid off the pineapple container. "Man, it smells good. Me … safe? I had nodded off on a couch probably full of bedbugs."

McNelly yawned and walked to a door. "Good night, gentlemen. Long, long day."

"Good night." I flopped down on the couch and fluffed up a red corduroy pillow. "You guys talk—I'll listen."

Keaka leaned on the bar, watching Eddie take his snack to the table. "Eddie, I don't know what's going on other than more of the same bullshit interference. It seems like someone is always watching out for the bad guys."

"Sounds familiar," Eddie said through a mouthful of rice.

"You're safer up here with us. Have you heard from Angie Marconi?"

Eddie wiped his mouth. "Yep. She made it back okay, but she said nothing about our Czech friends. I guess they're good. Ike, Angie said your folks are doing well, and they may take a pineapple tour tomorrow. When Angie called them, one marshal had arrived and joined them on their lanai."

"Thanks. As late as it is, I doubted I should call."

"Another thing."

"What?"

"It sounds like Hrubý will send his men back the day after tomorrow."

I pushed up on my elbows. "Oh? Why?"

Keaka yawned. "Why stay? They tracked down this shipment of gold coins, and our State Department guys kept it for now."

I stood and stretched. "Anyway, it's only a day earlier than planned. I'm sure Hrubý's staying until Monday since Angie will be here."

"Yeah, Hrubý's planning to leave when we do."

Keaka took the plate and placed it next to the sink. He walked over and patted Eddie's bald head. "So, Eddie … what do you guys think of Stepan Hrubý? I don't like to talk stink on people, but you all trust him, yeah?"

Eddie leaned back in the plastic chair, intertwined his fingers, then rested his hands on his belly. "He's a good man. Disciplined, and he's a bulldog for accomplishing his mission. Trustworthy, right, Ike?"

"I've had complete faith in his and his men's actions," I answered. "His motivations, though, might be muddier than we thought."

Eddie leaned forward, his elbows propped on his legs. "How so?"

I balanced my butt on the arm of the couch. "Our prisoner didn't bother to mention it earlier, but if you can depend on our guest in there, it seems Hrubý's family and the Tasevs have crossed paths before."

Keaka grabbed a chair and pulled it to the table. "Damn. I'm all ears, braddah."

"When Tasev held me at gunpoint, he talked a bit,

which he seems to like to do before mentioning even more tonight. He said his father made himself available in the 1960s to several organizations, including the Czech secret police. If believable, he said Hrubý's father played a role after the Prague Spring and the Warsaw Pact invasion in 1968. The communist government retaliated and had Hrubý's father and others killed. And … guess the assassin used by the new authorities?"

Eddie grunted. "No way."

"Yep. Karanos Tasev … Senior."

Keaka nodded. "That'll get your attention."

I grinned and stood. "Wouldn't it? And he—"

Eddie wiped his teeth with his tongue. "Sounds like you did the world a favor, Ike, when you choked the old goat."

Keaka held up his hands. "Wait, let me finish this. The gold coins are one thing, but Hrubý's real deal is getting revenge, right?"

"Danny, you remember when you came in the room right after Kharkov shot Tasev?" I asked.

"Yeah. Hrubý walked over and kicked Tasev on his wound and then said he wanted some alone time with him."

Eddie half-smiled. "Small world, huh?"

Behind us, hinges creaked, and Žák's door shut.

I nodded. "I wonder if he knows?"

"He does now." Eddie winked at Keaka. "And I don't picture Stepan offering details of his personal life to his men."

"Capturing the gold coins is something he's using to track down Tasev … and Kurić, of course," Keaka said. "Not that I blame him." He walked to the kitchen, then around the room, flicking off the lights. "Anyway, let's go to bed, guys. We're taking Tasev to the Honolulu jail tomorrow. They may arraign him at the district court as soon as Friday."

Eddie made himself comfortable on the couch.

I patted Keaka on the back. "Back to Maui, then?" I asked.

"Late tomorrow afternoon. First, I have a few things to show you on O'ahu."

****

Early the following day, the six of us loaded into the van. Žăk took the back bench seat and tucked the handcuffed Tasev next to him. Eddie sat in the front passenger seat to help his motion sickness—McNelly and I had the middle bench seat. During the drive down to Honolulu, there were very few words other than Tasev bloviating about something while I didn't pay attention. The daytime offered a panorama of gorgeous scenery, even while enduring the road's bumps and curves and Keaka's constant braking. But the ride … spectacular.

McNelly escorted Tasev into the Kaahumanu Hale, an unattractive modern court building next to the old Hawaiian structure guarded by King Kamehameha's statue. Keaka informed us the court had set tomorrow as an arraignment for Tasev, so we left it to the justice system to do its part.

"Okay, done and done. McNelly will join us later." Keaka pointed to the back seat. "It's time to get our brother here to Hickam. What's your name again?"

Žăk groaned. "Please do not—"

Keaka waved his hands. "Never mind. I'm just yanking your chain, buddy."

Žăk blinked. "My chain?"

"Nothing. There's a guy with a nice little two-prop plane waiting for us at Hickam to take you to Maui. It's nearly ten miles from here or thirty minutes … if we're lucky. Call Commander Hrubý and have someone meet you in Kahului. It sounds like you guys have only twenty-four hours left to have a real vacation."

"Thank you, Marshal Keaka."

Keaka grinned. "You're welcome, and call me Danny. Remember, I'm not officially a U.S. Marshal, only an adjunct worker. All right … let's get out of here."

****

We cruised to the airport much quicker than we thought—Keaka told Eddie he must bring good luck by turning the lights green. We said our goodbyes to Žăk, zipped through the security gate, and started our tour.

Eddie's stomach rumbled. "Where are we going, Danny? Your pastry was great but didn't last long."

Keaka grinned. "Your gut is always rumbling, but I'm taking you to the Punchbowl first."

"The military cemetery?" Eddie asked.

"Yes, something I want to show you."

In a few minutes, we approached a hill and traveled along a road corkscrewing up a slope. Older houses with untrimmed yards lined the incline, with a magnificent view of Diamond Head to our right. It certainly didn't look like an entrance to a national cemetery. We came to a last-second stop. Keaka reversed the van, then took a hard left onto the newer pavement, taking us under the canopy of eucalyptus trees. The overhead foliage dwindled, and we rode onto a circular drive with angled parking spots. We found plenty of spaces, and Danny picked one closest to a spectacular stone staircase leading up to a statue.

He guided us to the stairs, and we turned to find a flat lawn stretching into the distance. "Gentlemen, before you is the National Memorial Cemetery of the Pacific. We're in the crater of an extinct volcano that hasn't erupted for tens of thousands of years, if you're not familiar. If you look out on this field toward the city, you'll notice flat granite headstones for each of the thirty-five thousand people buried here. At the top of the steps on our right, the tall white statue is Lady Columbia, representing grieving mothers."

Eddie wiped his brow. "I've read about this place. It rivals Arlington … beautiful."

"It's spectacular," I said. "Thanks for bringing us here."

"You're welcome. I guessed you would enjoy this, yeah? Follow me." We strolled twenty yards, then veered to our right. "These side areas along the steps are called courts, and this is the first of eight courts as you walk up to the chapel. They show those men and women missing in action, mostly from the Pacific battles and the Korean War. But the one in front of us is the Vietnam court—twenty-five hundred men and women unaccounted for." He scanned the list of names, then pointed. "There … halfway down on the left… Hanalé Keaka, my father."

Eddie grasped his shoulder. "I'm sorry, Danny. You hadn't mentioned this before."

"Condolences," I said. "Your mother said he left y'all. I assumed divorce."

"Oh, he left … for the army. She never mentions the complete story. They didn't draft him, so he joined in 1967. She was furious with him for leaving her with three young boys at home when he could've gotten a deferment. We lived on the base but barely made ends meet while she worked in the mess hall. My dad trained in artillery and shipped out to Danang in December. Six weeks later, the North launched the Tet Offensive. During the worst fighting, the army transferred my dad's brigade to the front. The communists nearly destroyed Hue, but, in the end, we crushed them."

"And your dad?" I asked.

"They never found him. A building collapsed and burned around his platoon. Later, they found a few dog tags, but not his."

"Known only to God," Eddie said.

Keaka wiped his face. "Yes … known only to God." He jingled the keys and coins in his pockets. "Explore as you wish. I'm going to go to the altar at the top of the stairs. I'll rejoin you guys in a few minutes." He turned and jogged up the steps.

Eddie put a hand on my shoulder. "Ike, there goes a good man."

"No doubt." I looked down into his face. "I'm surrounded by good men."

Chapter Ten

Keaka rejoined us and promised a lunch of *laulau*, pork cooked in taro leaves, at the Pua´a Restaurant on Waikiki beach. We left the Punchbowl and took a leisurely ride down Ala Moana Boulevard in downtown Honolulu, west of the port where the captured *Müller* had docked. Keaka drove us down two backroads, then an alley where we ended up at an old parking garage entrance with two separate floors. Our van squeezed into the outside parking area, but I couldn't help ducking as the van skirted under the low abutment leading to the spaces.

We plodded back down the cement stairs, found a crosswalk, and strolled into the middle of the Ula Kapuna resort, comprising acres of shops, restaurants, bars, sand, bikinis, and a soaring, multi-story hotel. Keaka pointed to our left toward the ocean. The Pua´a Restaurant appeared straight ahead.

Keaka halted and threw an arm in front of Eddie. He motioned toward a tiki hut filled with puka and other shell necklaces dangling from a hundred nails on two rainbow-painted plywood walls. He glanced behind. "Come on … move to the left side of the kiosk and get off the sidewalk." We stopped at the bamboo counter, surprising the young woman behind it, her head down, typing on her phone. "Gentlemen, this kiosk has the best shell necklaces on Waikiki."

The sales clerk looked up and offered an affectionate smile, her face turning a lighter shade of pink like her t-shirt. "*Mahalo*, sir. I've been here for almost five years, but I don't remember you. My name is Noemi."

"Good to meet you, Noemi," I said.

Eddie frowned. "Danny, I'm sure this young lady has fine merchandise, but what do I—"

Keaka nodded. "For Doris. Don't you want something for her?" He scratched his chest and peered around me.

"Uh, well, not a bad idea," Eddie said. "Okay, miss, let me see the coral necklace, middle way up on the right."

"Great choice." Noemi handed him the string of coral-colored, rose-shaped stones held together by a gold chain. "This one is only one hundred dollars."

Eddie's eyebrows arched higher into his forehead. "One hundred? Wow. I don't know."

"Come on, Eddie," I said. "It's for your new—"

"Never mind." Keaka grabbed my left arm. "Time to go, guys. *Mahalo*, Noemi." He pulled me away, leaving Eddie standing, mouth open, and holding the necklace.

"Danny? Wait. Sorry, Noemi. I'll be back later." Eddie stuck the necklace in her face while watching us walk away.

Noemi's shoulders slumped, and she hung it on the wall.

"Danny, Ike. Hang on." Eddie's short legs pumped to catch up, the cuffs of his khaki shorts slapping against his knees.

I grabbed Keaka by the shoulder and stopped.

"Hold up."

He pulled away from me.

"What are you doing? Let Eddie catch up."

Eddie slowed, near panting, when he came up behind me. "What the hell?"

Keaka chewed on his bottom lip and fidgeted with the pack of cigarettes in his chest pocket. "Sorry, guys. We need to keep moving."

"But the Pua´a restaurant is to the left," I said.

A deep frown formed just below his hairline. Keaka pointed to a hotel nearby with a twenty-story mural of white clouds on a blue-sky background. "We're going in there." He grabbed my left arm again and Eddie's right, pulling us with him toward a back entrance.

Eddie's jaws clenched, and then he said, "You see a ghost, Danny?"

"No ghost … but scary. I'll tell you in a minute." Keaka slammed into the outer glass door, held the inside entrance for an elderly couple, and then we passed into the lobby of old-school black and red carpet, chrome-accented elevators, and fake palms scattered here and there. "This way."

We followed him as he shoved through tourists milling near an exit, then back outdoors and toward the beach. He stopped at another tiki hut, this one a small bar crouched in the shade twenty yards from the hotel. "Have a seat, friends." The outside bar had four round chrome stools supported by fake bamboo supports, offering a distinct wobble when we sat.

"What's going on?" Eddie asked.

Keaka ignored him and pulled himself up on the bar with his elbows. He smiled at the young man waiting for our order. "Hey, what you got?"

The bartender, who looked twenty-one barely, wore a white polo with the hotel's blue insignia and a name tag showing his name as Connor from Nashville. Conner cleared his throat and pointed behind him with a thumb. "The ones on the sign right there."

"Doesn't matter," I said. "I'm more hungry than thirsty."

"Gentlemen, I need to shut this down for my lunch break," Conner said.

Keaka pulled out his wallet. "Okay, Braddah Conner, give me three of the pale ales. Here's a twenty. Keep the change."

"Thanks? They're six-fifty each." Conner popped the tops and handed us our bottles, unlatched and lowered the bamboo and grass cover, then disappeared behind it. A door slammed, and he strode into the hotel.

"Tell us what's up. No more goofing," Eddie said while wiping his forehead.

Keaka rotated on the stool and surveyed the crowd. "I think we lost them, yeah?"

"Who, dammit?" Eddie wiped the condensation from his bottle onto his face, then guzzled a third of his beer.

Keaka took a swig and swiped his mouth. "Okay, here's the deal. I noticed these three big dudes pushing through the crowd a hundred feet behind us. They turned when we did and stopped two stalls from us while we looked at the shells. And not too far behind them strolled Wauna."

"Who?" I asked.

"Judge Wauna … retired now. I think he's fulfilling his greatest wish and works directly for the local underworld bosses instead of running interference for them at the courthouse."

Eddie tipped back his beer, swallowed hard, and slammed his bottle. "Let me guess. He served as judge over your cases when you worked on O'ahu, and what … he doesn't like you?"

Keaka smiled big enough to show the gap in his teeth. "He has a beef with me, one he's kept for decades. And not just me, but the Honolulu police, the FBI, U.S. Marshals, DEA, and probably the local mall cops."

"It's not like you to run away," Eddie said.

"Look, through back-channels years ago, I found out he's the force behind maneuvering me out of the police department back in the eighties. And coincidentally or not, Wauna had jurisdiction over the case where the ship's container of cocaine disappeared, along with the guys we arrested, including the one who killed my partner. A week after my partner's funeral, I stumbled across Wauna in the stairwell at the courthouse … uh … and I clarified what kind of human being I considered him to be. I pretended to have more evidence of his shenanigans just to spook him. Well, my fake evidence may have saved my life, but it wouldn't help me keep my job. They forced two other guys and me to resign, and that's when I headed to Maui."

"Over thirty years ago, and he still has a problem?" I asked.

"Maybe, maybe not, but it's a scab I don't want to pick." He pitched his empty bottle into the metal trash can to our left, then glanced behind us. "Eddie, do you think you could whip those big guys' asses?"

"I didn't see them, but I wouldn't like my chances. Now, when I was younger ..." Eddie slid off his barstool and dropped his bottle into the trash. "Finish up, Ike. This isn't a wine-sipping contest."

Keaka groaned. "Trust me, Judge Wauna would have no qualms now using his toughs against us, not even knowing you all. An association with me is not a good credential in his eyes. Anyway, I'm not sure if he noticed us, but it's awfully coincidental they floated along behind us the whole time."

I disposed of my bottle then touched Keaka's arm. "I think you might miss the forest for the trees?"

"In what way?"

"You say he's working for underworld bosses or something."

"Yeah."

"Would one of those be Miomir Kurić?"

Keaka moaned. "Yeah, I've considered it."

Eddie pulled my glasses off my face and handed them to me. "Clean these, Ike. How do you see?" He put a hand on Keaka's shoulder. "Come on, Danny. Let's circle back to the puka shell place—I want to buy the necklace for Doris now. I noticed three shops down on the other side is a little café with shrimp scampi and all kinds of Hawaiian goodies. We'll eat a bit, have another beer, and then get the hell out of here. How far away is the *Lanakila*?"

"Four miles, or twenty-five minutes in this traffic."

"Fine. We'll head back there and then board earlier than we planned. We can hang for a while and relax." Eddie winked. "Surely, the U.S. Marshals can protect us, can't they?"

Another gap-toothed smile shone. "Yeah, we're

safe," Keaka said.

"What time are we debarking?" I asked.

"Seven. It's the earliest McNelly could get free."

Our sidewalk merged into another, taking us back to the shopping area. A young woman in a luau costume pushed a purple orchid lei into my chest. I handed her ten dollars, bent over to let her place it around my neck, and she kissed my cheek.

Eddie groaned. "You notice she didn't offer us old guys anything."

"You'll notice I'm ten dollars poorer, too." I snapped my clip-on sunglasses into place on my spotless eyeglasses, and we followed the crowd to the shops. "So, only the four of us going back? Can you and McNelly handle it after dark?"

Keaka grinned. "No worries, braddah—McNelly pushes a few buttons, and we are on course." He winked. "At least in the dark, the helicopters will have a harder time finding us."

****

The near half-moon winked over the bay, disappearing and reappearing as low clouds hurried over us while we stood on the deck of the *Lanakila*. The night air warmed us for now, but it would likely cool as we journeyed into the Ka´iwi Channel between O'ahu and Moloka'i.

Late, arriving near eight o'clock, McNelly boarded, nodded, dropped a large paper sack at our feet, and joined Keaka in the control room. Someone had replaced the broken windows and removed the blood stains—the *Lanakila* was ready to go. Keaka had excused himself before sundown, his phone plastered against his ear for nearly an hour.

Eddie bent over and peeked into the sack. "Oh, dang. Ike, I smell pork … grilled, I'd bet. Are we getting a treat tonight?"

I inhaled a deep breath. "Yep, that's pork. Nice smoky smell, too. Let's take it down to the meeting room and set it up for dinner. I'm starving now."

Eddie grabbed the bag, and I followed him downstairs. He dropped the food on the table and pointed toward the cabinets. "Look for the paper plates … and if I know Danny, there's beer lurking here somewhere."

"Hey, these plastic knives won't cut any meat—"

"They don't have to," Keaka said, winking. He had stopped on the bottom step with the lower half of McNelly's body standing higher on the curved stairs behind him. "Those pork medallions are tender as my heart." He stepped aside to let McNelly pass. "We've got the skewers, more vegetables, and grilled pineapple. McNelly picked up our dinner for us from the *Pua'a* Restaurant. I didn't want you to miss these."

"They will amaze you," McNelly said while pulling out napkins from a drawer.

"Great job, sir." Eddie faked a concerned look. "You got any beer, Danny? Then it would be the perfect meal."

Keaka raised an eyebrow and scratched his forehead with a thumb. "Don't hurt my feelings, man. I have three things in my life … food, beer, and fishing. Women used to be up there, but priorities change."

Eddie smirked. "I understand … priorities."

McNelly nodded toward the stairs, and Keaka sighed. "Come outside. We'll eat up top where it's a little cooler. More intrigue is happening." He spun around and followed McNelly.

My gut bubbled, and I glanced at Eddie. "Well? What is it now, do you think?"

Eddie cursed while repacking the food bag, moving around me, and stopping on the third step. He turned back, showing tired eyes. "I don't know what to think. I'm tired of intrigue, and I want to go home, Ike, with my new wife and start a life with her." He blew out a sigh, took the last three steps, and passed through the doorway.

I hurried to follow and strolled onto the deck into a beautiful evening. The skies had cleared, and the half-moon hovered low over the Diamond Head crater—a postcard view. Keaka had spread the food and paper plates across the bench, with a Styrofoam cooler pushed up against the wall, filled with plenty of iced-down Primo.

McNelly joined us after starting the engines. He shook Eddie's hand, grabbed my shoulder, and offered his hand. "Thanks for your help, men. You've risked your lives for your department, the folks in Prague, and now us."

I shook his hand and nodded.

Keaka said, "Break open the cooler, braddah. We'll offer a toast to ourselves. No one else will."

I handed out three beers and kept another for myself.

Eddie popped a top first, then held up his bottle. "To all of us, Angie Marconi, and our Czech friends." We followed his lead and gulped a mouthful.

"Thank you, Eddie," Keaka said. His face offered no clues. "Eat up. McNelly wants to get underway."

McNelly grabbed a skewer and stabbed two pork

medallions, a tomato, onion, and a pineapple chunk. "Enjoy. I gotta drive." He pulled off half a medallion with his teeth and stepped into the control room while Keaka bit into a chunk of pineapple and headed forward to untie us.

Eddie and I decorated our skewers with as much food as they would hold, left our beers propped inside the cooler, and walked to the rail. Eddie swallowed hard twice. "Man, this is the best piece of pork I've ever tasted." He bit into the tomato, causing it to squirt juice and seeds. "Sorry."

I brushed off my O'ahu t-shirt and shot him a glare. "Red juice on my yellow shirt. Thanks."

"Any time." The aluminum stairs shook. "Hey, Danny. Away we go, huh?"

Keaka didn't respond while he loaded up a skewer. He pulled his beer from the cooler and plopped onto the bench next to the food. The engines revved, and we crept away from the port and into the harbor. The moon had disappeared behind the mountains, and the sea grew black as we glided into the channel.

Eddie and I finished eating and strolled to the cooler to pick up our beers. Eddie stabbed the last two tomatoes and asked, "Come on, Danny, what's up?"

Keaka hung his head and held his beer bottle between his feet. "Sorry, guys, I hope one skewer is enough, yeah?"

"We're good, but damn, you're not looking well."

Keaka picked up his empty beer bottle, handed it to me, and motioned with his head toward the cooler. I guessed he wanted another. "I'll be fine, Eddie. But do you guys sometimes wonder why the hell we're doing this? The justice system sucks … corrupted judges, lying lawyers. It's a two-tiered structure—those with connections and those without."

I shoved the empty bottles to the bottom of the plastic bag, then pulled full ones from the ice.

Eddie blew out his cheeks. "Spill it."

We had sailed at least a mile out from the port. Keaka swished the beer in his bottle, stood, then walked to the railing. He turned. "The Macedonian dude. He's out."

Eddie leaned with his palms on the rail. "Out? As in, out on bail?"

"No, I mean *out*. No bail, no nothing. Basically, a get the hell out of the country type of thing. The judge released Tasev to a Kosovar named Jakupaj, who will escort him to Honolulu International and get him on a plane to Kosovo."

The coastline distracted me while I watched the city lights recede into the night. I knocked back another slug of beer. "First, the man is a murderer, and there should be no extradition to Europe. The second is China. I bet this Kosovar guy is a fake. Tasev planned to go to Shanghai, remember? Then on to Dubai and Skopje."

Keaka nodded. "Could be. Obviously, Tasev and friends convinced a judge he needed out."

Eddie groaned. "Yeah, someone *convinced* a judge. Cha-ching goes the bank account. Now a killer with multiple victims walks free. And you're right, the rich and the connected live under a separate set of rules."

My hand slick from condensation, the beer bottle slipped, rolling onto the lower deck. "Crap. I'll get it. But don't forget a third category for what you guys are talking about," I said while walking to the ladder.

"What's that, Ike?"

"Rich, connected, or *blackmailed* by Miomir Kurić. Danny, you ought to find out who released Tasev— direct link there, I bet."

"Yeah, it's a given, and I already know," Keaka said. "The name is Judge Bernard Lee, and guess what?"

Eddie rubbed his temples. "I don't want to guess."

"They appointed Lee to Judge Wauna's old court," Keaka said.

Eddie rolled his eyes. "Whoever has that judgeship likes to make an extra buck?"

Keaka crossed his arms. "Yeah … it's always money." He and Eddie strolled back across the deck and joined McNelly in the control room.

I backed down on the metal stairs to find my beer bottle. The engines revved again, McNelly veered hard right, and we picked up speed.

Chapter Eleven

A silhouette leaned over the edge of the top deck. "Hey, Ike? You down there? Ike?"

"Yeah, I'm here." I shuffled across the deck to the bottom of the stairs.

"It's been half an hour. Danny thought you'd fallen overboard."

"Nah, I'm still here, searching for the bottle I dropped. I never found it, so I'm lounging on the deck near the edge, watching the waves. The blackness of the water is something. You can't see anything, and then you hear a splash, and foam will shoot over us."

"Hang on. I'm coming down there," Eddie said. "Hey, Danny. He's down here. All good." He stomped down the steps. "Ah, dammit, I cut my hand … and here's your bottle." The beer bottle whizzed by my head in two pieces, flying into the water. Eddie stepped onto the deck and surveyed his right hand. "Both pieces had wedged behind the ladder."

I shined my cell phone light on his hand. "There's hardly any blood."

"Is that supposed to make it feel better?" Eddie grabbed the ladder as we plowed through another wave. "So … enjoying the ride? I think I'm getting my sea legs." He walked to the deck's edge and grasped the shiny rail. "Wow, you're right. I can't see a damn thing out there." A fresh wave splashed him all the way to his

148

knees. "A little chilly, too."

I motioned to a spot against the rail. "Come over here." A square hatch rested on the deck where I had sat before, a cover giving access to the engines. "You feel the engines running?"

"Cool, huh? I can smell the diesel, too." He eased down onto the deck next to me. "You may have to help me up."

I shined my phone's flashlight behind him. "Look at these."

He noticed the five divots in the wall behind us. "Bullet holes?"

"Yeah. This is where I stood yesterday when the helicopter buzzed by us. I got lucky."

Eddie nodded. "We all did, except for Olan … but Danny especially."

"He lost his boat."

"But he's alive, Ike. They could've shot him, he might have died in the fire, or been eaten by a shark."

"True."

Our butts bounced, and foam sprayed over the deck.

"We must be out in the middle of the channel by now," he said. "Rougher than I would have guessed for a middle of the night sail."

"You never know—"

"Shh."

"What?"

"Be quiet a sec," he said.

"We're slowing down?" I asked. The pulsations beneath us grew quieter.

Eddie struggled to his feet. "I'll find out what's going on." He heaved himself onto the ladder's first rung, then stomped to the upper deck.

I stood, then steadied myself before taking a few steps toward the edge, but I saw nothing in the black void of water swirling around us. Moving to the port side, the water pitch black here, too, except for something else in the distance. A blinking light … dim, but we should have been too far away from Moloka'i to see any lights.

A hand touched my shoulder. "Hey."

"Braddah, howzit?" Keaka patted my cheek. "It's only me, yeah?"

"I didn't hear you on the steps," I said, frowning.

"What can I say? I float like a butterfly."

I took a deep breath. "So, what's going on?"

"We got a distress signal, an older version, then McNelly spotted something on our radar. A boat smaller than mine."

"Yours sank."

He frowned. "Did it now? Suck rocks, dude." He grabbed my wrist. "Come on, man, you're shaking, for god's sakes. We're not on the *Orca*, and a great white's not going to eat us." He let go of me. "Maybe it's a boat that lost power and needs help, yeah? This is a normal part of our job instead of chasing Chinese nationals and Europeans all over the damn place." He showed me his back and hurried toward the ladder, stopped, glanced at the deck, and turned back toward me. "Let's get this done. I want to go back to fishing … and you can go back to Virginia."

I flipped my hands over, palms to the sky. "Works for me."

He disappeared onto the upper deck.

A searchlight burst on from the aft side of the

Lanakila, illuminating dark waves, then I spotted it, a hundred feet away. A boat bobbed in the rough water, hardly large enough to be seagoing, rocking back and forth and floating haphazardly in the water, with no one standing on its deck. McNelly sounded our horn twice, and we waited. I caught the dim light again—it flashed red from the middle of the boat, near where I noticed the outline of the captain's chair.

Eddie called out before he climbed down the ladder, then strode toward me with a smirk. "Good job, Ike. I've never seen Danny so pissed. What—"

I held up a hand. "Stop. I don't understand what his problem is. All I know is he wants to fish and, it seems, will welcome us going back to Virginia."

"Not like him." Eddie glanced toward the other boat. "But, what the hell? How do you abandon a boat this far out? Danny said we're twelve miles from O'ahu and seven from Moloka'i. No one could swim so far in the dark."

"Maybe they stalled and then got picked up?

Eddie scratched his forehead. "I don't like this."

Our engines started again, and we eased toward the other boat. In half a minute, McNelly shut them down. Keaka scampered down the ladder and hurried over to us.

"Almost there," he yelled. He climbed over the rail and positioned himself, grasping onto the anchor chain. "Eddie, go to the storage bench behind the ladder. You'll find a rope. Bring it over, pitch it down … oh, and look for the duct tape."

Eddie hurried there and back, carrying a thick nylon rope and a roll of gray tape. "Watch out, Ike," he said. "I don't want to miss." He threw too high but near enough. Keaka tied one end to a cleat.

"Here we go." Keaka pushed himself against the *Lanakila's* hull, then crouched. The two boats bumped, and he leaped into the darkness. We heard a stumble and a grunt but no splash. "Made it," he called out. "Hey, Eddie, can you hustle up and tell McNelly we're good? If he's good, hurry back."

Eddie grunted and turned, headed to the ladder. He slogged up the stairs, cursing.

"Braddah Henry? Can you see me?"

"Yeah, yeah … mostly. What can I do?"

"Come join me. Wait until the other two get down here, though."

"Will do." Quick steps followed on the ladder—I guessed McNelly to be first climbing down, followed by Eddie's grunts.

McNelly hurried to the rail and called out, "You good, boss?"

"Yeah, we're tied together now. You have our parking lights on?"

"Hazards, too," McNelly replied.

"Give Henry two flashlights. Braddah, shove one in each back pocket and find a spot for the tape, then ease down on this side. It's an easy step but slick. We'll have a helluva time finding you if you fall into the dark water. Take off those sandals, too. Eddie, go to the storage bench and be ready with those rescue buoy rings."

"Again? Damn. All right, I'll be ready." He groaned and shuffled back to the bench.

I flipped my sandals behind me, threw one leg over the rail, then the other, and slid myself to the edge. Keaka had joined the two boats, but their bumping and bobbing were unsynchronized—the searchlight beam would dip and pitch, the side of the vessels going dark before again illuminating. I had to time this right.

"Coming?" Keaka stood six feet away, motioning to me with his hands. "We're drifting closer. I'll count down and say go."

"Okay. Let's do it," I said. A shiver slithered over me.

"One, two … jump."

I hurled myself forward before the light disappeared, stumbled, and fell headfirst onto the dark deck. Keaka hovered over me while I rolled over on my back.

"Graceful." He offered me a hand and pulled me to my feet.

"You said 'jump' instead of 'go.' "

"Same thing."

I pulled the flashlights from my pocket and turned on both. "Want one?"

Keaka cupped his right hand around his mouth. "Both of us are here, *Lanakila* friends. Hang tight while we explore, yeah?"

I found the blinking red light coming from a gray metal box about seven inches square. It dangled near a shelf under the steering wheel at knee level of the captain's chair. A splice connected the wires to the boat's ignition switch—tape held three C-sized batteries strapped across its top.

"Take a look, Danny." I squatted, and he peered over my shoulder.

"Well … not sure what it is. I first guessed a distress signal, but the wire splice … uh, don't start the boat, yeah?"

"You think it's rigged?"

"I'm not sure what to think, but it reminds me of an old eight-track player." Keaka spun back to the *Lanakila*. "Hey, McNelly," he yelled. "This may not be what it seems. Get the engines idling, and we'll make our visit short."

McNelly shouted. "What do you mean?"

"Just be ready." Keaka grabbed my shoulder. "Come on, braddah. The quicker we get off here, the better. Search those forward storage areas, and I'll go aft."

"I wish we had the moon tonight."

Keaka again turned back. "Hey, McNelly. One more thing."

McNelly had started the engines and shouted. "What? Louder, please."

"Can you adjust the floodlight? Shine it farther down on us where we can see better." The searchlight beam shook, passed over, then found us.

I threw my hands up in front of my face.

"Reminds me of a flashbulb from my dad's old camera. I see spots," Keaka said.

"Blink a few times."

I wandered forward and pulled open the lid to a storage bin, this one empty but two more to go. The second storage area under the seat behind the bow had an assortment of life vests—nothing else, so on to the third one. I lifted its lid and found a stack of transparent plastic, quart-sized baggies full of yellowish powder and definitely not flour.

"Hey, Danny." No answer. I glanced aft and found him crouching, his shaking flashlight pointed to the deck. "Danny?" I hurried to the back.

He shone his light on my face. "It's a body."

I pointed my flashlight at Keaka's feet and noticed an oblong pool of blood hugging the back of a man's torso, an orange cloth tight around his neck. He lay on his left side in a stretched white t-shirt bulging around the form of his belly, with tight jean shorts and one brown flip-flop. An auburn beard covered his face and throat, and a blue baseball cap had fallen from his head.

"Shot in the leg, then strangled with an orange scarf? Danny, do you think—"

"Yeah, I'm thinking the same, but this seems too coincidental. Tasev should be on a plane to Kosovo. If not, where would he be? Swimming?" Keaka touched the cloth. "And it's silk."

"His neck—you can see markings like strangulation," I said.

"Interesting. The marks aren't all the way around his neck." Keaka pointed at his own throat to show me.

"Number thirty."

"What?" he asked.

"On the cargo ship, Tasev said I would be his thirtieth victim."

"Glad you weren't."

Something tickled my toes.

"Ahh." I pointed the flashlight down, and three, inch-long bugs scurried under the body. "What the hell?"

Keaka snorted. "So, braddah, your first meeting with *elelū*, yeah?"

"What?"

"Cockroaches. *Blattella assahinai* … the Asian variety. They're keeping company with our dead guy here. Lucky for you, those are small ones."

"Nice. On another note, I found a whole storage container full of baggies. A pale-yellow color from what I could tell."

Keaka stood straight and blew out his cheeks. "Drugs? What the hell?"

"We need to move. I think it's a plant. The contraption is wired up to the ignition … I've already been in one explosion back in Alexandria. Ask Eddie."

"He told me." Keaka shut his eyes, rubbed his temples, then looked back at me. "Someone would have to know when we sailed … but you're right. I'll radio the location to the Coast Guard, and they'll get a boat out here. We must stay close, though."

"Stay? Why?"

"We can't leave this thing floating in the dark with a shitload of what might be cocaine, a dead body, and a rigged boat. Other vessels may pass it."

"Got it," I said. "Have you found any I.D. on the body?"

"Not yet, at least in his right pockets. Take a few pictures before we flip him."

I jerked my phone and snapped several body photos from different angles. "I think I should get a couple of pics of the cocaine."

"Yes, please, and another of the metal box."

I snapped four more pictures of the body before I backed up two steps. Without touching the still-blinking box, I took front and side shots of the gadget. I glanced to my left and noticed Moloka'i barely visible in the darkness, its mountains painting a black, irregular outline against the sky. Pinpoints of light showed here and there, plus a brighter area near the middle of the island that must have been a town.

I opened the storage bin holding our bags of powder, positioned my camera with the flash on, then stopped. Something flickered to my left, another pinpoint of light, but this one drifted off to our right. A vessel? I hurried with a picture and rejoined Keaka.

He had pulled the man onto his stomach and held a wallet and a square leather cover of the same size. "Found these. It looks like the Jakupaj guy I mentioned. This is getting weirder."

"Agreed," I said. "I got the pics. Now let's get off here. There's another vessel out there."

Keaka snapped his head toward me. "Where?"

I pointed straight off the starboard side. "Watch for a second. I noticed a glimmering of light a minute ago. It flashed three times, each time drifting to the right."

"Shit." Keaka grabbed my arm. "We've got company, man. Hey, McNelly," he shouted.

"Here, boss."

"We're coming back over. Take a gander on the radar. We may have guests."

"How do you know—"

"Go check, please."

"Got it."

Keaka shoved me in the back. "You first, braddah. Hey, McNelly."

"Here still."

"Henry is coming first. Be ready with the rope in case one of us can't jump like we need to."

Eddie's silhouette leaned over the rail. "I'll do it. Come on, Ike."

I either timed it better, or the waves were smaller. My leap to the *Lanakila* became more like a giant step this time. Eddie grabbed my shoulder from above, steadied me, and I climbed back onto the deck.

"Welcome back, buddy."

"Yeah, thanks. We need to hurry."

"What?"

"Let's get Danny over here first. Come on, Danny."

Silence from the small boat.

"Where is he?" Eddie asked.

"The flashlights. Look. That's what the tape's for. Danny's attached the lights to each end of the boat."

All quiet.

Eddie clapped his hands and yelled. "Danny, get your ass over here."

"I'm here," Keaka said. He swung a leg over the side.

Eddie put his hands on his hips. "Hell, man, let us help."

Keaka sat hard on the deck. "Woo … too spooky. I've untied us from the other boat. Come up top, guys. Let's see what McNelly has found."

"Look," I shouted. The glimmer of blinking lights now showed a row of six lights, moving faster back to our left.

Keaka shoved Jakupaj's wallet and passport toward me, then bounded up the ladder. I stuffed each in my waistband and hurried up the steps, with Eddie following.

Keaka yelled. "McNelly, get us out of here … now."

By the time we scrambled to the upper deck, Keaka stood next to McNelly, both men staring at the radar. Keaka motioned for us to join them when McNelly hit the throttle. The engines roared, and Eddie and I stumbled backward before getting our footing in the control room. Eddie plopped himself in one of the captain's chairs.

"Dang, guys, in a hurry?" Eddie leaned toward the monitor.

McNelly gave a sideways glance. "You noticed?"

The inside of the cabin flickered red and yellow, followed right away by a thunder-like rumbling, reminding me of a close lightning strike.

Keaka held his hand in front of his face and glanced aft. "Wow, braddah, we guessed right—that little boat just disintegrated. McNelly, slow to half speed and keep an eye on the other boat prowling around. Braddah, let me see those pics of the powder."

"Powder?" Eddie asked. "What kind of powder?"

I scrolled through the photos and handed Keaka my phone.

His forehead grew deep wrinkles as he used a thumb and a finger to zoom on the picture. "What do you think, Eddie? Show it to McNelly, too."

"The cocaine?" I asked.

Eddie blew out his cheeks, then frowned. "That ain't cocaine, Ike. Here, McNelly."

McNelly held the wheel with one hand, glanced down at my phone, and shook his head. "It's an explosive you're showing, Pierce—it's too yellow for cocaine."

Eddie slapped me on the shoulder. "We survived another one, my friend."

"Apparently."

McNelly chuckled. "It's what you make TNT from. That blown-up boat had enough explosives … I bet you couldn't find two molecules left to rub together."

"What is it with this bunch, Eddie? They like blowing things up."

McNelly switched hands on the wheel then pointed at the monitor. "Boss, the other object is still out there and closing."

Keaka blew an exhale. "What do you think? How big?"

McNelly raised his left eyebrow. "It's bigger than the *Miss Mio*."

Keaka's left thumb and fingers pulled on his bottom lip while thinking. "So, three or four-passenger capacity, yeah?"

"Right … but if I had to guess by watching it on radar, it's rigged for speed. Coming fast."

"Can we outrun it?" Eddie asked.

McNelly shook his head. "For a while, but not all the way to Maui."

Keaka scratched his chin and pointed at Eddie. "Old friend, you and Henry get below, break out the rifles again, and bring them back up here."

"I didn't know sailing in Hawaii would be such a delight," I said.

McNelly laughed.

"Not usually this exciting, braddah. Here's what we're going to do. We'll hit it hard and let them play chase. You think we can outrun them to Lana'i, at least?"

"Likely," McNelly replied, "but it'll be a tight fit."

"Good enough. Set a heading for Manele Bay. Turn our lights on nice and bright."

"Sir?"

"I want them to follow. Somewhere along the coast, we'll take a chance."

"For what?" Eddie said.

"A place to surprise them. All right, let's find out what they've got."

****

Eddie and I sat at the conference desk with Keaka, gripping the arms of our chairs as we bounced through the waves. Eddie appeared less than pleased. "Oh, Danny … dude, I may need to go back top. How much longer will it be this rough? I may barf up those pork medallions."

"Soon … if we're lucky. If they get too close, we have to shut down early."

"What do you mean?"

"Never mind for now. Let's get your mind off this. Pitch your phone on the table, Eddie. Call Angie Marconi, put her on speaker, and we'll get her up to date."

The phone rang twice, and a male voice answered. "Angela Marconi's phone. This is Stepan Hrubý."

I glanced at Keaka and rolled my eyes.

"Hey, Stepan, it's Eddie Stone."

"Good evening, Lieutenant Stone."

"We've run into a little difficulty, and it'll be late when we get back."

Keaka waved for Eddie's attention and whispered, "Tell him."

Eddie shook his head. "Can we talk to Angie?"

"Apparently not. Angela left this afternoon for Kihei to visit with Henry Pierce's family. Somehow, she left her phone in my room. Henry Pierce, may I have your family's cell phone numbers? I will contact Angela and let her know her phone is with me."

"Hey, Stepan," Keaka said. "Let us take care of it.

Henry can call his mom, and I'll call the marshals … I believe Trish is on duty tonight."

"Very well. We look forward to seeing you again. Everything went well?"

"Not exactly," Eddie said. "Our watchers got the Chinese freed, and somehow Tasev got released—"

Hrubý's voice burst with anger. "Tasev? That scum—"

"We know, we know," Keaka said. "It's the court in Honolulu. A new judge … but the old ways. Not only that, but we believe Tasev set us up, killed his minder, and is chasing us now in another boat."

Silence at first on Hrubý's end. "They are devils," he finally muttered. "I need to go. Angela is receiving a call from Alexandria, Virginia … the middle of the night there. Interesting. Please take care and ask her to call me." A click.

"I'll call my mom," I said. I dialed twice—straight to voice mail both times. My grandmother didn't answer either. "No telling what they're up to."

"All right. Let me call Marshal Myung." Keaka pressed the number and hit the speaker button.

"Trish Myung."

"Trish. Thank goodness. This is Keaka."

"Yes, sir. I've been trying to reach you."

"Oh? We're headed back—must have hit a dead area. What's up?"

"I'm at the hospital, sir."

Keaka grunted, staring at Eddie. "Say again?"

"I'm all right. It's Kai." Myung's voice broke. "Someone attacked her, sir."

Keaka leaned his chin on his hand and closed his eyes. "Another marshal …"

162

"Kai will make it, sir. She has a nasty lump on the back of her head, with four stitches and a slight concussion."

"Some good news, at least. Tell me what happened … wait, I need to let you know you're on speaker with Henry Pierce and Eddie Stone. Henry couldn't contact his folks."

"Angie Marconi is with Susan and Rita Faye. She agreed to stay at the condo when I rode with Kai in the ambulance."

Eddie drummed his fingers on the table. "This doesn't sound right," he mumbled and leaned toward the phone. "Trish, this is Eddie Stone. What's going on?"

"Right. Near dusk, Kai took a turn to sit outside in our vehicle, and she said she noticed two figures nosing around Susan Pierce's rented vehicle, the Nissan Sentra. They walked away when Kai approached them. Kai told me while investigating the parking area, someone from behind knocked her to the ground. A passerby yelled, and the two figures ran away. Kai was coherent enough to call me, so I called 9-1-1, and we headed to the hospital about forty minutes ago."

"Someone needs to let my mother know," I said. "I can't get hold of anyone there."

"I'll see what I can do," Myung said.

"Any I.D. on the perps?" Eddie asked. He glanced at his phone, shoved his chair back, and hurried into the restroom. He said hello, and pushed the door shut.

"Not much. The passerby describes one as rather tall, probably a male, and the other petite—a small male or maybe a woman. They both wore black caps."

"Interesting," Keaka said. "Please give Kai our

regards, yeah? We have our hands full right now. Long story, but we're near Lana'i with unknowns in another boat trailing us. We're headed to Manele Bay tonight, and we may not make it to Lahaina until morning."

"Be careful, sir. I heard of the helicopter story. Should I notify Kahului? They have the *Lehua* available."

"Kahului would be another hour before they would reach us. But no worries for now. You watch after Kai, Henry's folks, and Angie Marconi. Oh … if you talk to Angie, she left her phone with Stepan Hrubý."

"Will do, sir. I'll check in when I know more." Myung disconnected.

Keaka massaged his neck. He sighed. "Dammit. What have we gotten into?"

"I don't know, but I'm feeling a little *déjà vu* again."

Eddie left the restroom and came back to his seat, his mouth hanging open.

"What's up?" I asked.

"Doris returned my call. I left her a message earlier today. This time she told me she's in Shanghai."

"Shanghai? I thought she was settling her mother's things in Taipei," Keaka said. "They fled the mainland …"

"Yeah … Doris said Shanghai … something, something, her mother's estate … old business before the communists took over."

"Over seventy years ago?"

Eddie plopped into his seat while tapping his phone against his chin. "Yeah, seventy-three years. Her grandmother would have been nine years old. She's told me before her family fled from Guangzhou."

"Shanghai now. The story seems to be changing." I said.

"Yeah … something's not right."

Chapter Twelve

We approached Lana'i's southwest corner, near a harbor Keaka called Kaumalau. Our pursuers had kept pace, McNelly estimating we had a half-mile lead. I noticed few lights here other than along a pier, silhouettes of boats and sailing masts rolling gently with the waves. McNelly pressed the Lanakila closer to the shore, cutting down to quarter speed when we entered the small bay.

"Are they coming around the rocks?" Keaka asked.

"Not yet," McNelly answered. "But this is making me nervous."

"Right. Cut the lights and all stop, then drop anchor."

"Sir?"

Keaka smiled, showing the gap in his teeth. "You think they can find us on a moonless night?"

"Got it … and probably no radar for them." McNelly flicked off all lights except for the green glow from the radar screen. All grew quiet but for the sound of the anchor chain descending into the murky harbor.

Eddie returned from downstairs, bringing several rifles slung over both shoulders and a bag of ammunition boxes.

"Danny? You want one?" Eddie asked.

"Yep, and pull up the lid on the seat next to McNelly," Keaka replied. "You'll find a pair of night vision binoculars."

McNelly scooted over.

"These?" Eddie asked.

"Yes, sir. Give the binoculars to Henry, and you and I will get ready for target practice. McNelly will watch the screen."

Eddie handed me the all-black, metal binoculars, much heavier than they looked.

I stepped outside, and my vision improved, but everything through the binoculars showed with a green tint along the shoreline. "Now what?" I asked.

Eddie pulled a sleeve of saltine crackers from the bag of ammunition. "You need a snack?"

Keaka grabbed a handful and smiled. "I need Spam with these." He winked. "Come on, let's take a spot behind the rail. Braddah Henry, can you find the jetty of rocks on our left as you enter the harbor?"

"Yeah, I see it," I answered while fiddling with the binoculars' focus.

"If they follow us into the bay, they'll come around from the northwest and move toward us. If they pass us by, they'll stay on a heading of south-southeast."

McNelly called to us. "Radar shows they're here and slowing … almost stopped."

"I see zilch," I mumbled, then coughed, almost swallowing half a cracker.

"You might as well have a seat, Ike," Eddie said. "Leaning over the rail doesn't help."

"What? Oh, right." I crouched, then looped my legs around a vertical support guardrail, resting my elbows on my knees and peered through the lenses. "Still nothing, Danny."

McNelly had leaned back in his seat, chewing on

his right thumbnail. "Hey. They've pulled past the rock outcropping. They're coming."

"I can make out a few lights but no human shapes," I said.

"Dammit." Keaka checked his rifle, then used the chrome rail crossbeam to support the gun barrel. Eddie did likewise. "They must have seen us pull in the cove. Eddie, tell me what you're thinking."

"I think I'm feeling a little trapped. Hey, McNelly?"

"Yes."

"Are we certain this is the right boat? If they get close, I'll be glad to use the entire bag of ammunition and hope one of them is Tasev. But I got to be sure this isn't a random family in a boat."

McNelly slid from the captain's chair and poked his head through the doorway. "Nothing is one hundred percent, but maybe ninety-nine percent? The echo signature is the same as the one that's been following us."

"It's a small boat," Keaka said. "They'll have to get closer before we can verify."

"Any chance we can get help from Lana'i City?" Eddie asked.

Keaka shook his head. "Not soon enough. Only rough trails lead down here. It's near impassible during the daylight even."

"Listen," I said.

"What did you hear?" Keaka asked.

"Nothing. Their engine stopped."

"Your hearing is better than mine, young'un," Eddie said.

The green light vanished from the control room,

and McNelly joined us at the rail. "I've lost them along the shore, boss."

"Honest? It's treacherous there. What do you see, braddah?"

"Yeah, people hugging the shore."

Keaka fidgeted with the gun's sling. "This is damn unusual. Are they trying to sneak along the shore and surprise us?"

"Just what I'm thinking," Eddie answered.

"No boat movement," I said. "So, here's what I'd suggest—give them a few minutes to get close, fire up the engines, and we leave them behind."

McNelly nodded, and Keaka smiled.

"Not bad, kid," Keaka said. "McNelly, how long would it take to throttle up out of here?"

"Less than ten seconds, but the anchor is the problem. It's sitting on the bay floor, about thirty feet down. Starting the anchor motor up and pulling it will take time, and don't forget the noise it would make."

"True." Keaka motioned for me to hand over the binoculars. He scanned the shore, turning a hundred twenty degrees from left to right. He pulled them away from his eyes, rubbed his forehead, and looked down. "These things give me a headache, braddah. Come over here and help me out."

I pulled myself up on the rail and shuffled over, my feet and calves tingling after sitting so long. "What do you want me to do?"

"Look over my right shoulder, then ten degrees to my right. Can you make out shapes?"

I skimmed straight ahead and to the right—nothing came clear. I noticed a glowing human figure back to the left, then two more. "Three … I think. They are moving slowly. It looks like one large adult and two kids."

Keaka shoved a cigarette into the space in his teeth. "Kids? I only saw two figures earlier. Both looked like adults to me."

"We can't shoot at kids," Eddie said.

McNelly took the binoculars from me. "Yeah, it's three … but, my god, the one figure is a monster. Huge. But there's something else I don't understand."

I noticed Keaka light his cigarette, inhale a long draw, then try to blow the smoke away from us. "Sorry. I needed that. What don't you understand?"

"First, what luck to find a spot to wade ashore unless someone knows this bay … at night?"

"It can't be luck." Eddie waved his hands and ducked under a cloud of Keaka's smoke.

"Nope, luck has nothing to do with it. And second?" Keaka asked.

"Who's watching the boat?" I asked.

Keaka grinned. "Yeah? That boat holds four people at best, but that's a helluva load to transport between these island channels."

"I got it," Eddie said. "We pull our anchor while we pin them down on the shore with our rifles. We might delay them. McNelly hits it, and we head for the ocean. They'll be way behind."

Scratching at the beard growth on his neck, Keaka raised an eyebrow and winked at Eddie. "You're a sly old man, but don't get smart because I already thought the same thing."

"Sure, you did."

"How close can we get to their boat?" I asked.

"They have a small draft—ours … not so much,"

McNelly answered.

"And?" Keaka asked.

McNelly frowned, running his fingers through his graying hair. "A guess, but we can't go closer than thirty feet."

Keaka chuckled. "We head that way, then make a wave on the way out of here."

McNelly smiled. "Got it." He jumped back into the captain's chair and flipped a switch.

The anchor engine groaned, and the chain grew tight, pulling the anchor from below. A noise crackled near the shore.

Keaka pushed me toward the cabin, then grabbed Eddie's arm. He glanced through the binoculars. "Shoot away, my friend. Those aren't crickets chirping. Point to the left and keep them busy."

Eddie's gun butt slammed against his shoulder. "Oh, damn. It's got a kick." He aimed and took another shot, echoed by three shots from the shore.

"Ready, boss?" McNelly asked. "The anchor is in."

"Geev 'um."

The engines roared, and I stumbled to the deck. Eddie fell back, still holding his rifle and aiming at the sky.

"In here, Eddie," Keaka called to us. "God, men, can't you two learn to hang on?"

Eddie struggled to his feet, staggered into the control room, then laid the rifle with the other guns secured under the windows.

"Eddie," I yelled.

He weaved his way back through the door. "What?"

I pointed my right index finger to his left sleeve

and poked it into a circular ripped piece in the material. "Lucky man."

Eddie pushed my hand away and grabbed his shirt. "Well, shit."

Keaka ignored us and shouted to McNelly. "Take us as close as you dare, then hard left. They'll get a good bath if anyone is on the boat."

"Will do."

Keaka pointed at us. "Guys? Please grab onto something this time."

We made our own waves in the near calm bay, splashing toward our prey. Forty feet away, the *Lanakila* pitched to our starboard side. Keaka shouted. "Aim for the rocks." He grabbed onto the seat. "Ready?"

"Yes," McNelly shouted.

"Now."

We pitched back hard to port. Eddie lost his footing and sprawled on the deck once more. I looped my right arm around the rail and caught his foot with the other. Keaka slid toward us and grabbed an arm.

We straightened again, and McNelly let out a shout. "Splash one dumbass."

"What happened?" I asked. Eddie struggled to his feet, then the three of us crowded next to McNelly while he and Keaka high-fived one another.

"Someone stood in the boat. Our maneuver rocked him enough, and he fell into the water."

"Great job, man," Eddie said, straightening his clothes.

We passed the jetty of rocks and hit the rolling sea.

McNelly grinned. "Boss? Manele Bay?"

Keaka patted him on the back. "Nope. I think we're

good now. Let's head home—Lahaina in fifty minutes. A bath, then I'll fix my nachos for you guys. Deal?"

****

We arrived at the Lahaina docks after eleven p.m. and another very long day. I showered and joined Keaka and Eddie at the Hokele bar, watching the pedestrians, many of them weaving down the sidewalk after too many drinks. The noisy restaurant guests spilled over into the bar's seating area, as seemed to happen every night.

Malo appeared from the kitchen, whispered to his brother, and ten minutes later, he brought out a pile of tortilla chips covered with roasted pork, pineapple, and a spicy sauce full of diced mangoes. We devoured them along with a beer but waved away a refilled plate.

Eddie patted his gut and leaned back in his chair. He wiggled both shoulders to loosen them up, then belched. "Excuse me. Danny, I'm not a big fruit and meat fan, but that was damn good."

Keaka rubbed his tongue across his front teeth. "I'm damn glad it was damn good."

"Thanks for getting us home safe," I said. "I never expected a trip to Honolulu would be like fighting pirates all day."

"Me either, braddah, but here's the deal … our safety is an illusion. Those guys tracked us the entire way, they knew of our route from Honolulu, and someone booby-trapped the little boat. Then, they were going to shoot us."

"You're not powerless, Danny," Eddie said. "You have the U.S. Marshals—"

"I know it, and I've already made the call. The island is on alert … but for who or what?"

"Tasev is involved somehow," I said. "I'm still confused about how he had a judge cut him loose, then he killed his minder ... the body we found."

"All we can do is stay attentive, yeah? I've alerted the police on Maui, along with airport security. Outside of that, what else? Eleven small airstrips are scattered around Maui, and those are the ones we know of. Plus, a score of helipads dots the island. He may have already gotten on a plane, gone to Honolulu, and then who knows where or who."

Eddie rubbed his eyes and groaned. "I've got to get to bed. But what do you mean?"

"Kurić, or Kurić's people. It might be Tasev is long gone, but others in the organization are trying to get to us. We took a bunch of their gold coins. And if you want to make yourself crazy, what of the Chinese and this General Shai?"

Eddie shook his head and rose from his chair. "I'm leaning toward Kurić. The helicopter attacked us yesterday before any of these Chinese and Tasev issues came up. Anyway, I'm going to go bang on Hrubý's door and find out if he knows anything."

I offered Keaka my hand. "Danny, thanks again. We couldn't have made it without you."

"And vice versa, but friends take care of one another. Sleep well, and let me know first thing about your family. The last info from Trish is that Kai is alert and doing better. McNelly messaged me, and he and I are driving down to Kihei."

"Great news," I replied. "Have a good night, and if you hear something first, call me."

Eddie hadn't waited, and I found him strolling across the courtyard, heading for the last room on the first floor at the northeast corner. By the time I got there, Hrubý had opened the door and had a hand on Eddie's shoulder.

He nodded. "Henry Pierce, welcome back. Eddie Stone mentioned your escape this evening. Please come in." Eddie and I stood in the entry, watching Hrubý pull on a windbreaker. "And the U.S. Marshal … Kai? Many things are happening. We must be extremely cautious."

"Kai is recovering, but where are the guys? And what have they been up to?" I asked.

Hrubý gathered his wallet and change. "They are jumping bars down in Maalaea. I hope they take a taxi back to their rooms."

Eddie smiled. "You mean bar hopping?"

Hrubý hesitated, then chuckled. "I suppose. Unfortunately, they have their Toyota, and Angela took the Jeep to Kihei. I have no transportation and still have heard nothing. Commissioner Bates called Angela's number earlier. I spoke with him for a few minutes."

"Really? That would be in the middle of the night in Alexandria. Did he say the last time he had talked to Angie?" Eddie asked.

"No, he did not say and offered nothing about the timing of his call." Hrubý stared at us for a moment. A scream from the restaurant, then a chorus of happy birthday. "Well? Are you ready?"

Eddie glanced at me. "For what?"

Hrubý scratched his chin. "Kihei. Give me your keys or come with me. I am taking Angela's phone to her, and I guessed you would be curious concerning the Pierce family."

I sighed. "Yes, yes, of course. But you'll have to

drive no matter the rental agreement. I feel like a zombie. It's been a day … again."

"As you wish. Eddie Stone, what will you do?"

Eddie shook his head. "Sorry, guys, I'm out. These last three days have been endless, and this old guy is exhausted. Ike, when you get back, you'll find me passed out on the couch. Wake me up, though." He shuffled into the courtyard, then stopped with his back to me. "Be careful."

****

Hrubý eased onto the highway, turning right out of a residential neighborhood. I struggled to stay awake, but he, apparently, didn't feel in a quiet mood. We wound our way through the dark mountains, with the ocean to our right, stars glimmering off the water. We descended the last hill, lights flickering in a line along the coast. A glow from Kahului and the airport runway shone through the darkness to our left.

I pointed ahead. "Maalaea Harbor and the ocean research center. Your men are there?"

The car slowed. "Correct. Along with several bars, apparently. Should I check on them?"

"Normally, I would say yes and join them, but not tonight."

"Very well. The intersection is ahead, and I believe I make a right?"

"Yes, we came this way the other day," I answered.

"As did Angela and I when going to the ʻĪao Valley."

We passed a car parked on the right side of the road. A couple appeared to be sleeping on the hood. "Cheap place to stay, I guess."

"Or get robbed," Hrubý said, giving me a glance.

"I thank you for accompanying me."

We drove another five minutes. "Have you been this far?" I asked.

"No. You should guide me."

"We're on Highway 310. Stay to the left up here, then we'll take Highway 31. It's a little faster than going through town."

"Very good."

Too tired to even rub my eyes, I used all my energy to talk. "Can I ask you a question?"

"I cannot stop you."

"It seems like you and my boss are getting along well. What are your intentions?"

Hrubý laughed. "That is your question? You sound like my late father-in-law."

"Oh? I hadn't realized you'd been married before."

"Not everyone needs to know everything," he said, half grinning. "I have a daughter and two grandsons in Munich—my son lives near Salzburg, Austria. He has married twice but no children. And, to answer your question, I have good thoughts of Angela, but either of us would have to give up much to live in another country."

"You've talked of it?" I asked.

"Briefly, but do not jump to a conclusion. Angela and I care for one another, but as far as any ongoing relationship … we will see."

"Do you mind if I ask what happened to your wife?"

He drew a breath, then hit the brakes hard as a light turned red. "I do not discuss it with most people, but I will tell you if you do not bring it up with my men. I want them to know me as their commander, not a

177

friend."

"I won't. By the way, Lipoa Street is where we turn for the medical clinic. Three miles. It's a half block from my mother's condo."

"Thank you." He sighed. "Yes, my wife, Valeska, a Slovak, grew to adulthood in Bratislava. We met at Prague University and married in 1988. Her father served as a minor communist official in the immigration office but lost his job after the Velvet Revolution, the end of the communist government."

"Shouldn't that have been expected?"

"I suppose. Unfortunately, her father, mother, and Valeska's younger brother moved in with us at our two-bedroom apartment, three kilometers from downtown Prague. Our daughter, Dominika, was born in January 1990, then our son, Valentýn, eleven months later."

"A bit crowded."

"Indeed. Finally, the economy recovered enough, Valeska's parents found an apartment, and I received an offer for a position in the police department where I've been since."

"Thirty years."

"Yes, like Angela."

"And your wife?" I asked.

He gave me another side glance. "Murdered … in 2007."

"My god."

"Death by misadventure, the records show." He slapped the blinker to turn right. "Hit by a car after stepping off the curb."

"And it wasn't an accident?"

"I recognized the car." We pulled into the near-empty urgent care parking lot. He turned the key and handed it to me. "My old enemies. I had gone back into the restaurant for my umbrella … it should have been me."

"Stepan, I'm sorry."

He shook his head. "No need."

"Thank you for sharing this. Does this have anything to do with the Tasevs?"

Hrubý pulled the door handle and placed one foot on the ground. His glare appeared to signal I had gone too far. "How do you know? Who gave you the information?"

"I didn't mean to upset you, but you should know Tasev told us his father and your father were enemies, and he's pissed off at me for killing his old man."

"It is much more involved." He pulled himself out of the car, bent over, and peered around the doorjamb. "The old man killed my father, and I believe his son is responsible for my wife's death. Know you have made a mighty enemy, Henry Pierce. The Tasevs are relentless and never quit … but neither do I." He slammed his door, then reopened it. "One more thing. You did the world a favor when you choked the old man Tasev. He was one of the vilest men in Europe— hundreds of people he assassinated. I am always in your debt, Henry Pierce." He slammed the door again and left me sitting alone.

The car's lock relied on my fob, so I right away typed a message telling him I wanted to check on my folks and Angie Marconi. A five-minute walk and I found the carport where my mother had parked. A rubber seal drooped on the glass along the Nissan's front passenger window—someone must have inserted a tool partway until Kai had interrupted them. The car still locked, I noticed a packet of my mother's favorite gum on the console. The cupholder held a Diet Coke can with pink lipstick staining the edge. I didn't see Marconi's Jeep.

Worry pushed away my exhaustion. I hopped up the stairs two at a time to the third-floor landing. On my right, nighttime shrouded the Haleakalā slope except for scattered lights along the lower third of the summit. Flickering fluorescent lights glowed overhead, lighting the condominium's exterior hallway. I approached the fourth door on the left and found the outer door barely hanging from its hinges and with its screen pushed inward. I peered through the door's smudged window into the darkness. The only light inside the condo filtered through the lanai's sliding door. After knocking twice, I called out, but no answer. The doorknob turned, but the second lock had the door secured.

My phone vibrated. Hrubý's message told me Kai was alert, complaining about a headache, and wanted to go home. I called, but it went straight to voice mail, then sent a text message and told him I had found no one at my mother's condo.

A man passed me, plodding in heavy sandals and dressed in Hawaiian cargo shorts, a red t-shirt, and a white unzipped hoodie with the hood pulled loose over his head. He glared.

"Hey," I asked. "Are you staying here?"

He shuffled to the stairwell and stepped down once. He stopped and turned halfway to his left. Without looking, he said, "Just visiting."

I eased toward the stairs. "Have you seen three women together on this floor?" A tap of light footsteps behind me preceded a sweet, flowery smell drifting nearby—a familiar scent.

He stepped down to the first landing, then spun toward me. "I cannot say."

A shadow reflected onto the wall of the gray-painted rough cedar, showing a short arm holding something in both hands. I froze as the man on the stairs ascended from the landing. The shadow behind me shifted closer, raising its arms. I pivoted a half turn and burst toward the figure, knocking it to the ground. A crowbar sailed toward the rail, and several heavy steps pounded on the stairwell as I rested on my attacker's gut, holding weak arms against the ground. A familiar Czech voice echoed down the hallway, followed by scuffling noises.

My attacker whined from under me … a female voice. I pulled back the hood, partly repulsed by the face. "Nika?"

"Funny seeing you again, Ike. This position seems familiar." Nika Campbell, the woman we noticed at the resort's hot tub and whose colleagues had tried to kill me last winter.

"As in, I'm not dead, and you're trying to finish what Charlie couldn't?"

The noise behind me had stopped. I glanced to my right to see Hrubý standing over the man in Hawaiian shorts and hoodie, now face down on the cement walkway.

He grinned. "Ah, must you always be the one to get the girl? So, you know one another?"

"Yep. She has friends in low places and an unpleasant habit of wearing sweet perfume. Stepan Hrubý, I would like you to meet Nika Campbell, the young woman we've discussed."

He stepped closer and stared down. "Should I say, pleased to meet you, Ms. Campbell? If memory serves, you are still batting zero, as my American friends say, in ending the life of Henry Pierce? Yes?"

"Ike, let me up. God. The Kurić people have been horrible … forcing me to do things."

"Sure, they have." I pulled her up and forced her arms behind her. "Stepan, you don't happen to have any rope?"

"I do not carry rope with me … unfortunately."

"Who's your buddy this time, Nika?" I asked.

"What buddy?" she asked, smirking.

I nodded toward the stairwell.

Hrubý groaned. "*Hovno.*"

"He escaped," Nika said. Only a sandal lay on the top step. "Yeah, Ike, you were so excited to see me that you and your friend here didn't notice him slip away. Fantastic job, guys."

I couldn't help myself and twisted her wrist a bit. "But we have you and your friend's shoe."

"He's not Cinderella, and he drives a Porsche, not a pumpkin."

Hrubý stepped forward, grabbed her left bicep, and loomed over her. "Stop your inane banter. We destroyed Kurić's organization in Virginia and Prague. Now it is your turn. Henry Pierce may be reluctant, but I will gladly slap away your red lipstick … and what's this?" He caught her chin and turned her head. "Interesting. It looks like you've gotten a well-placed slap already."

Nika yanked her head away, then shook it to get her long hair out of her face. "So, fellows, how do you want to do this? I scream rape, and you let me run away?"

Hrubý used his right index finger with his thumb and pinched her plumped-up lips together. "This is what will happen. We have made friends with the U.S. Marshals here, and your rape story will not be an issue."

"Let's call the police, Stepan," I said. "Nika has an outstanding warrant in Virginia with abetting a felony attack … on me."

"In time," Hrubý said. "Let's take this woman to the emergency clinic where the marshals are waiting. I'm sure it would interest our friends if this were the perpetrator who attacked Kai."

Nika's easy tears had vanished. She raised an eyebrow and smiled. "You may not have a choice," she said. "Ike, didn't someone tell you that he would do the same since you took someone away from him?"

I grew cold, then felt my face flush hot. "Stepan, we've got to find my folks and Angie."

"What? Yes … yes, I know. Are you well? Your face …"

I stared at Nika. "Someone has kidnapped them."

She let out a squeaky giggle. "You'll never win, Ike."

Exhausted, frustrated, and consumed by rage, I couldn't stop myself. My right fist already clamped in a ball, I struck her, hitting her nose and popping it to the left. Nika fell back against the rail and slid to the cement deck, out cold. I stared down at my hand, still in a fist, with blood on my knuckles. My mouth hanging open, I glanced at Hrubý and shook my head. "I hit her. I've never done that to a woman."

He grabbed my hand and tapped it several times to

release the tension. "Henry Pierce, as you said, this young woman has a warrant in Virginia and will now have another charge of aiding in an attack on a U.S. Marshal. She is seemingly aware of a recent kidnapping, plus she has a new attempted assault on you with a deadly weapon."

Wiping my face, I gave him a sideways glance. "I need to get away, Stepan. I'll kill her if they harm my folks and Angie. I mean it … I might kill her."

Hrubý gave a slight smile. "I doubt it. Go to the emergency facility and find Danny Keaka—tell him to get the police up here right away. Nika Campbell might offer information for us, plus something even more valuable."

I blew out my cheeks, then rubbed the back of my neck. "More valuable?"

"Come now. Do you not remember our group discussion a few days ago? We discussed Ms. Campbell's possible parentage."

"Right, right. Sorry, I can barely think."

"So, who has the bigger, how do you say, bargaining chip?"

I shook my head, unable to focus. "Bargaining chip?"

"Yes. The people who may have kidnapped your family and Angela, or the people who hold Miomir Kurić's daughter?"

Chapter Thirteen

I charged through the automatic double doors at the
clinic's entrance, finding Keaka and Trish Myung
seated in the waiting room. Keaka's toothy smile was
long gone, and Myung had fallen asleep with her head
rigid against the beige plaster wall. McNelly slapped
his wallet against his hip, staring into the vending
machine.

I bent over, panting. "Danny, call the police. I hit a
woman."

McNelly shoved his wallet back into a pocket and
joined us.

Keaka leaned forward in his chair and grabbed my
wrist, his movement causing Myung to wake. "Slow
down, man. What's going on?"

I closed my eyes. "Stepan and I tangled with the
perps we think attacked Kai—they were outside my
folks' condo. The guy got away, but Stepan is still
holding the woman … the smaller figure Trish saw. It's
Nika Campbell, Danny. Nika Campbell." Three
unfamiliar people hovered in the waiting area, watching
and listening.

Keaka let my wrist drop, stood, then grabbed my
shoulders. "Outside." The four of us stepped back
through the sliding doors and away from the entrance.
"Nika Campbell? The young woman associated with
Kurić?" he asked.

"The one and only, and Nika all but admitted the kidnapping."

McNelly grinned. "And you hit her?"

My face flushed hot again. "I couldn't handle the attitude, and I knocked her cold. She said the same thing as Tasev—I took something of his, his dad, so he would take something from me."

Myung waved a hand. "Hang on. Stepan is outside your mother's condo? I'll go check."

I stared at the sky. "But the police … we know of two crimes—"

Keaka grabbed my arms and pulled them back down to my side. "Henry, settle down, yeah? Myung, McNelly, please assist Stepan. Cuff Campbell and gag her if you must, and if she's still unconscious … all the better. Put her in your car and head five miles south of Makena. You'll see a sign for Palauea Beach. Once you turn, the path to the beach is on the right, and to the left is a dirt road. Follow it a mile and a half, and you'll come to a shack. If he's there, you'll find the green helicopter with a marijuana leaf painted on it."

McNelly smiled. "Ano?"

"The one and only. Get his ass up and tell him what's going on. He always likes a little intrigue."

"Got it."

"Tell him, Danny says, '*Puu Kahua*.' It's a helipad right in the middle of Kaho'olawe. The passcode is *Kikaliki*. There's a tin building there with a kitchen and some beds—it's rustic, but we can contain her."

"Kaho'olawe? Isn't it restricted?" I asked.

Keaka gave me a cockeyed grin. "Braddah, think for a minute. If we hand over Nika Campbell, what do you think the authorities will do with her? Lock her up, then extradite her to Virginia?"

My eyes filled with tears. "No … no, somehow, Nika would go off our radar again."

"Right. Now, McNelly, no matter what, I don't want Campbell released unless I'm the one banging on the shed's door. MAX-1 security. Understood?"

"Got it. Passcode is *Kikaliki*." McNelly motioned with his head. "Come on, Myung."

"And tell Stepan to get down here pronto," Keaka said.

"What should I do?" I asked.

Keaka had pulled his phone from his pocket and seemed to be thumbing through his contacts. "I think Marshal Barnet will sit with Kai. Somebody needs to be here. I don't want the one guy who got away to come back and finish the job."

"Stepan and I have excellent descriptions."

"Good, I'll let my friends know. You go in and tell Kai to sleep well while I make my call. We'll check on her in the morning."

"Thanks, Danny."

"But be prepared. We'll do our best for your family and Angie, but I'm not giving up Nika Campbell. It may sound cruel … but no bargains."

****

"Hey, Ike. Sorry, buddy, we got to get going."

I blinked and pushed up on my elbows. Keaka's conference room. Several pairs of legs stood around me while I rubbed my eyes. "God … my head. Eddie? When did you get here?"

"A few minutes ago—time enough to make coffee, and the best part? Danny had Irish cream."

I slung my legs to sit up and then took the cup from

him. "Tastes great. What time is it?"

"Seven."

A ray of sunlight mirrored off the harbor into the U.S. Marshals compound in Kahului. Hrubý and his three men circled the conference table, sipping coffee and devouring a bag of bagels. "Did you get a white donut, Eddie?" I asked.

"Nah, just a big raspberry bagel this morning."

"Where's Danny?"

Eddie gave a sly smile. "Fell back asleep after he picked me up. He's on the floor in his office. I bet he didn't sleep two hours last night." He thrust a blueberry bagel in my face.

"Oh, right, my head's clearing." I smeared cream cheese on one half, shoved a piece in my mouth, then chewed while talking. "We got here two thirty this morning—Danny pushed me toward the couch and told me to sleep. He looked like a zombie."

"The zombie lives." Keaka peered around his partly open door. He shoved his fingers through his thick gray hair and nodded. "Stepan … men. Let me freshen up in here, and we'll get started. Eddie?"

"Yes, sir."

"Coffee, please? Stepan, you guys make yourselves at home." He shut the door.

Eddie poured the coffee, and I excused myself to the hall bathroom. After washing my face, I stared in the mirror. Those three women … all important in my life and now missing. The kidnappers had offered us nothing. Had Tasev already killed them in retribution for his dead father, or did he want something else? If alive, where would they be? Maui, another island, headed to the mainland … or Europe even?

Someone pounded on the door. "Henry Pierce. Please come out. Danny Keaka is ready to start."

"Be right there, Vitaly. Ask Eddie to warm up my cup."

It seemed I always came in last to these gatherings, so I chose the one empty seat facing Keaka. He leaned over in his chair, his crossed arms supporting his head on the table. "Have a seat, braddah."

My heart and head pounding, I rubbed my temples. "First, anybody got any pain relievers?" I asked. "Second, Angie and my folks aren't hiding in this building, so sitting here won't help."

Eddie slapped down two pills and pushed my cup closer to me. "Ike, we need to talk through this … figure out a plan."

My eyes filled with tears. "I only want to find them."

"As do we," Hrubý said. "Henry Pierce, I cannot imagine your feelings right now, but we must have some patience."

I slugged back a fourth of my cup, then stood. "I'm going. Text me your plans."

Kharkov slapped the desk with both hands. "Sit down. I received a message last night of my father's passing, yet here I sit. I could not help him, but I will help you."

"Yes, and where would you be off to?" Talích asked. "Our schedule had us leaving this evening, but we have delayed our flight to help you."

"I will help, too," Žăk said.

My knees gave way, and I dropped to a squat next to Eddie. My shoulders shook—I broke down completely.

Eddie gave me a minute, then pulled at my elbow. "Have a seat, buddy."

I slunk into the end chair, then stared down at my lap. "My dad would be furious with me for letting this happen." I glanced up to see Kharkov hiding his face while weeping. I grabbed a tissue and wiped my nose. "Vitaly … I'm sorry about your dad. You should go home."

Kharkov leaned his forehead into his hands. "Arrangements are complete, and I have eight days until the funeral. I want to be a part of this today."

My hands shook when I picked up my coffee cup. I took a deep breath and spewed an exhale. "Thanks for staying, guys. Besides figuring out this kidnapping, maybe we can knock another leg from under Kurić."

"Exactly," Hrubý said. "Our first concerns are Angela Marconi and the Pierce family … but many other opportunities present themselves."

Keaka's frown disappeared. "We're thinking the same, Stepan. We rescue our friends first, then the fun starts." He pulled out his phone and began typing.

"Fun?" Talích asked. "Perhaps I cannot translate the meaning."

"Lieutenant," Hrubý said, "an American figure of speech. But would it not be 'fun' to capture, maybe dispose of Karanos Tasev, a key player in the organization, as well as neutralize Kurić's daughter?"

"I see. Yes … yes, you are correct. Fun."

Eddie leaned toward me, and I tilted back. "Ike, listen for a bit," he whispered. "Let Stepan and Danny work out a plan. But today, you and I are a team. Angie is my best friend, and your folks mean the world to me, too. They'll be safe."

"I'm counting on it."

He nodded. "I told you we would find Angie in Prague, and we did."

I couldn't help a chuckle. "And you ended up shot and face down in the mud."

"Uh, gentlemen?" Keaka asked. "Would you like to share with the rest of the class?"

Eddie straightened his back, raised an eyebrow, and said, "Just preaching patience, Danny."

Keaka nodded. "Patience, we will need. These kidnappers have contacted no one. I'm unsure what it means."

"They might still be on the move," Žǎk said. "How do we know they haven't left the islands?"

"Yeah … we can't know for certain," Keaka answered. "I have a watch out at the airports. We have tried to restrict small airfields, and they can't filter through a big airport because we would identify them."

"I believed you as only a consultant to the U.S. Marshals," Hrubý said. "How do you do these things? I cannot operate in such a manner in Prague."

Keaka shoved another unlit cigarette into his mouth. "The governor fishes with me, and let's say I have other connections, too. Anyway, I should tell everyone I received a message from Marshal McNelly. He, Marshal Myung, and our dear Nika Campbell had a restful night on the red desert flatland of Kahoʻolawe. Trish Myung presented, forcefully, a dose of Nyquil to Ms. Campbell after she complained about her sore, probably broken, nose. Poor thing … she gets a little overwrought."

"Good," I said, finishing my coffee. "Nika should grow to like the taste."

"She may have to," Keaka said. "So, Braddahs Eddie and Henry, we're going to find your family and Angie Marconi, and we will rescue them alive. Stepan and I talked earlier—"

"Did you sleep at all?" Eddie asked.

He raised an eyebrow. "A bit. Your snoring the entire way from Lahaina kept me awake."

Žăk raised his hand. "From our conversation with Tasev at your Coconut Castle, it seems he is filled with information. Although his reactions to us may cause his death, it would be ideal to have him alive for what he knows."

"Thank you, Mr. Žăk," Hrubý said, "but that will be his choice. If he remains alive, we will need to deal with the logistics of his travel back with us. There would be no chance for anyone to free him this time if we have our hands on him."

"Understood," Žăk responded.

"We'll take him to Kaho´olawe first," Keaka said. "He and Ms. Campbell can reminisce. I'm not so sure about his return, though. He's murdered people here …"

Hrubý clenched his jaws.

Eddie held up a hand. "Let's capture him first, then talk consequences later."

"Agreed," Keaka said while rubbing his baggy eyelids. "Can we move on now?"

The room remained silent.

"All right. Let me tell you about my hunch—the West Maui Mountains. If you walk to the other end of the hall and look out the window, you will find a mountain range to our west, a range you've passed as you came to this office from Lahaina or going down to

Kihei. It is a beautiful, rural area, with hiking trails and camping, waterfalls, and so on, but it can be perilous. The mountains are also home to a multitude of hiding spots, including caves and lava tubes. In the last dozen years, the U.S. Marshals and other law enforcement have acquired several drones to survey the area, find missing hikers, and other activities."

Eddie scratched his face, then rubbed his nose. "Danny, do the 'other activities' include tracking any peculiar activities, as in the criminal type?"

Keaka crossed his arms and used his feet to push away from the table, bumping into the wall. "We have isolated two areas. One is a straight up and down drug consignment area—helicopters flying in and out, back and forth … to Moloka'i, mostly. The D.E.A. has an operation currently to track these shipments. Beyond that, I've ignored it and left it up to others to coordinate as needed."

"You said two areas. What's the other?" I asked.

Keaka scanned the room, frown lines heavy at the corners of his mouth. "The Trail of Death, or so it's called, winds through the area. We have pictures, but they are hit and miss of seeing anything. Collecting pics of all the goings-on there has been inconsistent."

Talích wiped his mouth. "What is hit and miss?"

Keaka gave a sideways glance at Hrubý. "We've lost two drones over the last five weeks. I don't know what the hell they've armed themselves with, but something like a shotgun blast that can go remarkably high."

"They don't want to be seen," I said. "You're playing whack-a-mole if you have no surveillance. Can you get any satellite images?"

"That's a string I can't pull. Oh, an occasional still photo, but not much help."

"Who are they and them?" Kharkov asked.

Keaka smiled. "Good question. At first, I guessed it related to the drug trade I mentioned. These two suspicious areas only three miles apart are the most concerning, but a mountain separates them, which is not easily passable. The groups aren't necessarily connected, but I thought it odd when I told my D.E.A. contact that he only seemed interested in the drug trafficking side. The rest didn't whet his interest, even though he surely knew the trail through the wilderness had the stupid nickname. At that point, though, I wasn't aware of all the Kurić crap going on."

I swallowed the last of my bagel, then asked, "And all this means what? Seems you're pointing us to this area, thinking Tasev and friends have taken their captees there?"

"Yep. Vitaly?"

Kharkov straightened himself in his chair.

"The large screen behind you, and the keyboard and mouse are sitting next to it. Jiggle the mouse, and the screen will come on. I'm going to have you drive for us."

Kharkov glanced toward Hrubý, panic covering his face. "Where are we going?"

For the first time today, Keaka's gap-toothed smile showed itself. "Not literally driving. I want you to control the screen."

Kharkov shrugged, leaned forward in his chair, pulled the keyboard into his lap, then wiggled the mouse.

The fifty-inch screen lit up the dark corner of the

room. An app already ran in the middle of the display, showing western Maui from ten thousand feet.

"Good job, sir. Zoom in and find the name Puʻu Kukui below the West Maui Forest Reserve shown right there in the center. Puʻu Kukui is the highest peak on west Maui, about six thousand feet, and we consider it the second wettest spot in Hawaii. It's gorgeous scenery through there when not hidden in the mist." Keaka wheeled closer to Kharkov and pointed. "Okay, now go north and a little west from there. Find an object called the ʻEke Crater."

Kharkov moved the mouse.

"Stop. Stop there. Take the elevation down to two thousand feet. Ok, see sort-of-a circle? It's the extinct crater with the eroded remains of a volcanic cone sitting there in its middle. 'Heaven's Gate,' as the old Hawaiians referred to it. Does anyone want to guess what it's good for?"

Žăk had craned his head, trying to get a look. "It seems flat compared to the other terrain and conducive for helicopter landings, I would guess. And it would appear to be an ideal place to watch the goings-on in the entire valley."

"Bingo," Keaka replied. "But not completely flat. It's roughly five hundred feet across, so only an expert pilot could comfortably land on a misty day. A rough path normally takes hikers to the top, but I've been told heavy rain has damaged the trail in two places. Anyway, go down as far as you can on the map, Vitaly. Right there, yeah?" Keaka moved past Talích closer to the display, then pointed. "See here at the top and to the right. It's the so-called Trail of Death's starting point. The trail hugs this mountain for a thousand feet down, takes a hard left, and then disappears under the canopy of trees. Two waterfalls come and go at various times of the year, depending on the weather. It's all explored, of course, but we discover surprises now and then. Old records show a large lava tube up here a half-mile through these trees. I've seen black and white pictures of its discovery in the 1890s. The park rangers monitor it, and, supposedly, a bamboo bridge leads over a stream to the tube's entrance."

"Lava?" Kharkov asked.

Talích sneered. "Hardened lava, Mr. Kharkov … it's cooled."

Kharkov turned toward us briefly and rolled his eyes. "I guessed that."

"Yeah, it's like twenty thousand years old," Keaka said, smiling.

Hrubý glared. "Let us finish."

Eddie stood, stretched, then scooted his chair, forcing Žăk to stand and move out of the way. He shoved a finger onto the screen. "Come on, Danny, this is the second time you've mentioned lava tubes. Is this where you think our friends are?"

"I do."

"Why?" asked Hrubý.

Keaka poured more coffee. "I asked my contacts for info on this area, and I received a call about five this morning. It concerned a young man whom the authorities heliported into Kahului yesterday evening, taking him into surgery right away. Rescue personnel found him at the bottom of a small ravine off the trail I've mentioned. Apparently, he slipped and tumbled thirty feet or so into a rocky area. He stupidly hiked by himself, but he had enough smarts to send an SOS to a friend farther down the mountain."

Grabbing half a cinnamon bagel, Keaka bounced it against his hand a few times, took a small bite, then swallowed. "He'll be fine, it sounds like. After surgery, he told them he had seen a man hiking along the trail. Our injured guy called out, but no one heard him, or the man ignored him. Right after that, he said two middle-aged women, an older woman, and another man followed. Even from a distance, he said the second man towered over the others."

"It's them," I shouted, standing and stepping toward the door. "So … let's go. We know where they are now."

"Braddah—"

Eddie threw his hands in the air. "Ike, what are you going to do? Go in with guns blazing through rocks and waterfalls into a lava tube?"

"We're wasting time," I said.

"Come on, man," Keaka said. "We're almost done. Give me ten more minutes, and we'll head out."

Hrubý leaned his elbows on the table and held his head with his right hand. "Henry Pierce, please have a seat. We are all anxious, but it seems Marshal Keaka has knowledge of their location, and so far, it sounds as if they are alive."

I shook my head. "God, I can't imagine my grandmother trying to walk through there."

Hrubý pointed. "By tonight, we will be successful, and they will enjoy the rest of their stay in Maui."

I slumped into my seat and flipped a hand toward Keaka. "So … tell us your plan. Let's get this done."

Chapter Fourteen

We loitered in the tourist parking lot next to an orange Jeep at the ʻĪao Valley park's entrance. It had been stripped, including the license tag, and Hrubý could not be sure if it was Angela Marconi's rented Jeep. The cool wind swirled around us, a slight mist blowing through the valley. The iconic ʻĪao Needle thrust into the sky, its volcanic base covered in lush, green vegetation. Behind us, the flat dry isthmus connecting the two parts of Maui remained bathed in sunshine.

A dozen motorcycles had parked on a graveled area serving the Kamaka Trail's head. Keaka chuckled after telling us the name translated to 'imminent death,' but no one else cared for his humor. He told us advanced hikers, who we were not, used the path for hiking farther into the valley and away from the day-to-day tourists coming to view the rocky spires surrounding us.

The Kamaka Trail extended well beyond the state monument, going three miles to the base of the ʻEke Crater, where we would find the connection to the so-called Trail of Death. We had stopped by a sporting goods store in Wailuku, bought hiking equipment, then changed clothes in the portable bathrooms sitting at the parking lot entrance—not a pleasant experience.

We wore heavy hiking boots, cargo shorts, and

long-sleeve cotton shirts of assorted colors. Our camo backpacks weighed near twenty pounds each after Keaka insisted we pack water and snacks, a light jacket, rain gear, and a gun chosen from his arsenal.

The worn path followed a stream for several hundred yards. Beautiful clear water bounded around us to the left and right, sometimes over the black boulders and smaller rocks strewn through the narrow gorge. Palm fronds and ferns swatted us as we ducked through the undergrowth. I brought up our group's end and noticed two couples pass us, headed back to the parking lot—no one followed us.

Eddie, Kharkov, and I had the most trouble maneuvering. Eddie flopped once on his rear end—Kharkov fell twice, once soaking himself. I avoided the water, but not a fern that slapped against my left eye, blurring it for several minutes.

An hour into our journey, Keaka stopped and leaned against a lava outcropping next to the trail. The others found similar spots, but Eddie and I searched for someplace dry to sit.

Kharkov climbed to our right, finding the only beam of sunshine we'd seen since leaving Wailuku. He spread out his hands. "Ah, warmth. We should move away from the stream, Marshal Keaka. I see more sun ahead."

Keaka dug in his pack and pulled out a protein bar. "Come on, everyone, have a snack, and drink your water. This has been the simple part. And, Mr. Kharkov?"

"Yes?"

"I hate to disappoint you, but the sunshine is temporary."

"Unfortunate."

Hrubý stroked his head. "We have come well over a kilometer, yes?"

"Yes, sir, a little more than a mile," Keaka replied. "Good guess."

"Not a guess. We have had extensive wilderness training along the banks of the Vltava River, except for Mr. Kharkov, of course."

"Of course." Kharkov glanced toward me, giving a slight eye roll.

Hrubý grinned. "And fortunately, or unfortunately, I trained with Soviet troops in the Crimea, where I met Kharkov's adopted late-father. Soon, the government ordered three Czech specialty units to Kabul in late 1988. All my previous training did me little good in the desert."

"An ugly war," I said.

"Yes … as the Americans have found." Hrubý removed his black cap and scratched his head. "Thankfully, I remained there only nine months before my government brought us home. They believed we would aid in repressing the Velvet Revolution in Prague, but that was not to be." Hrubý's face flushed bright red. "Jakeš, Urbánek, and, of course, Gustáv Husák … I hate them all."

Hrubý's men were stoic. From what Žák had mentioned, Hrubý had been reluctant to reveal personal information over the years. His conversation with me in the car about his family, and now a brief mention of his early military career, had made Stepan Hrubý a fascinating man.

Eddie groaned and glanced at his watch. "Eleven thirty? And we've only come a mile?"

Keaka pointed. "What's the matter, Eddie? Those old feet aching?"

"Hey, my feet aren't much older than yours. Besides, it's not the feet, it's the heavy boots."

Žăk leaned back against a boulder and held up his right foot. "You will appreciate these by the end of the day, Lieutenant Stone." He dropped his foot too hard into a puddle, splashing his sunburned face.

Talích gulped the last of his water and wiped his mouth. "These are excellent boots. I can pay you when we return, Marshal Keaka."

"No, no," he replied, shaking his head. "You'll earn them today."

Eddie grumbled. "And you promise a helicopter ride back? I don't want to be trudging back in the dark, especially if we have Ike's granny with us."

"Yes, a helicopter ride back. My buddy, Ano, will handle it," Keaka said.

Žăk shoved his trash into his pack. "Can he maneuver through low clouds and an uncertain landing site?"

Keaka drenched his hands with his remaining water, then dried them on his shorts. "Oh, yeah. He did it in Vietnam, and I've seen him do it here if the lieutenant can ensure our getaway is safe?"

Talích nodded toward me and answered, "I will be ready."

"One more thing," Hrubý said. "My apologies for not mentioning it."

Keaka zipped up his bag halfway, then stopped. "Yeah?"

Hrubý stood, holding his pack by one strap. "As I parked outside your office, I received a call from

Prague … an associate of mine."

"Go on."

"According to my source, Tasev and his superior have communicated. They have noted my men and I are absent from Prague and are pursuing a mission halfway around the world. I am not pleased our location is part of a conversation among our enemies. Our days in Hawaii have also caused questions within our Police Presidium."

"Tasev may know we're tracking him," I said.

"Correct, no surprise, but we have a great opportunity here. A successful resolution to this situation would help us upon our return to Prague."

"Got it," Keaka said. He finished zipping his pack and hoisted the backpack's straps over his shoulders. "All right, men, let's get on with it. Pack your trash and then take a whiz if you need to, and off we go. We'll rest again in a mile and a half at Camp Maluhia."

"A camp?" Eddie asked.

"Right. It's a park rangers' building a half-mile from the crater. Then, we'll have a ten-minute walk out in the open to 'Eke. Lieutenant Talích?"

Talích's black caterpillar eyebrows arched into his forehead. "Yes, sir."

"You and Henry keep your ankles well."

****

On we plodded over a more challenging trail to the northeast. The heavy scent of moldy vegetation and wet earth encircled us. Without the gushing stream flowing next to us, it became easier to hear the occasional grumbles about the climb. I remained the last in line, losing ground to the front because of Eddie's ever-slowing steps.

He halted and bent over, hands on knees. "Oh, damn."

I stepped closer, straightened his backpack, and bent over to see his face. "What's up?"

He stared at me with his mouth open. "Ike … tramping up these trails is hell on me."

I nudged him with my elbow. "You're as studly as ever, Eddie."

"Old studs and young studs aren't the same. You'll find out."

We both stood straight when Keaka called us. "Eddie?" The others stopped and turned. Keaka passed by Hrubý, who followed. Hrubý's men dropped their packs, used them as seats, and they welcomed another break.

"I'm alive, Danny, but you're right. This is tough on a middle-aged man who likes his donuts and coffee."

Keaka lifted one strap of Eddie's backpack and slid off the other. He laid it near Eddie's feet, then dropped his own next to it. "Middle-aged? Maybe late middle-aged. Don't get discouraged, buddy—I've been pushing us hard. But we're only ten minutes from the camp."

"Really? We've been trucking it," Eddie said.

Hrubý stepped closer. "Danny Keaka, is there a key to the shed of which you spoke? I will take my men, and we will settle there until you arrive."

Keaka unzipped his bag and pulled out a yellowed envelope. "Good idea, and here's the key." He handed it to Hrubý. "These days, if it's not occupied, vandals come along and break windows and so on, even with a park ranger coming by twice a week. Try the generator out back and to the left. I suggest you and the others have guns ready … and lock the door behind you."

"Understood."

"If someone is there, mention my name—if they don't know me, take whatever measures you need to clear it. It's federal property—"

Hrubý waved a hand. "We know what to do." He turned away, plodding toward his men.

Kharkov glanced back and gave thumbs up with both hands, and soon they disappeared around a bend in the trail.

I had an ugly thought. "Could Tasev know we're close? The hostages might be in trouble."

"Anything's possible, braddah, but I've told no one except the helicopter pilot of our location. Two others in the Kahului marshals' office are aware of the situation, plus McNelly and Myung know we're on the hunt."

Eddie groaned and picked up his backpack. "But Tasev's not a dummy. He's bound to have a lookout or two near the lava tube if that's where they are." He took two steps, then stopped. "Well? Let's go. We can't let our European friends have all the fun."

The quick rest appeared to put a spring back in Eddie's step. In five minutes, the ground leveled off, and we headed around another turn. A stronger breeze greeted us, with a light mist filtering through the thinning trees and undergrowth. Still walking in the rear, I pulled my backpack to my front, pulled the zipper, and fished for the dark-green poncho I bought earlier in the morning. I tried slipping it over my head while walking, but with no success.

"Hey, wait up a minute," I said. "I'm trying to stay dry."

Keaka stopped, then slipped his backpack off his

shoulders once more. "It's too late. Eddie?"

"What? We're almost there, right?" Eddie asked. He pulled out the poncho, slipped it over his head after watching me, rolled up his safari hat, and dug into the bottom of his bag. Out came his pistol, and he slipped it into the leather holster strapped around his gut.

"You're thinking ahead of me," Keaka said, "but why'd you choose a .22? You needed a .44 like me." He flaunted his gun and smiled. "Yours is only enough to piss off a mongoose."

"I wanted to carry something light, and trust me, I can make a .22 hurt," Eddie said.

"This .357 is good for me," I said. "Its grip is better than the one I have at work."

Keaka chuckled. "All right. We've compared our guns, now let's get going." He pulled his pack and stared at Eddie. "Well?"

Eddie's jaw muscles unclenched. "Just a second. I want to run something by you guys."

I shifted my pack and adjusted the plastic hood farther down my forehead. "Like what?"

"Stepan Hrubý."

Keaka wiped his eyes and pulled his hood over his head—mist covered it right away, water dripping on his nose. "Yeah … Stepan's been my concern the whole time."

Eddie pulled a sleeve from under the plastic, wiped his forehead, then covered his head. "Don't get me wrong … it's nothing bad. I trust that man with my life, but we need to watch him."

"Why?" I asked. "He and his men will make this go much easier."

"I know his skills, Ike, but it's the emotional part

of this."

"Yeah, yeah, revenge on Tasev?" Keaka asked.

Eddie nodded. "Revenge can be a motivator, but it can also cause a loss of focus."

Hrubý wouldn't appreciate me telling his story. "Guys, keep this between us, but when he and I rode down together to Kihei, he opened up to me. He admitted his dad and Tasev's dad had a history, and he believes the older Tasev responsible for Stepan's parents' deaths. He also blames Tasev, Junior, for his wife's death many years ago."

"Wife?" Eddie asked. He slipped a hand under his hood to scratch his head.

"Right, and Hrubý has two grown kids living in Europe. He believes his wife's death occurred during an assassination attempt … on him, from a hit-and-run driver they never found."

"I don't blame him for his anger," Keaka said, "but Eddie is right. We don't need old emotions bubbling up today. If the brain gets foggy, then trouble follows."

"Even as much as he's done for us," I said, "we have to keep our thumbs on him."

"This has to go perfect today, guys," Eddie said. "We can't risk Angie and Ike's family getting hurt because Hrubý wants to settle old scores."

"Agreed," Keaka said. "Let's get to the camp before Hrubý makes his own plans."

****

A clearing emerged, opening to a flat plain leading to a plateau on our left. The heavy mist dripped from our hoods, a gusty wind blowing it back in our faces. My hiking boots grew heavy as the trail changed from rocks to mud.

I glanced at Eddie, who blew out beads of collected mist as they dropped onto his nose and rolled onto his mouth. He noticed me watching, then blew the drips toward me. "Nice weather."

Keaka grabbed my arm, stopped, and pointed. "Look about, friends. ʻEke Crater or Heaven's Gate—we're standing in its middle. The plateau over there is the volcanic cone, and it's the place we'll depend on Lieutenant Talích to set up his camp."

Eddie raised a hand and shielded his face as if looking into the sun. "You say it's three hundred feet to the top?"

"Yep."

"It disappears into the mist," I said.

Eddie winked. "You and Talích say your prayers. Falling will be a quick way to get to … Heaven's gates."

Keaka nodded toward the edge of the jungle. "To the right, guys."

Eddie stepped calf-deep into a puddle. "Damn. I made it all this way, and now the inside of my shoe is wet."

"I'm ready to get those long pants on," I said, "and the heavier cotton shirt."

"Me, too," Keaka said. "We're nearly three thousand feet up, and my phone said the temperature is sixty-five degrees. I hope the park rangers filled the propane tank in the last few weeks, and let's hope Hrubý's guys have started the heater."

We passed a cell tower and then pushed back under the tree canopy, sheltering us a bit from the moisture. The path stopped abruptly at the base of three cement steps, leading up to a wooden structure covered in tin and stilted a foot off the ground, hunkering under a blanket of thick ferns. Two skinny, vertical opaque glass windows stood as sentinels on each side of a rotting plywood door, painted gray, but peeling in irregular chunks. The park rangers had positioned two chunky brass locks above the tarnished doorknob. A light glowed through the right window.

Keaka grabbed the knob, then stopped. "Locked? I'll use my other key." He pulled out a ring of jumbled keys, thrust one into the top security lock, and twisted it using both hands.

I snickered. "Come on, Danny, you could blow on the door and open it. I don't know why you'd need to worry with two big locks."

He twisted his head back toward me and grinned. "Watch this." He leaned with his back against the door. A metallic squeal assaulted our ears until he got an opening wide enough to squeeze into the building. "Come in, gentlemen." He slapped the back of the door and smiled. "The plywood covers a three-inch-thick steel door, braddah. The frame of this little hovel is steel. It's here to stay. We dressed it down a little to keep away nosy visitors."

Kharkov stood in his underwear near the floor heater. "Please, Marshal Keaka, shut the door. We are trying to dry ourselves."

Talích, Hrubý, and Žák had changed except for bare feet. They had scattered their soiled white socks in front of the space heater that also warmed the kitchenette, where two cabinet doors hung open, showing a shelf of plates, cups, and a stack of plastic utensils. A short hallway led to a room with a bare mattress on the floor flopped next to a small lamp sitting on a pine nightstand. The hallway led into a darker room with a toilet, a distinct smell floating toward us.

"This is a tight fit for seven men," Kharkov said.

"And if you need to relieve yourself," Žăk said, "you will need to find a private tree. This toilet does not flow."

Keaka dropped his pack, then sighed. "Hell. Hang on, guys. Let me go check." He pulled the heavy door behind, then shoved his way through the ferns to the left side of the building, his curses leading the way.

Kharkov pulled on his long pants and buttoned his shirt. "A welcome stopover," he said, "and what is this called ... rural, yes?"

"Rustic," Eddie replied.

The door squealed again, and Keaka's head peered around the frame. "Braddah Henry, please try to flush now." He turned again and disappeared.

"Why me?" I asked.

"You young guys have to figure out the mechanical stuff," Eddie said.

I gave a glance at Kharkov and thumbed toward the bathroom. "Hey, Vitaly, you're the technical one."

"A simple device, Henry Pierce. Even you can figure it out."

Eddie buttoned his long pants and stared. "Ike, go. Danny's waiting for you to let him know."

"Fine." I stuffed my nose in the crook of my arm and pouted my way down the hall. I reached and pressed the toilet's lever. An easy flush followed, and clean water filled the bowl. "It works," I yelled to the crew, "and now I get first dibs."

Groans floated through the hall, and Eddie yelled

back. "Don't take forever like usual."

Shutting the door brought a quiet moment. I don't think I had been entirely alone since my second day in Maui. It amazed me how I had gotten here. Eight months ago, I finished a job as a patrolman at Mt. Vernon, then made my way to Alexandria, Virginia. A detective position in a middle-sized city—a perfect spot, I thought, to move ahead in my career. And because of that decision, I couldn't be sure my mother and grandmother were even alive.

Someone pounded on the door. "Ike Henry Pierce?" Žăk asked. "Please finish and come out. There are six other men with needs."

"It's Henry Ike," I replied through the door while washing my hands. I tripped over the threshold, and Žăk struggled past me.

I grabbed his arm and whispered. "If we're mixing up names, should I mention yours?"

He glared and shut the door in my face.

Eddie squatted on the floor next to the space heater, the heating elements dark as someone must have unplugged it. "Ike … you're white as a cloud."

Anxiety again swept over me like a flood. My face grew hot, and the room spun. I went down to one knee, lost my breath for a moment, then rubbed my pounding forehead. "Sorry … again. I'm mostly distracted until I remember my folks … hoping they haven't been …"

Eddie stepped toward me. "Stand up, buddy."

He helped me, but I didn't look up from the floor.

"Look at me, Ike, right in the eyes." He cupped my chin and pulled my face into his. "I'll bet your mom, granny, and Angie are doing okay. Remember, Danny has Nika Campbell as a bargaining chip."

Keaka grinned. "Right, and all of you should know we have leaked her capture to a few contacts."

I ignored him and stepped away from Eddie. "What if they aren't even in the lava tube? This whole trek seems like a wild guess. Maybe they've taken them somewhere else."

"What is the saying … do not borrow your troubles?" Hrubý said. "We will pursue Tasev—"

Keaka waved a hand. "We're here to rescue three women and, if possible, capture Tasev."

Talích emerged from the bathroom and stopped next to Žăk, who stood in the hallway.

"Good luck, Lieutenant Talích. Your skills are near those of Mr. Žicăn's."

"Thank you, Mr. Žăk, but we all know I could never outshoot him."

Hrubý brushed a cobweb out of a window and stared at the opaque pane of glass. "Killing Tasev is also a priority."

"For whom?" Keaka asked.

Hrubý adjusted his belt and holster once more. "He has murdered many, just like his father did, but the old Macedonian used politics as a veneer for his killings. His son doesn't care—he grew to adulthood with death all around him. But I will stop him."

Eddie grunted. He glanced at Keaka, then stepped closer to Hrubý. "Stepan, look. We know of the Tasevs' actions. Ike accidentally took care of the old man, and his son will get his reward, too, but the hostages are more important. Tasev's death isn't worth Angie's life, is it?"

Hrubý heaved a groan. "You are correct. Angela's life is more important." He spun away from the window and pointed at Keaka. "But understand something, Marshal Keaka. We have never been this close to Tasev's capture. If the chance arises, I will handle him, with or without your permission. You had him once and let him get away."

Keaka pointed back. "We followed the legal process I swore to uphold when I became a cop. Obviously, the same protection racket in Honolulu helped with Tasev's bail. A crooked judge did it, not me. And listen carefully, Stepan. You and your men are guests here on vacation in Hawaii and the United States, and you'll follow the law as well. And yeah, the law sucks sometimes, but I won't hesitate to arrest you."

Eddie crossed his arms. "We're wasting time."

Hrubý glared. "Do not interrupt."

Eddie stepped closer. "I'm not your underling, and I'm telling you how it is. The pissing match is over. By the looks of Lieutenant Talích's pack and equipment, I'd say he's ready. Right?"

Talích's furry eyebrows arched. He stared at the ceiling, seeming to concentrate. "Yes, Lieutenant Stone … supplies, rifle, scope, communications. I am good to go, as you say."

"And you, Ike?"

"Climbing has never been my favorite activity, but my Army Ranger dad insisted I learn. So, yeah, I'm ready."

"Good. It's past one p.m., and you need to get this show on the road," Eddie said.

"What show?" Kharkov asked.

Eddie sighed and glanced around the room. "And let me tell you guys something. If those three women get hurt because of somebody trying to be a hero, I will shoot you in the ass. Understood?"

Keaka adjusted his backpack, grabbed the door handle, and half-turned toward us. "I'll take our climbers to the base of the ʹEke Crater … show them the path. The rest of you relax. We don't all need to stand out in the rain while these guys climb." He nudged the door open.

"I choose to accompany my subordinate, Marshal Keaka. In fact, I insist," Hrubý said.

Keaka opened his mouth but stopped. He stepped outside, Talích and me following, leaving Hrubý behind while gathering his gear.

Chapter Fifteen

"This isn't what I expected," I said. Talích and I had marched up a narrow ridge for a hundred yards, rounded the first corner, then advanced directly into a twenty-foot-tall blockage of jumbled ferns and moss-covered boulders. More debris had fallen over the edge and landed forty feet below near a pool of clear water where Keaka and Hrubý stood, looking up.

"It's never as expected." Talích dropped his pack, knelt, and unzipped the heavy bag. "What did you imagine?"

"I guessed we would climb the whole way … literally. This is a skinny, counterclockwise path to the top … and how far is it? One hundred fifty feet?"

"Marshal Keaka said the top of the cone is only one hundred meters. This is not Mt. Everest, but it is dangerous with the rockslides. Now help me with the hooks."

I pulled my phone from my pocket. "Good signal, still."

"What?" Talích's eyebrows relaunched themselves. "Should there not be a signal? I can see the cell tower from here. Now please help me. I cannot do this alone."

He twirled the rope and swung his hook over the top of the pile, then yanked. The rope pulled back quickly, and the hook followed, landing at my feet.

I stumbled backward. "Uh, I'm going to stand a

little farther over here."

"Wherever you like, but once I have caught something, I want you here pulling with me unless you want to climb over this mound?"

"I'll pull."

"And if you are aching to use your phone, message Marshal Keaka to move away from where they are standing. Debris may fall their way."

"All right." I messaged him but received nothing back. "I hope he got it."

Talích tried again, with the same result.

"Be more careful," I said, grabbing the hook's rope. "If those boulders fall the wrong way, they'll crush us."

He looped the rope from his hand to his elbow and gave me a side glance. "I am aware of the physics, Henry Pierce, and I do not intend to kill us." He pointed above. "You try it. The blame can be yours."

I held the looped rope in my right hand and whirled the hook with my left. Heaving it upward, it disappeared over the top, clattering twice against the rocks. I pulled, and it stuck.

"See? That's how you do it."

Talích glared and spun his hook as if at a rodeo. "Shut up and watch. Yours is on the edge—I will place mine better." He pitched it, and it flew left, disappearing behind the largest boulder. He pulled on it, the rope giving way at first but finally catching onto something. "See? And mine is in a better spot for dislodging the blockage."

"You're going to pull the biggest boulder? How?"

"You notice the length I used?"

"Yes."

"We will maneuver down to the trail's curve, and both pull on the ropes from there—we need leverage. If it falls, it will not affect us unless a boulder knows when to turn right."

"Like the big round boulder in the movie."

Talích tilted his head and smiled. "Yes, one of my favorites. Let us try." He pulled on leather gloves and braced his feet. "Get behind me and pull when I say so."

Two feet of rope stretched behind him. I pulled on one leather glove, wrapped the cord around my hand, and steadied myself.

"Okay. Ready," I said.

"On my count, we will yank and then pull. *Jedna, dvé, tah.*" He yanked, but nothing happened. He glared. "Can you please help, Henry Pierce?"

I rolled my eyes. "I still haven't learned Czech. Let me count." We grabbed hold. "One, two, pull."

We tugged, tumbled forward, and both landed face down in the mud. A rumble and small stones scattered past us, plant debris floating to the ground.

Pushing up on my elbows, I found Talích sitting on his rear, leaning against the side of the mountain. He wiped his face and grinned. "I think it is not packed as tightly as we assumed."

I stood and helped him up, then pointed up the trail. "Look. Not much left of the blockage."

He sighed. "And I almost went over the edge."

"Yeah, and my rope and my hook are gone," I said. My phone vibrated. I yanked off the glove and pulled the phone from my rear pocket. "It's Danny," I said. "He thanks us for the avalanche we sent them and asks if we are well."

Talích frowned. "You warned them?"

"Yes." I typed a few words and pushed it back into my pocket. "I told him we would move on."

He slid his pack on and slung the rifle strap over his right shoulder. "My equipment is intact. We need to go faster, though."

"Agreed," I replied, then repacked my bag and hurried up the steep embankment. Heights rarely bothered me, but a look to my right, and my stomach fluttered. I stopped, choosing to stare at my feet.

Talích had moved away when he noticed me falling behind. "Henry Pierce? Are you ailing?"

Straightening up, I licked my lips and took a deep breath. "I shouldn't have looked down."

"I have avoided doing so after a similar feeling. This corkscrew-type ascent with this unstable ledge can play havoc. Stay near me and keep your eyes left. I will watch for us in front."

"Deal." We shuffled forward, turning hard to the left. "It's definitely not a nice, round circled trail."

"You are correct. The satellite pictures are misleading—it is an oblong hill, and the trail is uneven. I noticed the warning sign at the bottom, noting only experienced hikers should attempt this, but it should be closed to the general public."

"It's not for the faint-hearted. Danny said he would let the park service know about the rockslides. I guess it's common."

A chuckle, and he peered over his shoulder. "And since I'm staying on top of this hill, you must descend by yourself, Henry Pierce."

"I've no choice."

"Even if you are escorting any unknown hikers we

217

may find?"

"Yes, well, not likely," I answered. "No one else would have made it past the last slide. How much farther do you think the second slide is?"

"Marshal Keaka told me one in the middle and another near the top. But we must stay aware. After we go to the top—"

"Right. Make sure no one is up here when Danny's friend lands the helicopter in the field."

"Correct." Talích stopped again and dropped the backpack at his feet. "We should drink."

"Sounds great. Want to try my flavored water?"

He arched an eyebrow and frowned. "Not really."

"You'll be okay up here by yourself? It might be two or three hours, and these skies aren't looking any friendlier."

"Yes, I am prepared with appropriate clothing, plus this." He pulled a smaller canvas bag from his backpack.

"It looks like a book cover."

He smiled and shoved it back into his bag. "It is the correct size, is it not? It is a pup tent, I think you call it, although I am not sure what it has to do with dogs."

"Good, you'll stay dry." I opened a package of crackers and gave half to him. "Can I ask you a question?"

"When have you not asked questions, Henry Pierce?"

"Is there a Mrs. Talích?"

Talích shook his head in the light mist falling on us. "In my job? It would be a marriage in name only—I would never be home. I have had two serious female acquaintances, one of which led to an engagement, but work interceded, as always. And my colleagues … do you think any of them have married?"

"No, only Commander Hrubý," I answered.

"Yes, which is news to all of us, although he had mentioned his son before. I would never have guessed one or both Tasevs might have been involved in the death of the commander's wife."

"He seems convinced. And he mentioned his own father, too. A Valentýn Hrubý."

Talích frowned, zipped his pack, and pulled the straps over his back. "That is his son's name, too, but the commander does seem convinced of his wife's assailant. Now, I think I see one more turn, maybe two, and then we should be at the top."

"Good deal." I shoved the last cracker in my mouth and followed him.

Talích halted. "And there it is—twenty meters."

I peered over his shoulder and noticed another slide blocking the path. "It looks smaller than the first one. You'll have to use your hook."

"Yes, and this one is mostly mud, but see the boulder sitting on top? It is perched like a golf ball on a tee."

"And?"

"And we are in a dangerous place. My rope is not long enough to pull the rock and still give us distance for safety."

"Can we go over it?" I asked.

"I cannot fly."

"Look up," I said, pointing over his left shoulder. "The ridge there with the ferns whipping around it? Twenty feet to the top on our left."

"Yes. Talích removed his pack and placed it

between us. He knelt, then glanced at me. "I will climb it. I have the gear."

"Right, but go lightly and have your gun ready. I can send you more equipment after you settle."

"Very well. Watch me pack again so I do not forget things. I have my hammer and hooks, my pistol holstered to my left, and you will momentarily send my rifle and scope." He lifted his left arm to show me the BMG 50. "What else?"

"Deodorant? I smell something."

Talích scowled. "I used my deodorant, but we have been very active today." Another breeze, and he wrinkled his nose. "It is you."

I couldn't help holding my nose. "I don't think it's body odor … at least, a living body."

Talích's frown flipped, and his eyebrows arched. "Yes, definitely flesh. A boar? There are many wild ones here."

"I don't think so. A boar wouldn't be climbing a trail this high, would it?

"Doubtful."

"I'm getting a bad feeling about this. Let me get past you—I want to see something." The path had widened, and we stood side-by-side while gazing at the boulder sitting on top of the debris. I pulled a piece of bamboo from the pile and shoved it into the dirt. Talích brushed away soil as I loosened it.

"Careful, Henry Pierce. Dig lightly, or the pile might shift and squash us like insects." He dropped his pack and knelt on his hands and knees, lowering his head to near ground level. "Halt." He grabbed the bamboo stick from me, shoving aside a handful of dirt. Something has emerged from the pile. "A boar doesn't have a thumb and four fingers."

I pinched my nose. "It's not animal, and there's a turquoise ring on the pinkie. I would guess dead for a couple of days. The skin is discolored, and the hand has swollen from bloat."

"We have no way to know who it is unless we dig them out."

"Which might start another slide."

"You are correct. Leave it for now. Message Marshal Keaka and Commander Hrubý and tell them they will have to arrange the removal of this body. We are not equipped nor have the time."

"Agreed," I said. "It would be nice to know—"

"Not now … it is time to act. Look up to our right."

"Rocks, rocks, more mud. And?" I asked.

"And the area slopes inward. I can climb easily to the jut of rock and stake and climb the rest of the way over the top."

"There's enough room for two on the rock shelf, but it would be easier for me to send your gear from there rather than here."

Talích scratched his chin, then patted my shoulder. "This is what I will do. First, I will climb with nothing—the backpack and equipment will unbalance me." He dropped everything at my feet.

"That works, but let's tie the rope around your waist. We'll use it instead of me trying to throw it up." I pulled it tight in a small knot, and he turned and started up the slope right away. "Looks like you're doing good," I yelled, light debris peppering my face.

Talích slipped down a bit but held on with no problem. "I am fine," he yelled back. He inched his way to the outcropping, placed his arms up to his elbows on the black volcanic stones, and pulled himself onto the black lava shelf. On all fours, he crawled to the edge and waved, pushed up to a kneel, then cupped his hands around his mouth. "Henry Pierce … do not come up … the earth is not compact." He stood, then balanced before tiptoeing and peering over the edge above him.

"Are you certain?"

"Very certain." He brushed off his jacket and pulled the hood over his head. "It is getting wetter," he yelled. "The wind is worse on top, but I do not appear to have company. Hurry with my equipment." He untied the rope and held it in his gloved hands.

I wound my end through the backpack's straps and wiggled the cord.

"No," he yelled. "Send my rifle up at the same time. You must hurry. The edges here are shifting."

I untied my knots and looped the rope around the rifle and backpack. "Okay, ready." I lifted both items over my head and waited for a tug.

Talích sat, then leaned back against the embankment. He kicked at the rock with both feet, seeming to get a foothold before pulling. "How many pounds do you think?"

A curtain of rain blew over me, drenching my face even with my hood up. "Thirty pounds, I'd say." The pack lurched out of my hands and disappeared into the clump of ferns to my left. "What do you think?" I asked, coughing through the moisture.

"Not too bad. I need to pull before it finds a place to hang." The pack jumped toward him in spurts. Fifteen feet, it spurted upward, halfway, and he stopped.

"Are you hung up?" I asked.

"Resting. I am afraid to change positions without dropping them or me falling. One moment." His arms remained outstretched while he shook his head twice to shake away the rain. "All right. Now I go."

A second burst of energy brought the pack up near Talích's feet. The butt of his rifle showed first—he leaned toward the edge to grab it. Dirt and stones fell toward me.

"Easy," I yelled.

Talích nodded and tried another time. The rifle came over the edge, and the backpack's left strap showed itself. He pulled it over without resistance, then fell back against the hill. He gave me a thumbs-up, stood, and untied the pack from the rope—it slithered down toward me.

"Wish me luck." He sought momentum, swung the pack forward, then backward twice, and threw it over the edge above him, followed by his rifle. "All good here," he shouted.

"Great. Now, how do you go the rest of the way?"

He shook his head while setting his hands on his hips. He looked to his left and pointed. "That way." The ferns quivered as he plowed through the undergrowth, moving out of my sight. Apparently, he had found a path.

All movement stopped.

"Talích?" No response.

Our trail vibrated beneath my feet, followed by a splintering crack and a rumble. The mountain's face near Talích's path dissolved into black mud, hard lava, and plant bits, tumbling onto the ledge where Talích had been resting. The mass slowed, then gathered more debris as it collapsed toward me. I grabbed my backpack and scrambled back down the path, a deep rumble following me. Around the corner, I stopped and turned. Debris slid by me and shot over the side. The trail up to Talích had disappeared. One minute passed, then two.

My phone vibrated. "Pierce."

"Ah, Henry Pierce. You are alive," Talích said before coughing several times.

"As are you?"

"Yes, I began unpacking when a sound like thunder came from the top, and a portion of the mountain disappeared."

"It passed me on the trail."

"Oh? Can you find your way to the bottom?"

"I could jump, but yes, the trail is intact … so far."

Talích breathed heavily in the background. "Excellent. I am assembling my tent on the northwest side of this plateau, then I will open my hand warmers. After that, I will ready my rifle. I look forward to trying Marshal Keaka's superb scope."

"Sounds great. Are you sure you're alone?"

"I have scanned the area and have seen nothing other than scattered trash left behind by others."

"Even better. All right, we depend on you to keep us safe."

"Understood … and I confirm my escape will depend on Mr. Ano's helicopter. I cannot climb down."

I slowed, rounding another turn with a steep drop-off. "Right, no other options. Remember, Danny said the chopper had army green paint with a marijuana leaf painted on a door."

"Yes, yes, I remember the description. Oh …

Marshal Keaka."

"What?"

"I talked to him before I called you. The mudslide missed them again, but a body landed near Commander Hrubý. It must belong with the hand we saw."

"Has to be. Well, fingers crossed for you, Lieutenant Talích."

"Go careful, Henry Pierce."

****

With my backpack much lighter, the walk down became more manageable. I kept my eyes to the right, and on my seventh turn, flat land finally appeared, stretching out to where Hrubý and Keaka waited, one standing and the other kneeling.

Eddie had joined them. He waved, then cupped his hands. "Hey, Ike, did you learn to yodel?"

"No," I shouted, "and I'll thank you for talking me out of doing such a thing again." A minute later, I stood in the light rain between him and Hrubý.

Eddie patted my shoulder. "Glad you made it."

Hrubý showed a slight smile and wiped the moisture from his face. "Lieutenant Talích is well, correct? He said so."

"When I left him, he said he was setting up camp."

Hrubý nodded. "We are thankful."

"Did he tell you the helicopter is his only escape now? The trail near the top has collapsed."

"Yes, he emphasized his departure needs," Hrubý said.

Still squatting, Keaka motioned with his head. "Braddah Henry, welcome back. Please come here."

The odor returned, and this time with the entire body visible. "God, Danny, that body is broken seven

225

ways to hell."

Keaka grimaced. "It's extreme, isn't it? The head's bent backward and the left foot laying on the shoulder blade—I'd say at least seven ways."

"You should be a coroner."

"No thanks, and I don't know about the face." Keaka stood, then stretched his back. "I've called a buddy in Wailuku to pick up the body, and he'll get it to the coroner in Kahului."

Eddie had stepped closer. "You think it's a hiker?"

Keaka shook his head. "I doubt it … no gear."

"An associate of Tasev?" I asked.

"Could be," Keaka answered. "He's unarmed, though, if it means anything. Help me push him over onto … what I think is his chest."

Eddie and I gagged simultaneously but did as asked. The body rolled over, its head flopping forward onto the ground.

Keaka checked the body's back pockets, then pulled a wallet from the left side. "Nice leather bifold." He checked the different slots—the right side held credit cards, then he pulled out the contents from the left side. "Driver's license, I guess." He stood again and handed me the rectangular piece of plastic. "What language is it?"

I rubbed off dirt and squinted to focus. "It's Cyrillic."

"I know, braddah, but that's not a language."

"I can't read Cyrillic. See on the bottom right. Is it a word? Kumanovo?"

"What of it?"

"A city? But this face on it definitely isn't Tasev."

Eddie crossed his arms. "Stepan? Want to help?"

Hrubý brushed my arm as he grabbed the square plastic piece. "Yes, it is Macedonian script, and, yes, the word is Kumanovo, a small city near Skopje … close to Serbia. It has a reputation."

"For what?" Eddie asked.

"For everything. Gentlemen, Lieutenant Talích has signaled his readiness, and I, likewise, have signaled my men to join us. Mr. Kharkov is bringing a blanket to cover this body and will return to the cabin. Mr. Žăk is more than ready to proceed."

Eddie's phone buzzed.

"All right," Keaka said, frowning. "The lava tube is a twenty-minute walk on the trail … thirty if we have to go off the path and climb through the brush."

"Agreed. We cannot go wandering off the trail—"

"Guys," Eddie said.

Keaka ignored him. "With five men, we should split and move in from two directions."

Eddie shouted. "Guys … listen to me."

Keaka grabbed his pack. "What?"

"The text message on my phone. Unknown caller."

"Do you need a car warranty?" I asked.

"Shut up, Ike."

"So, what is it?" Hrubý asked, seemingly exasperated by all the talk. "Tell us."

Eddie wiped his mouth. "It says 'Hurry.' "

Chapter Sixteen

The five of us slogged along a crooked route of pebbles and mud into a jungle of dense undergrowth that appeared untrimmed for months—not a regular hiking trail for typical tourists. I walked behind Keaka, and Eddie behind me. Hrubý and Žăk walked faster, vanishing into the darkness twenty yards ahead.

I skipped a step and tapped Keaka on the shoulder. "Danny, you need to slow them down. It's the Trail of Death, after all. Hrubý will go storming into the lava tube—"

"Come on, guys. You're acting like Stepan's the enemy," Eddie said. "Let's not go down that road. I'm a little concerned about his rationality, but he's a good man."

"You know what I meant," I replied, "but you heard Hrubý. A bullet through Tasev's head would make his day."

Keaka turned and walked backward a few slow steps. "You're both right. Our friends are not the problem here, but I don't want Hrubý going vigilante on us. He's a good man with a hardened heart for Tasev, not to blame him, because Hrubý's no different from us. Things happen to us over the years that cause darkness in our souls. We try to stay out of those dark corners, but the shadows are always there." He turned and strolled down the path.

"Philosophy from Danny Keaka," Eddie said, winking. "Well, my soul is a nice mocha color." He patted my back. "How about you, Ike?"

Keaka turned back toward us and grinned. "Somebody once said, 'I have no desire to peer through the windows of men's souls.' And that's the end of my philosophy lesson for the day."

"Deep, Danny."

He winked. "Our friends will have to slow in a couple of minutes. The bridge should be coming up."

"What bridge?" Eddie asked.

"*Ohe Uopo*, the Bamboo Bridge. I haven't seen it, but I've heard of it, and I think I hear water."

"Me, too," I said, watching Hrubý and Žăk duck under bent and broken bamboo stalks before disappearing into the heavy underbrush.

"We should find a beautiful, tall waterfall a quarter of a mile northwest of here—the stream flows across our path. Someone built a bridge many years ago, and some say Kamehameha built the original himself."

Eddie chuckled. "That's a damn old bridge."

"Yeah? And 'old' is what I mean by slowing down. From what I've been told, it's rickety enough when only one person crosses it. If Hrubý doesn't think first, they might take a cold bath in the stream, plus foul up our crossing over."

We followed Keaka into the shady bamboo forest, pitch black at first, but my eyes adjusted. The path changed into small steppingstones, most broken and partially buried. Water flowed somewhere in front of us, getting louder as we approached. Everything dripped, but the thick foliage sheltered us from the heavier showers.

Keaka pointed. "Down there."

The path transformed into purposeful, manufactured steps. The stones became rectangular concrete blocks under our feet—old and stained but steady. Bamboo handrails ran parallel to each side, sections splintered here and there.

"I hear voices," Eddie said.

Keaka pointed. "Me, too, and notice where the path evens out? A few steps beyond should be the bridge. Hang here a second." He hiked first one leg, then another over the rail, then shoved into the growth.

The voices grew louder, and two hiking boots appeared on the bottom step, then a body bent halfway under a broken bamboo stalk—Žăk's face appeared with a big smile. "Lieutenant Stone, Detective Sergeant Pierce … welcome. We have come to an impasse and need direction from Marshal Keaka." He glanced behind us and quit smiling. "And he is where?"

"I'm here," a voice called from behind. Keaka emerged from the thickest stand of green bamboo, pushed through a broken piece of the rail, and stepped down toward us.

Eddie scratched his head. "Danny? How did you get behind us?"

"I did a little exploring. Why not?

Žăk squinted. "This is an odd time—"

"Never mind." Keaka nodded to our left. "Let's go, guys."

"You won't tell us how you came that way?" I asked.

"I took a wrong turn. Let's go." He jostled past Žăk and hurried out of sight.

"Someone seems a little embarrassed," I said.

Eddie chuckled and pointed at Žăk. "Lead the way, sir." Žăk stepped away, and Eddie grabbed my arm. Leaning closer, he said, "I think our friends are getting a little tense."

"I noticed," I replied while slowing again, "and I am, too."

"I don't blame them, mind you. This is getting a little too much Indiana Jones for me," Eddie said.

"Yeah, a big boulder reminded me this morning."

"Stick close, though, Ike. Those three women are the most important people in our lives. We're here for them, not these guys. We'll get them free and go home. Hrubý and bunch can get their revenge and keep hunting all the gold coins they want, Danny can go back to fishing, and we can be normal detectives."

A bamboo stalk scratched my face. "Ouch. It all sounds good, Eddie, but all this hokey-pokey, as you used to call it, seems to control us rather than the other way around. And how did we get to Maui in the first place? Didn't someone want to get married here?"

Eddie frowned while adjusting his backpack. "Yeah … that guy."

"Right. Come on, or we'll lose Žăk, and I don't have a clue on how to get out of here."

The bamboo grew even thicker as we walked along the path. We stepped down while turning in a half-circle, water rushing ever louder below us but still not visible. Pale-yellow flowers enveloped us.

"Whew, that's a powerful scent, Ike. It reminds me of Doris's lei they gave her at the airport."

The overhanging plants hid Žăk's torso, and I saw only his feet, occasionally his legs, while moving steadily along the path. He hesitated, and we almost caught up before he disappeared to the right.

A few more steps down, Eddie and I stopped.

"The bridge," Eddie said.

Ohe Uopo stretched before us. Three connected sections crossed the surging river—the first two portions from our side appeared newer and held steadfast in the rushing water. They connected to a final segment that diverged into two parts that angled away from one another. A challenging feat to build, judging from the complicated construction. The third segments had lost most of their rails, and the bamboo footings and crossbars lacked upkeep—several splintered slats hung vertically, pointing down to the river. I couldn't see the other side, making it difficult to judge the last span's length. At a distance to our left, the hissing sounds of a waterfall flowed through the ravine.

Keaka, Hrubý, and Žăk stood near the edge, Hrubý seemingly upset.

I touched Žăk's arm. "What's up?"

Žăk frowned and motioned with his head. "You and Lieutenant Stone should get into the conversation."

"Great," I said. "More wasted time."

Eddie stomped past me and grumbled. "Talkingest bunch of damn people. Let me handle this, Ike." He stopped at the edge of the drop-off and yanked his hood back. He placed a hand first on one of Hrubý's shoulders, then Keaka's. "So, gentlemen, do you have this figured out? You're having a séance … what's up?"

Hrubý gave Eddie a sideways glance, grabbed his hand, and brushed it off his shoulder. "Marshal Keaka and I are trying to plan a strategy."

"Well, let's go. That's my strategy," Eddie said.

"It's past three o'clock, so we have about an hour and a half to get back to the hill, mountain, or whatever the hell it is, before it turns dark." He pointed over my shoulder. "Do either of you believe we can go back up the trail in the dark with Rita Faye?"

Hrubý pulled back his hood and stepped toward Eddie, his head cocked and his eyes leering over him. "Do not interfere in this effort, lieutenant—"

Eddie's fist connected with a noticeable smack— Hrubý fell backward. Žăk grabbed Eddie's arm and twisted it behind him.

I looped an arm around his neck. "Steady, Žăk. We don't want this to get uglier."

Keaka yanked his gun from its holster and backed onto the bridge's first span. He pointed first at Hrubý, then Žăk. "Commander … Mr. Žăk."

Hrubý pulled himself to a kneeling position, then wiped blood from his lip. He waved a hand. "Let him go, Mr. Žăk, and you, Henry Pierce."

Eddie pulled away and nodded toward me. "Ike, get over here." He walked several feet out onto the bridge, and I followed. He pointed at Žăk. "Young man, however tough you think you are, or however much training you've had, you touch me again, and I'll make sure you never have kids. And Stepan, the only interference I've seen is from Europeans who want to chase and kill each other over those damn stupid coins. Again, if any of you or your men gets one of those women hurt … I swear I'll ring your necks and enjoy doing it." He walked farther out.

Keaka holstered his gun and pointed at Hrubý. "You're a better man than that, Stepan. Remember, you're on a temporary visa here. I'll be glad to slap all of you on a plane to Prague. You guys have been a great help, but you need to put aside your hate for Tasev and make better decisions. Your men expect it, too."

Hrubý slapped the wet earth, then stood. Wiping off his hands on his pants, he said, "My apologies, Lieutenant Stone, Marshal Keaka. I have not set the correct example."

Eddie leaned on the bamboo rail. "So, what the hell are you two so fired up about? And make it fast. I'm tired of this damn drama."

Keaka pulled the backpack's straps over his shoulders. "Eddie, the other side of this bridge turns into two paths. My contact has led me to believe the paths are simply part of a circle meeting at either end of the lava tube. I had hoped we would split up and meet in the middle. No one in there can escape."

Eddie clapped his hands twice. "Sounds great. Let's do it." He stepped farther onto the bridge. "Okay, we'll take one side, and the three of you take the other. Ike? Let's go. Those ladies are our responsibility."

"Sounds good," I said. I grabbed onto a bamboo rail while trying not to look down. "Of course, we're all assuming my folks and Angie are even there."

"Wait," Hrubý yelled to us. "The other side—"

"The other side, what?" Eddie asked.

Keaka blew out his cheeks. "Slow down, friend. Those split spans are narrow and weak. Go slow, and the two of you do not cross on the third span simultaneously. Understood?"

Eddie glanced at me. "Got it. You good, Ike?"

I nodded and turned toward Keaka. "Danny, my phone's signal is dropping in and out. We'll try to let you know when we're in position."

"Sounds good, braddah. If you don't hear from me in thirty minutes, we'll meet back here." He pointed toward the bridge spans. "Eddie, I mean this in a good way … since you're a little … chubbier … take the right span. It looks stronger."

Eddie's jaws unclenched, and the corners of his mouth slanted upward. "Load limit, huh?" He motioned to me, shuffled a few small steps, and turned. "Come on, Ike. I'm not waiting on them if we get to the tube first. We'll treat it like when we hunted down Rijad Kastrati in Prague."

"You keep bringing that up. Kastrati found us first."

"Same difference." Eddie straightened up, then stepped forward, passing over the seam between the first and second spans.

"You're doing good, Eddie." Keaka squatted, staring down at the rickety infrastructure.

Hrubý and Žăk stood behind Keaka, both grimacing while watching us.

Eddie gave us a behind-the-back thumbs-up. "Moving slow, Ike." He shuffled his feet forward as if on ice. "There aren't any obvious breaks … yet."

I had to shout as the rushing waters grew louder. "It wouldn't show a break if they aren't at the tube and never came this way. We've spent all this time—"

"Danny seemed pretty certain." Eddie stopped at the division between the second and third sections of the bridge. "Stay back, buddy. I'm going to walk a few feet and see what happens."

I peered over the side and drew a breath. "We're about fifty feet above the water, and it's moving fast." I squinted as if it would help. "How do we get into these messes?"

"Don't know, and quit looking down. I know we need to do this separately, but I don't want us to lose sight of each other. I'll keep going, and you stay put as long as you can, then head this way. We have to take a chance."

"I know, but it's dark as hell under this tree canopy." I heard nothing but rushing water and creaking sounds from the bridge's braces. "Eddie?"

The creaking stopped. Eddie shouted through the roar. "Ike? I can barely see you. Come on, you'll have to move closer to keep up."

"Okay." I looked back, but too quickly, bashing my backpack against the railing. The rail gave a bit, and I leaned to the left. Surprised at how little distance we had covered away from our colleagues, I waved and shouted. "Hey, Danny. We're moving forward … and the bridge shifted."

Keaka returned my wave and yelled. "I see. We've lost sight of Eddie."

"He's there."

Eddie bellowed. "Come on, dammit. Keep up."

I crossed the seam onto the third span, the bridge shuddering. Water gushed against the boulders beneath us, crashing hard against the bank, then heading back into the channel to our right. The waterfall must be near—a cloud of mist had grown so thick I had trouble breathing. I pulled my phone and tried the flashlight, but its beam caused a halo effect in front of me, blurring things worse than without the light. I couldn't see Eddie now or hear him. Nothing else to do but move ahead.

"Eddie?" My folks … how would they have crossed this? Marconi, more than likely, but my family?

My hand slipped off the railing, and I leaned hard to my right before recovering my balance. The rails disappeared on both sides, giving me a floating sensation in the blackness. Three feet in front of me, the bamboo decking vanished. I dropped to all fours, inched forward in a crawl, then slumped hard when my right arm fell into space, my head hanging in the emptiness. I pulled back, feeling for anything to my left, and guessed I'd found an opening in the decking, one into which I hoped Eddie had not disappeared. I crawled ahead on all fours, sometimes crossing over more gaps, most patched with odd-sized bamboo pieces.

My phone vibrated, but it would have to stay in my pocket. In front of me, slender silhouettes of vegetation appeared ahead, and I saw, or believed I spotted, handrails leading to solid ground. Coming up to a stooped walk, I ducked under thick ferns, water dripping from the foliage like a hard rain. Finally, hard ground—the plant overhang vanished, and the rocky edge of the riverbank came into view.

"Eddie?" I called out, almost panting. "Eddie!" My heart sunk. I yanked my phone from my pocket, remembering it had vibrated—a message from Keaka wondering how we were doing. I replied: *I'm safe but haven't found Eddie*. The text message errored.

What to do? Eddie wouldn't have gone on without me. If he had dropped into the river, my friend would have been lost. I would have to crawl back to the damaged part of the span and see if his body sprawled across the boulders.

I dropped my backpack on what seemed to be a path, smashed into the brush on my right, then leaned against a boulder to relieve myself. A tear dropped onto my cheek. Marconi, Eddie, my family—could they all be gone? Turning toward the bridge, I used the raincoat's sleeve to wipe away mist and tears. I shivered, thinking of crawling along on the bridge with the surging, rolling water sweeping under me. My backpack would stay behind this time, its weight a hindrance … but what happened to it? Turning in a circle, I hadn't wandered far from where I had been. My pack had vanished. Someone else was here.

A chill fluttered down my spine, like someone tickling my back with a feather. I unsnapped my holster, pulled my gun, and marched back onto the muddy path that took a left turn past a jutting hunk of brown lava. Another step and my rain jacket pulled tight against my throat. I jerked backward and pulled away, my gun ready.

"Woah there, Ike. Where are you headed without your bag?" Eddie thrust the backpack into my chest. "You looked like you were walking the plank."

"Where the hell did you go?" I slid the pack's straps over my shoulders. "I called several times."

His eyebrows bowed upward, and his mouth hung open. "Huh? You know my hearing's bad." He shoved his phone in my face. "Danny sent me a message … said you had made it. Why didn't you send one to me?"

I faked a grin. "Well, I … I thought you drowned."

"Me? Not quite. I tried to yell about the hole in the decking. I guess you didn't hear me."

"Nope, but I found it."

"I noticed you were pissing on the rock, so I waited

here with your pack. You walked right by me."

"Wow … anyway …. Danny and crew are crossing?" I asked.

Eddie yanked his yellow plastic hood back and scratched his head. "Right, and, supposedly, Žăk has crossed … Hrubý is next."

"Good, and you still want to beat them there?"

He pulled his hood over his bald head. "Yep."

We walked a hundred yards when Eddie threw his arm against me, reminding me of how my mother used to hold me when she made a quick stop in the car. "Listen."

"What?"

"Not sure," he said through clenched jaws.

"You said you had bad hearing."

"Maybe my imagination is better than my hearing." He pointed. "Look near those groups of banana trees."

"And?"

"Past where the bamboo leans hard over. You see the round, orange-looking light?"

"Right. I see it."

"It has to be the lava tube."

"You're right," I said.

Eddie shoved past me before I grabbed his sleeve. "What?"

"Think about it, though," I asked. "Wouldn't you suppose someone would be on watch?"

He swiped his face of moisture. "A trap? Maybe, but we're out of choices. Message Danny and tell him we're in position, and then it's time to do our thing."

I typed away, sent the message, and blew out a deep breath. "It went through. So, yeah, time's up. Let's get closer. You stay on the left side, and I'll try to push through the bamboo stand on the right. I think I can see better from there."

"Got it."

Eddie pulled his gun and hustled near the entrance, hiding in the shadows under dripping palm leaves hanging over the ragged, black and brown lava tube. He shrugged, so I assumed he had seen no one.

I rammed my way into the thick bamboo stand with stalks a third the size of my thighs. A gap emerged a few yards outside the tube's entrance. An engine noise had grown louder on my right, where I noticed a wooden, toolshed-sized structure nestled against the lava tube. This had to be the energy source for the light inside the tube, which meant someone had to have brought fuel to keep it running.

I waved to Eddie. He returned the wave with his gun, pointing the pistol at the entrance. Presuming he wanted me to move ahead, I escaped my bamboo hideout and stepped nearer the shed. The gate hung loosely, with the rotted bottom of the wood-slat door hanging free, the top hinge holding it crooked to the frame. I never welcomed surprises, but I knew I had to look inside. My dithering did not please Eddie, judging by the face he made. He pointed at the shed, and I puffed up my courage.

I grabbed the top of the gate, yanked hard, and it popped open into my cheek—a nice smack to the face. Inside, the old gray generator chugged away, with two upside-down gasoline canisters tossed in a corner. I jerked my phone and triggered the flashlight, aiming directly at the far corner behind the engine.

Another body, male, leaned back against the corner in a sitting position, his head tilted to the right, looking as if sleeping. An orange cloth hung loosely around his neck. I backed away, escaped the shed, and got Eddie's attention. I typed a message and waited for his response.

He shrugged, the message erroring. I tried to make a motion of someone with a broken neck, but it didn't help. Eddie glanced at his phone again, looked up, and pointed directly at the lava tube.

I pulled my gun, slunk along the edge of the bamboo stand, and pressed against the tube while peering around the corner. The lava tube was a long tunnel, the bottom flat, with rough, irregular rock jutting along the edges to the far entrance. The orange light came from a series of flood lamps spaced along the inside wall, likely for any hikers or tourists finding their way here.

A car-sized protrusion of jagged lava almost hid what appeared to be a sitting area, forming a u-shaped divot into the side of the hill. I noticed two pairs of feet, of which both the right ones jiggled up and down … like my mother and grandmother did when anxious. I gave Eddie a thumbs-up and made a 'V' sign with my fingers, trying to tell him I had seen two people. He stooped and shuffled toward me.

Standing straight again, he peered around the rock, his head directly under my chin. "Two people?"

"Yes. Look toward the left and down. I see one pair of feet now—the other person has moved, I guess. Women's shoes and feet with nervous twitches like my folks."

Eddie whispered. "Anybody else?"

"Don't know."

He pulled his phone. "Ike, remember the message I

got earlier. The one that said 'hurry'?"

"Yeah."

"Watch this." He typed something and sent it, then shoved me back against the tube's outside wall.

Someone stood and crept toward the other entrance, her back to us.

"It's my mother." I moved past Eddie, but he grabbed my arm.

"Hang on, man. We still don't know who else is in there." He stepped one foot into the entrance. "Dang. This lava tube looks like a picture from my last colonoscopy." Eddie's phone vibrated. "Look at this." He shoved his phone in my face.

"What?"

"I asked, *who is this*?"

I took it from him and chuckled. "*Your boss. Get your ass in here*."

"Come on." I pulled away and darted inside. "Mom? Granny?"

They came around the corner and smothered me like a sandwich.

My mother wiped her face. "Ike, my God. We were so scared."

"And … cold." My grandmother leaned her head into my chest and sobbed.

Marconi stared, both hands on her hips. "Dammit, Lieutenant Stone, it's about time." She smiled briefly, then locked an arm with Eddie. "We have news."

"Tasev?" I asked.

My grandmother pulled away, then brushed my cheek. "How'd you get so many scratches?"

I shrugged.

"Explain the unknown phone number to me,"

Eddie said.

"I guess I lost mine—"

Eddie shook his head. "Stepan had it in his room."

Marconi turned a bright shade of red.

"They grabbed ours," my mother replied. "We took someone else's."

My grandmother nodded. "They're wicked men, Eddie … crazy as bed bugs."

"You think they're coming back?" I asked.

Marconi waved her hands. "Hang on, hang on. One thing at a time. Susan, Rita Faye … we need to tell him."

My mother grabbed his right arm, pulling him closer. "It's not good, Eddie."

Marconi stayed to his left, my grandmother and I close behind. We rounded the corner where my folks had been sitting. The area had three slatted benches placed haphazardly on top of large lava chunks that served as end pieces, supporting the boarded seats. Behind the third bench, sitting on the ground and leaning against the tube's wall, a woman sat knees up with her hands behind her, I presumed tied with something. Someone had gagged her with another orange cloth.

"Doris?" Eddie yanked away from his escorts, hurried to her side, and knelt.

Chen looked away, not responding.

Eddie grabbed at her gag, but Marconi jerked on his shoulder … hard.

"No, Eddie. Leave her."

"What? Dammit, let me untie her. What's going on?" Eddie grabbed Chen's wrist.

I touched his shoulder and nodded toward Marconi.

"Eddie, listen to them."

Chen jerked her hands away from her husband.

He stood, his mouth open, looking back and forth between Chen and Marconi. "Angie? Why is my wife bound and gagged, and why aren't you doing something about it?"

My grandmother stepped between them and put a hand on Eddie's chest. "She's one of them, Eddie … she's one of them."

Eddie stepped back, his face showing as much fright as anger. He wiped his face, his hands trembling. "What do you mean? One of who?"

Marconi took his hand. "Please sit down." She pointed toward a bench.

Eddie bounced onto the splintering seat. "One of who, dammit?" he asked again while Doris refused to make eye contact. My mother and grandmother eased down next to him.

I remembered our colleagues, pulled my phone, and messaged Keaka that we stood inside the tube and had found a surprise.

Marconi stood behind Eddie, wrapped her arms around his shoulders, and rested her chin on his bald head. "My best friend … I'm so sorry. Doris Chen, aka Diu Liang, is an agent, a contact for the Chinese government, a PLA unit, or whatever you want to call it. She's hooked in with the two Chinese men they found on the ship."

"One of those men we detained had the name of Liang," I said.

Eddie turned, his mouth still gaping open.

Chen tried to straighten herself against the rocks, tears streaking her cheeks.

"She isn't already married to him, is she?" I asked.

Eddie rose to his feet and shouted. "No … no, this can't be right. Doris … Doris? Nod or something."

Chen bowed her head.

My mother grabbed Eddie's hand and pulled on his sleeve until he eased back down to the bench. "Let Angie finish, then we'll figure this out."

There was a noise on our left, and Danny Keaka appeared, his gun pointed. "Braddah? You confused us."

Hrubý and Žăk stalked in, guns ready. Hrubý's face burned red. "Where is Tasev?"

Keaka holstered his gun. "He's not here, Stepan. Put your guns down."

Žăk did so.

Hrubý's right arm dropped, his gun pointing at the ground. "That's Eddie's wife."

"That's Doris?" Keaka asked. "I thought she—"

"Taiwan," Eddie whispered. "Shanghai … now here. It's another nightmare." His jaws clenched while staring at Chen. He pointed to Marconi. "Angie, your turn."

Hrubý's face lost its color. "Where is Tasev?"

Marconi grabbed his gun hand. "Sit down, Stepan. Unless you want to walk back in the dark, listen to me, and then we'll get out of here."

Hrubý's complexion blinked red again. Marconi led him to a bench, she pointed, and he sat.

Eddie had turned away, his hands covering his face while Chen fidgeted, leaning against the ancient lava.

"All right," Marconi said. "The moldy smell in here is awful and is ripping my sinuses. I'll just give you the basics."

"We've found two bodies today, Angie," I said.

"Two? Wait, wait, you'll get me off track. In Kihei, we were out on Susan's lanai, the front door open but the screen locked, when we heard a crash … someone kicked the screen in. In comes the tall, surfer-looking guy in sandals, and guess who else?"

"Nika Campbell," I answered.

"Uh, yeah … good guess. Nika Campbell spouted off, and even though the surfer kid had pulled a gun, Susan gave her a good slap."

I grinned and glanced at my defiant mother.

"The little bitch deserved it and more," my grandmother said, nodding. "They tried to kill our boy."

Marconi smirked. "Yeah, she asked for it. Anyway, three men showed up, grabbed us, and stuffed us into a van, then they brought us into the mountains. We walked forever—"

"Tasev?" Hrubý asked.

Marconi sighed. "No one identified himself as Tasev, and we saw no fedora. I don't think two guys spoke much English, and the other one muttered and grunted like an animal. Huge guy, I bet near seven feet tall and four hundred pounds. He didn't seem all there, if you know what I mean. Shaved head, jet black mustache and goatee, and those eyes … black pupils against the whites … damn creepy. They looked like they would pierce steel."

"Well, irrational, psycho or otherwise, I found a man in the shed," I said. "The body I saw wasn't a big man."

"Killed him, right?" Marconi asked.

"Wasn't an accident."

"The dead guy made the mistake of loosening Rita

Faye's hand ties after she complained. The big guy shot him in the leg and dragged him outside. Only the monster man came back."

My mother wept, breaking Eddie out of his trance. He patted her hand, and she stared at me. "So scary, Ike. We thought—"

I nodded. "We're safe now."

"Are you sure?" my grandmother asked.

Marconi lowered herself next to Hrubý and locked eyes with him. "Next thing we know, in walks Doris with two Chinese men—"

"Busy damn place," Eddie said.

"The two Chinese guys barely spoke to the big man. They handed him something on a fob, then they left. Doris offered nothing, acting like she didn't even know us."

I glanced at Chen, who returned a frown.

Marconi shot her a glare. "The big guy mumbled something as they left … it didn't sound like Chinese or English or anything else I know of. Anyway, he vanished from the left side there, and we haven't seen him. The dead guy's phone fell from the big man's pocket on the way out. It's the one I used to buzz you."

"I suspect they know we have Nika Campbell," Keaka said, "and he chose to not harm you."

"What do you mean you have her?" Marconi asked.

"Ms. Campbell is a guest at a *pastoral* hideaway," Keaka said. "Very safe."

"What is with so many people coming and going to this isolated area?" Žăk asked. "We found no one on the path or after crossing the bamboo bridge."

"What bamboo bridge?" Marconi asked.

"We didn't cross a bamboo bridge, Mr. Žăk," my grandmother offered. "It's metal with a new wood slat deck."

Eddie and I turned toward Keaka.

"Danny? Is there another way in here?" Eddie asked.

He shrugged. "I don't know. My directions came from a buddy in Kahului. He told me he knows these mountains like the back of his hand."

Marconi rolled her eyes. "He needs to wash his hands, but congrats on finding us. It's something, at least. I'll show you how we came in, Danny, on our bridge when we walked under and around a waterfall. Beautiful. But once past there, you'll have to get us the rest of the way."

"Agreed." Keaka stuck an unlit cigarette in his mouth.

"All right, Angie, my turn," Eddie said. "How and why did you tie Doris's hands?" He pushed the toe of his right boot against Chen's ankle. "And how was your grandmother's funeral, the new love of my life? Taipei, then Shanghai … Timbuktu? You're stacking up the miles."

Marconi stood and shuffled to the opening where Eddie and I had entered. "Did anyone else hear something?"

Žăk joined her. "The generator and rain. What do you hear?"

"It sounded like a helicopter."

Hrubý stood, pulled his gun, and stationed himself at the other end of the tube. "Stay opposite me, Mr. Žăk, with eyes opened wide."

Marconi straightened her bangs. "Stepan, where

are Kharkov and Talích? I hope they're together."

Hrubý drew a deep breath, then sighed. "Doing their assignments—Kharkov remained at the camp while Talích held a position on top of the mount. He is to keep a landing site secured for Mr. Ano."

Marconi gave Eddie and me a sideways glance and shrugged. "Are they both armed, Stepan? The monster guy may have headed their way."

Hrubý unzipped his rain jacket and reholstered his gun. "This is worrisome. Lieutenant Talích should be fine. Mr. Kharkov …"

"Another good reason to get out of here," Eddie said. He cut his eyes at Keaka. "Angie, fill us in on Doris, and we'll hit the trail, *your* trail."

We all stood.

"Let me finish," Marconi said, waving her hands. "So, Doris's Chinese friends leave, and, as I said, the monster man blows a gasket with the one guy and apparently murders him outside, then he leaves, too, after he and Doris have a whispering session. He handed her a fob of some kind, then yanked the orange scarf from his pocket and threw it at me."

"Why?" Eddie asked.

"No idea."

Eddie shook his head again while staring at the ground. "Doris … hooked up with these people."

My mother interrupted. "Doris had fed us claptrap like she's a prisoner, too. We went to leave, and she grabbed at Angie … the wrong thing to do."

Marconi beamed a smile, then held up her right hand in a fist. "Sorry, Eddie, but I didn't believe her. Doris had her bag, and she pulled out rolls of duct tape as if she's going to keep us here and like we were going to just stand here and get taped up. I decked her."

My grandmother giggled, then wiped her mouth. "This ground is hard. Doris bopped out like a whipped cage fighter. We used the tape on her, gagged her with the orange cloth, and she woke up a couple of minutes before you guys walked in."

"Enough of this," Eddie said. He knelt next to his wife and wrenched the cloth from her mouth. "Doris … spill it."

Chen pursed her lips, dried blood shimmering on her right ear lobe, then she looked away from Eddie. "I have nothing to say. You all, as always, are over your heads."

"We aren't the ones tied up right now," Eddie said. "So, how did you worm your way into the city's police lab?"

Chen sneered. "I'm good at my job, and where else can we control criminal evidence? Besides, I only followed orders."

Eddie stood, keeping his gaze on her. "That's a damn old excuse. Who gave the orders?"

"It doesn't matter." Chen struggled to move her feet, then fell back against the rough wall. "He's dead now, and others have vanished."

"Rijad Kastrati," I said.

She sneered again, ignoring me while staring at Hrubý. "It seems you and Tasev have a history, Stepan. Surely, you've told everyone."

"Our 'history,' as you say, is not your concern. It would appear you have more important things to worry about."

"Your mother, Doris," Eddie said. "It's not real … just like our marriage."

"They required our marriage as a part of my work. And my mother died in 1984. Chinese funerals are long." She chuckled.

Marconi stood, crossed her arms, and smiled. "I guess it's a big joke, Eddie."

Eddie turned away, his jaws clenching, then unclenching. "I'm a damn fool," he said. "I imagined someone would be interested in me after all these years … a damn fool."

"Not your fault," Marconi said.

Keaka caught my attention, stepped behind me, and unsnapped his holster.

I nodded. "So, what's the end game, Doris? Why did you come back? Eddie said he got a call from Shanghai. Did you think he wouldn't notice?"

She offered another scowl, nothing else.

"Shanghai keeps coming up, doesn't it, everyone?" I asked. "The Chinese men we detained were Shanghai bound, Tasev's plane ticket to Europe showed a departure through Shanghai, and last but not least, Shanghai is the home of Lieutenant General Shai and his PLA unit."

Chen snapped her head toward me. "How could you—"

Eddie growled. "Hush, Doris. You might learn something."

I smiled and nodded toward Hrubý. "The lieutenant-general in Shanghai who likes old Yugoslav gold coins."

Hrubý offered a smirk to rival Marconi's. "And guess who has those now, *Mrs.* Stone?"

Chen fidgeted, and she mumbled. "I know."

I bent over and picked up a loose stone. "Hey,

251

Doris. Watch out." I tossed the rock toward her—her hands flew to her face.

She rolled toward Eddie and grabbed at his feet. A gunshot burst to my right—Chen screamed. Keaka lowered his gun as Eddie stumbled back against a crumbling hunk of lava. Chen rolled over, grabbing her left shoulder.

Eddie kneeled, then unzipped his backpack. "Hang on, Doris. I've got bandages." Eddie ripped her sleeve and used it to wipe the blood. He wrapped her shoulder with gauze and tied the bandage under her armpit, then pulled her wedding ring from her finger.

"He tried to kill me, Eddie."

Eddie pointed at Keaka. "If Danny Keaka wanted to kill you, you'd be dead. It's not much more than a scrape."

"Sorry, Eddie." Keaka thrust his pistol back into its holster. "I caught a hand moving."

Eddie glanced at me. "Ike?"

"I noticed she had loosened the tape around her wrists. I wanted to see if she would react."

Hrubý nodded. "She did."

Eddie shoved Chen's wedding ring into his left pants pocket. "Anybody got ibuprofen? She'll moan all the way back if we don't kill the pain."

Žăk cleared his throat. "I will have one in my kit."

"Give it to her," Hrubý said. "We need to go … now."

My mother propped her foot on a bench to tie her shoe. "No one answered Ike's question."

"Which one?" Keaka asked.

"Shanghai," Hrubý replied. "This all seems centered in Shanghai."

Chen swallowed her pill, then Eddie and Žăk helped her to her feet. Chastened a bit, she stared at me with teary eyes. "You're correct, Detective Pierce. All Asia flows through Shanghai. It is like Prague for Europe."

I pulled up my hood and helped my grandmother with her jacket. "It seems to me that the Chinese and the Kurić organization are not only associates but are working together as allies."

"Let's talk more," Hrubý said, standing, "on our way back."

Doris frowned. "I'm not talking more without an attorney."

Eddie grabbed the roll of tape, pulled Chen's arms behind her, and bound her hands together. She gasped from the pain in her left shoulder. "Relax. It'll be sore, and you might need a stitch," he said. "Danny's an excellent shot for an old man."

Keaka showed his missing tooth with a big smile. "Angie, show us the way back."

Chapter Seventeen

The nine of us pushed ourselves, trudging along a well-worn path. My grandmother looked exhausted, no surprise, and Chen complained endlessly about her wound. The jungle of ferns and bamboo grew even darker as we drew closer again to the sound of moving water. Marconi, Keaka, and Hrubý led us up a hill, each trying to function as the lead, all three jostling along the improving pathway. I stayed in the rear with my folks—Eddie and Žăk escorted Chen, or Diu Liang, as Marconi had called her.

I spotted a glimmer of light in front, and the heavy growth opened right away to a flat plain of tall grass and scattered bushes. The mist grew lighter, and to our left in the distance, I saw the plateau where Talích camped, watching over us. We passed a copse of bell-shaped Hitachi trees, and the roar of a waterfall signaled our arrival farther up the stream than where we had crossed earlier. A bridge with steel rails stretched over the water, this one newer and better quality than the so-called bridge we had risked our lives to cross.

I shouted. "Hey, Danny."

He stopped and let the others pass by. Nodding to my mom, he slipped near my grandmother and adjusted his pace with hers. "What's up, Braddah Henry?"

I pointed. "Um, you see the bridge up there?"

"Yep."

"I'm getting the feeling this is actually *Ohe Uopo* bridge, not the one we used you said Kamehameha must have built."

"Forgive me, braddah?"

"Where did you cross?" my grandmother asked.

"It reminded me of the Frost poem, Granny," I replied. "The two paths diverged …"

Keaka grunted. "Hey, I just followed our Czech friends down into the ravine. It must have been the old way to go."

"They chose badly."

My grandmother slowed even more. "Ike, how much farther? I don't get kidnapped very often—I'm worn slick."

Keaka offered the crook of his arm. "Two-thirds of a mile, Rita Faye, and the ground will be flat. There's a helicopter landing area ahead, and Ano confirmed he's fifteen minutes out. His old bird can hold three passengers. I would like you and Susan to ride out of here first if you're up to it. Otherwise, it's a long walk to the parking lot."

"Works for me," she replied. "This old bird has never been in a helicopter."

Keaka glanced at me. "This won't be too exciting. Ano's copter is old, like him, but he keeps it in decent shape … unlike him. He'll take you to a pad in Makena, south of Kihei. After, he can drive you to your condo."

My mother waited for us, grimacing. "Momma? Did I hear something about a helicopter?"

"Yep," I said. "Danny's arranged for y'all to fly out of here."

As Keaka passed her, she grabbed his sleeve until he stopped. "What happens then? I would rather

Momma and I not be alone at the condo."

She was right, so I offered, "Check out of your room. Eddie and I can sleep on the floor for a couple of nights—Granny can have the bed, and Mom, you use the pull-out sofa."

All but Eddie, Žăk, and Chen had stopped on the trail.

"No, no. Susan and Rita Faye can bunk with me," Marconi said. "I have the two-bedroom suite plus a pull-out."

My mother's face burst into a smile. "Great. We only have tonight and Sunday before going home."

Marconi returned her smile. "It's settled then. You stay with me, and we'll have at least one good day tomorrow." She glared at Hrubý. "Right, Stepan?"

Hrubý shrugged. "Why is it up to me? Tasev is loose. He seems to do as he pleases. And, as a side point, Talích and Kharkov have not responded to my texts or phone calls."

Marconi blew out her cheeks. "I hope they're okay."

"We will know soon."

Žăk and Chen had stopped on the other side of the bridge.

Eddie strolled toward us with a scowl on his face. "Faster, folks. The skies are getting darker again, and the guy's helicopter won't be much fun in a storm."

Keaka typed away in a conversation with someone. He held up a hand. "Ano is nearby. He offered to drop you off at a different helipad north of the Wailea resorts. You could walk to your condo from there."

Marconi nodded. "If our feet still work."

"Susan, Rita Faye." Eddie pointed toward Žăk.

"Why don't you two join Mr. Žăk? I need to talk over a couple of issues with these folks."

My mother frowned. "Gladly. I'm tired of all this business. Come on, Momma."

Eddie shook his head and waited. "Let them finish crossing. I've got info out of Doris."

Marconi smirked. "Did you charm her out of it, Eddie?"

"Not funny. Come on, let's keep walking." He adjusted his backpack, and I noticed Chen's orange cloth gag had caught in one of its zippers.

"Why did you save the cloth, Eddie?" I asked.

Eddie's eyebrows arched. "I assume the others we've found were tested for DNA. Danny?"

Keaka's frowned. "Uh, I don't know."

"Good lord." Eddie rolled his eyes and waved a hand in front of his face like shooing a fly. "Anyway … back to Doris."

"We haven't had time to offer our sympathies," Hrubý said. "We must—"

"No, no, I appreciate it, but don't worry," Eddie said. "I'm tough. I just want to get home first before I figure out what I'm going to do."

Keaka nodded. "You're strong as nails, Eddie, but not invincible."

Marconi smiled. "We'll take care of him."

Eddie wiped his bald head. "Okay, okay, I appreciate it all, I really do, but first things first. Doris stayed tight-lipped until my harping on jail time loosened her up a bit."

"Curious," Hrubý said, stopping again. "Others associated with the Kurić organization have taken their own lives rather than offer information."

"True," Eddie replied, grabbing a rail and glancing at the stream. He let Marconi pass him. "Remember, though, those other folks had a family to threaten. Doris doesn't."

Keaka nodded. "We get that."

Hrubý signaled for Žåk and Chen to move ahead, then we stopped in a semi-circle in front of Eddie.

"Right. So, Doris said she's been part of the organization for years, outside any of the shenanigans in Alexandria. I know she came from Taipei to Illinois on a student visa, finished her degree, and got engaged to a fellow from Beijing. It caused a helluva fight in her family in Taiwan, and it turns out they were right. Doris admitted to me her fiancé worked for his government and had come to the U.S. to connect with other spies, or whatever you want to call them. He gained tenure at a little college outside of Chicago and cast out a web of visiting Chinese students to gather information for his mission. He charmed Doris for a while, but he broke off the engagement, eventually. It didn't seem to matter, though, as money drove the whole thing, so he sent her to D.C. It sounds like General Shai in Shanghai has his tentacles all over the place, sometimes overlapping with Kurić in Europe."

I shivered, either from the dampness or a thought. "As we've said, a direct connection between Kurić and Shai is the worst possible news."

"Right," Eddie replied, rubbing his hands together. "Doris pleaded she knew nothing of the coins. Her major interests are forensics, and she's been overseeing the labs for five years now."

Marconi dug into her raincoat pocket and pulled out a piece of nicotine gum. "Damn. You think she's fixed any evidence over the years?"

"We'll have to go back and check any cases involving Rijad Kastrati and his bunch … and maybe the Serb, Aleksandr Stanich, too," I said.

"You've got a mess back home, yeah?" Keaka shoved another cigarette into the gap in his teeth. "It may take a while to sift through."

"No doubt," Eddie said. "And I asked Doris about this fob after I pulled it from her front pocket. It's a key used at Ronald Reagan Airport." He held it up to us. "Obviously, to a locker." The stubby key seemed to be brass with a dark patina. Its beige knob showed red letters of *RR* with numbers in small black lettering.

"What's the number, say?" I asked.

"The number? What difference does it make?" Eddie dropped the key back into his pocket.

"Maybe nothing, but you know Doris is likely the person who rented it, and the airport is only five miles from our office … it seems pretty convenient."

"But why did our monster-sized kidnapper get it from the Chinese men and then pass it to Doris?" Marconi asked.

Eddie shrugged, then pulled the key back out of his pocket, bringing it closer to his face. "The locker number is gate 61, locker 398."

"Awesome," I said.

"What?" Eddie asked. His eyes grew enormous. "Oh, shit. The Chinese unit … PLA 61398."

Hrubý spat over the bridge. "General Shai and Shanghai. The clues keep slapping us in the face, do they not?"

I took a step, and Eddie threw his arm in front of me. "Ike, Angie. Those first two numbers?"

Marconi's neck showed splotches of pink. "What now?"

Eddie shoved the key in front of her face. "Sixty-one."

"So?" she asked.

"Our flight," he replied, "in March to Vienna."

Marconi slapped her hands against her hips. "And?"

Eddie dropped the fob into his pocket. "The airline we flew?"

"Yeah?" I asked.

"And the gate number?" he asked.

Marconi groaned. "I can't remember that stuff, Eddie."

"We left from the series of gates numbered in the sixties," I offered.

Eddie grinned. "Bingo. This locker is in the terminal where the European flights leave from."

****

What looked like a giant green mosquito buzzed overhead, white marijuana leaves painted on the pilot's door. Ano passed twice over the plateau from where Talích camped before the helicopter spiraled down in three tighter circles, making a soft landing into tall grass a half-mile from the bridge we had crossed. I caught up with my folks and pulled them close.

"Time to go, Mom," I said. "Don't look down after you get in."

Her brow furrowed. "I'm too exhausted, Ike. I'll probably fall asleep."

"Just don't fall out."

My grandmother sighed. "Anything will be better than walking."

"Right," I replied, escorting them closer under the rotating blades while Marconi followed. "Danny said it's only ten minutes to the landing pad."

My mother inhaled and stopped in a mud puddle. "Ike. Ike, look," she said before covering her mouth. "Is he our pilot?"

My grandmother turned toward Marconi. "Maybe we should walk."

A man had pulled the pilot's door aside and unbuckled. He slid from his seat and smashed his two red cowboy boots on the ground.

Keaka came from behind and whispered. "Don't let his looks fool you. Too much weed, but he's got a chest full of medals from Vietnam—three Purple Hearts among them. He served in the medical corps, and one of his friends told me he rescued over sixty soldiers from the battlefields during two tours. He's a very skilled pilot … and a hero."

The tension vanished in my mother's face, and a tear crept down her left cheek. "Thanks, Danny. My husband, Henry, was a helicopter man for the Army Rangers. They crashed in the Grenada invasion, but he and another man survived."

Keaka grinned and waved toward Ano, who lumbered our way. His patched jeans slid over the top of his boots, and he wore a black-and-red, seersucker shirt he had unbuttoned halfway down his chest … not that it needed to be buttoned. His long, silver beard covered his front, flowing and fluttering in the air currents from the slowly rotating blades. Long, silver hair flowed past his collar, topped by a black and red Maui College baseball cap.

Ano cupped his hands and called out, "Hey, Keaka,

how in the hell did you get all those pretty women to stand so close to you?"

Marconi grunted, turned to her right, and motioned for Hrubý, Žǎk, and Eddie to come closer.

Keaka extended his hand. "Women always like to stand close to me."

"Oh, bulls … uh, sorry, ladies." He pulled off his cap, exposing the pink skin of his bald pate, and then nodded at my mother and grandmother. He towered over Keaka and stood an inch or two taller than me. "I'm Jimmy Lee Anderson, folks. Danny likes to call me Ano."

"Because it sounds Hawaiian?" Marconi asked.

Ano snorted and slapped Keaka on the back. "I guess that's part of it. It actually means Army Nurse Operations. He never believed I looked like a nurse. Weird, huh?" He grinned and dropped his cap on the crown of his head.

"I'm Rita Faye Henshaw, and this is my daughter, Susan Pierce. My grandson over there … Detective Sergeant Henry Pierce, aka Ike, and that's his boss, Director Angie Marconi, and her second in command there, Eddie Stone. Oh, and the lady is, uh, Eddie can explain later."

Eddie rolled his eyes.

Ano again removed his cap and pointed. "Good to meet you, Rita Faye, Susan, Ike, Angie, and Eddie … if I've remembered everybody's names. Rita Faye … it sounds like you're from my part of the country?"

My mother spoke up. "Rocky Gap, Virginia. You?"

"Kingsport, Tennessee."

"Well, shoot, we're practically neighbors," my

grandmother said. "Should we call you Jimmy Lee or Ano?"

"I'm used to Ano." He pulled his cap tight. "I haven't been back home since 1970, though, after I got drafted in sixty-eight. My ma and daddy died while I flew choppers in Nam. In seventy-three, I got out of the service and never got closer to home than Maui."

"Hey, Ano, two more here," Keaka said. He thumbed toward our Czech colleagues. "This is Commander Stepan Hrubý, Czech law enforcement I told you about, and this is Mr. Žák … or just Žák." He winked.

Ano nodded, then shook hands. "Good to meet y'all. Danny caught me up. I'm impressed."

Hrubý offered a slight smile. "You are kind to say, Mr. Anderson … Ano. We appreciate your services today and have been told of your exploits in Vietnam."

Eddie offered his hand, too. "Thank you for your service, Ano."

Ano's forehead wrinkled, and the smile vanished. "It's called duty. I loved those guys."

Hrubý nodded, then glanced at Keaka. "Mr. Ano, did you notice our man, Lieutenant Talích? He is on the plateau, watching over us."

Ano crossed his arms, frowning. "Well, we need to discuss. And to answer your question, I found no one on top."

"Wait … what?" Keaka asked.

"It wasn't thirty seconds after I contacted you last time that a black helicopter whizzed by me. The dumbass almost collided with me in the gorge coming through here."

"And no Talích?" Hrubý closed his eyes for a

moment.

Ano tilted his head and scratched the back of his neck. "That's what I meant. I saw a tent, and I found a spot to land like Danny had told me. I intended to bring your man off there, but he wasn't around."

"Shit." Keaka rubbed his eyes.

Žăk yanked his phone from his pocket. "Still nothing from Mr. Kharkov, Commander."

"Anyway, I grabbed his backpack and a gun and put them in my copter. The gun had been emptied … shells scattered everywhere. It looked like a hell of a gun battle." Ano hustled to his helicopter, ducked low under the blades, and pulled Talích's things from the rear seat. He brought them over, laid the backpack at Žăk's feet, then pushed the rifle toward him. "I didn't bother with the tent."

Hrubý's face grew pasty. "This is distressing."

Žăk's hands disappeared inside the backpack. He stopped, shut his eyes, and removed his arm from the pack. He held an orange cloth.

Hrubý bowed his head, hands-on-hips. "My God. They have him."

Marconi put her arm around his waist. "We don't know yet, Stepan. Let's find Kharkov. It could be they're together."

"But look," I said. "My folks need to get back if you're still up for it?"

"You bet," Ano replied, flashing his teeth in a big grin. Both upper cuspids were missing. "Ladies, let's load up."

"Wait," Keaka said. "Ano, could you squeeze two more in there?"

"Four passengers? Hmm. I guess so if three of

them can claim to have skinny butts. The back seat will be tight, but it's only a few minutes."

"Are you talking about Doris?" Eddie asked, then glared at his wife.

Chen tried to back away. "I can walk," she said. Eddie caught her arm.

"I'm going, too," Marconi said, clutching Chen's other arm. "You come with us, Doris."

"Hang on," Keaka said. "Ano, one more favor."

Ano stroked his beard. "I can't keep up."

"I'll make it up to you. A six-pack of Primo?"

"You always go cheap. So, what am I supposed to do?"

"A U.S. Marshal will meet you at the Wailea helipad, but I don't know who yet."

Ano tilted his head. "And?"

"The marshal will drive our three friends to the Kihei condo, help pack up Rita Faye and Susan, then follow them to Angie's suite in Lahaina."

"And this other lady here? What do you have in mind, as if I couldn't guess?"

"Puu Kahua."

"Dammit, Danny, are you trying to get me in trouble? How many times can I fly and land in Kaho´olawe?"

"I've got you covered, buddy. Drop off Ms. Chen—"

"No, it's Stone now." Doris cast a smirk at Eddie.

Eddie clenched and unclenched his jaws. "Not for long."

Keaka rubbed his stubbly face. "Watch out for her, Ano. Tie her down in the back seat if you need to. Drop her off at Puu Kahua and let marshals McNelly and

Myung take her. Then we need you back here one more time."

"Okay, I'll handle it. Come on, ladies. I'm on a tight schedule, apparently. Back in forty-five minutes, Danny." Ano motioned them to follow, then he helped my grandmother in the front. Marconi eased into the back, and Ano shut her door. He stepped to the other side, pushed Chen into the helicopter, then grew animated. He leaned into his copter, curses flowing from two people.

Eddie grunted. "He's taking care of Doris, I guess."

Ano pointed inside the cabin and barked another curse. He turned and offered a grin to my mother, helped her in, slammed the door, then hurried to the pilot's seat. The copter blades engaged, picking up speed. The helicopter lifted away, rose to our right, and disappeared through low-hanging clouds.

Hrubý and Žăk picked up their guns and backpacks.

"No lingering for us." Hrubý checked his ammunition. "Mr. Žăk, please locate Mr. Kharkov—I assume he remains in the cabin. Lieutenant Stone, would you be willing to help?"

Eddie nodded. "Of course." He pulled on his backpack and unsnapped his holster. "Mr. Žăk, let me carry your pack, too. You won't have to fuss with it, and you can keep your gun hand free."

"Excellent," Žăk replied while picking up Talích's rifle. "We can return for Lieutenant Talích's pack."

Hrubý shook his head. "No, I will take it … and Mr. Žăk?"

"Yes."

"Do whatever is needed." Hrubý stared at Keaka,

looking for a response.

Keaka nodded. "Agreed. My preference is to capture Tasev or those other guys, but in these circumstances—"

"No more talk," Eddie said. "Let's go, Žăk."

Žăk turned right away, leaving Eddie to catch up while carrying both packs.

Hrubý glanced back at us. "Gentlemen, let's find the lieutenant."

****

We drew closer to the broken body Kharkov had covered for us earlier in the day. The wind had pulled the covering away from the man's legs, the left one showing itself twisted to the right at the knee.

"Leave it." Hrubý motioned forward with his head. "Marshal Keaka, look ahead of us, one hundred meters. I believe I see debris from another slide. Can you?"

Keaka double-stepped his way past us and nodded. "I didn't notice it earlier. I don't like this."

Hrubý set off, trotting toward the rubble, carrying backpacks and a rifle.

"Come on, Danny," I said, "keep up."

Keaka yanked my sleeve. "Leave him. Walk slow. If Talích is there, we need to let Stepan find him."

The sun surprised us with a peek through the clouds, warming me instantly, at least for a minute. Keaka guided us off the trail and toward Hrubý. Despite our slower pace, we soon found Hrubý kneeling in the grass. The packs had fallen over next to him. He unshouldered the rifle, placing it longways in front of him.

Now fifty feet away, I noticed the debris was a body. I saw Talích's muddy hiking boots, the toes

267

pointed upward. I jogged ahead. Dirty, seemingly asleep, with one thing amiss … a bright red opening glowed below his right eye.

Hrubý had bowed his head and covered his eyes with his fists. He seemed aware of me kneeling, then pulled his hands down without looking up. "He's gone," he muttered. "Shot. At least the bastard did not strangle him."

"I can't think of a thing to say, Stepan. I should have stayed up there with him."

Hrubý shook his head vigorously. "No." He opened his mouth and turned toward me, showing red eyes and a tear-streaked grizzly face. "Then you would be dead, too. See the death wound?"

I glanced down, then turned away. "Yes."

"I believe it is from an old ZB30, a Czech automatic. It is the same kind used against us by the helicopter when we sailed to Honolulu. The back of his head—the bullet went through. Otherwise, his head would have exploded like Marshal Olan."

Keaka stumbled to a halt, placing his hands on our shoulders. "Damn, Stepan, I'm sorry. He seemed like a top-notch guy … and very brave."

Hrubý pushed up from his knees and stood, as did I. "Yes, one of our best." Hrubý heaved a sigh. "Tasev's body count continues." He wiped his face.

"Lunatic," I said.

Hrubý nodded while talking. "I suppose, Henry Pierce. But like his father, Tasev's victims always serve his purpose to an end while formulating his next plan in that defective mind. And, yes, he is a lunatic on a mission, a never-ending one."

My phone vibrated. "It's a text message from

Eddie. They found Kharkov alive. Eddie says it looks like he's been in quite a fight, but other than several bruises, he appears to be fine."

Hrubý gave a guttural groan. "Thank God."

Keaka glanced around my shoulder. "Eddie is asking about Talích."

Hrubý grabbed my wrist. "No. Let me. I'll call Žăk." He walked away from us, leaned on a boulder, and pulled his phone. He pressed the screen, waited a moment, then began talking.

Keaka yanked my sleeve again. "Go slow. Stepan needs a few minutes."

The sun shone through the clouds, longer this time. We removed our rain jackets and lifted our backpacks. A five-minute walk to the cabin, and we ducked under the ferns hanging at the entrance. The front door swung ajar, and Keaka shoved his way in, bumping into Eddie. Žăk chose not to face us, leaning on the bar and supporting himself with his elbows. Eddie hovered over Kharkov, pressing a wet cloth against his cheek.

I motioned Eddie to hand me the cloth, then knelt. "Let me, Vitaly," I said. "There's swelling on the other side above your eyebrow. If you don't want to repeat yourself, you can tell us what happened when there's a better time."

Kharkov grabbed the wet cloth and tossed it on the floor. "When is a better time? Mr. Žăk has lost his brother, and now Lieutenant Talích is dead. And for what?" He wiped his face. "Some of the worst people in Europe are our enemies. Are Mr. Žăk and I next … then Commander Hrubý?"

"They are evil people, Vitaly. We've helped stop some of it."

Žăk turned abruptly. "We must keep going, Mr. Kharkov. My brother is dead, and I will not surrender to them."

Kharkov began to speak but looked away instead.

"What happened here, Vitaly?" I asked.

Kharkov stood, then steadied himself. "Three men came in—none Tasev. Two were smaller men, both with neck tattoos, and the other man … a giant … and not pleasing to the eye. I do not know if they could be Tasev's associates—it did not come up. They burst in a half-hour ago, and apparently, I surprised them. They grabbed me, but I broke away, ran into the bedroom, and picked up the steel torch I noticed in the corner. The large man caught me, but I beat him on the head with it. He yelped and stumbled out the door. The other men fought me for a minute, then followed the big guy. I found a kitchen knife for a weapon and waited for them to return, but they did not."

"Did they say anything?" Eddie asked.

Kharkov gave a quick shake of his head. "The smallest man asked who I was, but I did not answer. He had an accent, but I could not make out his origin. The larger one never spoke except in grunts. They dressed shabbily and were soaked."

"Were they armed?" Keaka asked.

"I never saw a gun."

"Thank God," Keaka said. "I feared we had lost you, too."

Žăk held up his phone. "Vitaly, the commander needs us. We are to pack our gear, then find him. He wants us to make a sled to pull the lieutenant's body to the helicopter's landing site. Marshal Keaka?"

"Yes."

His chin quivering, Žăk looked away. "The commander wants … a body preparation—"

"A funeral home or mortuary?" Keaka asked.

"Yes, yes, I believe that is it."

"Let me call a couple of people. I know of a funeral service in Wailuku a friend of mine owns. But I need to call the coroner, too. We need to have him examine the lieutenant's body before you return home."

Žăk sighed. "I see."

"But first," Keaka said, "look in the bedroom closet. There may be a canvas cot in there. Break it down and use it for a sled."

Žăk nodded. "Mr. Kharkov, are you able to help?"

"Yes, I am well enough."

They both headed to the bedroom. A jumble of noises drifted down the hall, accompanied by Kharkov's curses. Both men reappeared with a legless cot, its canvas material wrapped around one of its supports, and a musty aroma drifting around us.

Žăk grabbed his things. "Marshal Keaka, please relay to Mr. Ano that we will meet him near his previous landing spot. Commander Hrubý would like to escort the lieutenant's body to its destination. Mr. Kharkov and I will rejoin you for our walk to the parking lot, then take our vehicle back to Maalaea, where we are staying."

Keaka offered his hand. "All good, Mr. Žăk. I'll contact Ano. We'll be waiting."

Chapter Eighteen

A hoped-for quiet Sunday, our last full day in Hawaii before tomorrow morning's departure. I rolled over in damp sheets and noticed the digital clock blinking 12:00 a.m. Fumbling for my watch, it said a few minutes after seven. The fan above me churned away, flicking the beige curtains against the wall. Silence came from the living room—no noise from the air conditioner, and I couldn't hear Eddie's snores and snorts. Had he made coffee and sat on the lanai?

I touched my feet to the floor, much like stepping onto a bed of nails. My leg muscles ached from yesterday's hike, with blisters on my ankles, heels, and on the outside of my big toes. I hadn't noticed a problem until we got back to our vehicles the previous evening, heaving myself into the back seat of Keaka's blue Ford and yelping when Kharkov stepped on my left foot. We had stopped at a convenience store south of Lahaina, bought a lotion, and Eddie and I hobbled around the suite until falling asleep after the late news.

I pulled on my yellow and green shorts and found my green t-shirt that read *Maui nō ka ʻoi,* supposedly, *Maui is the Best*, although the street vendor had told me the words were for tourists. No matter. With our adventures, I didn't feel inclined to do laundry. I had one change of clothes left for tomorrow's flight, a thirteen-hour journey, including stopovers in Denver and Atlanta. Someday I'd return here, hopefully without all the peripheral hokey-pokey, as Eddie would call it. I even missed my cruddy, gloomy apartment in Alexandria.

I crept into the unlit suite and found Eddie face down on the couch. I touched his shoulder. "Eddie? Hey, Eddie?"

He coughed into the pillow and flailed his arms. "Ike? God, it's hot in here." He rolled over and threw back the covers, showing faded blue pajamas he had told me his late wife had bought him years ago. His belly shook when he pushed up to sit. "Is the air conditioner dead? What's going on?"

"I figured you had turned it off and had already made coffee." I pulled back the curtains, opened the lanai doors to get air flowing, and pressed random buttons on the air conditioner's controls. It roared to life. "Huh. There must have been a power outage. The clock on my dresser blinked midnight." Pointing to the kitchenette, I said, "Look. The clocks on the coffee pot and oven are blinking, too."

Eddie whipped his sheets like a tablecloth. "My sheets are soggy."

"Mine, too."

"Well, a bathroom break, and I'll change clothes. You make the coffee, but no fancy crap. Make mine black, and of course—"

"Irish cream," I said, "but I don't think you left much the other day."

"There's enough." The bathroom door slammed.

I found three coffee pods for today and tomorrow. After the first cup, I started the second, then pulled a chair away from the lanai's table. This day showed cloudy, not the usual sunshine peeking over Haleakalā. The breeze felt much cooler than the last few mornings—cooler outside than inside. I shut my eyes and listened to scattered voices and the gentle bumping of a boat against the dock. This is what I had hoped for the entire week. Nice and peaceful.

Eddie kicked my chair. "Hey, excellent coffee."

"There's only one coffee pod left, but you can have it in the morning. I'll get something at the airport."

"All right, if you're good with it. I wouldn't be able to wait that long." He sipped his drink. "So, what's for breakfast? It's past seven thirty. I bet things are opening up."

I grinned and replied, "Look in the breadbox."

"Breadbox? Did you go to the bakery already?" He raised an eyebrow. "It's the young woman who works there, isn't it? Did you get something for free?" He winked.

"Nope … and nope. Go look."

A grin covered his face, and he hurried to the kitchenette. "Awesome, buddy," he called out. "First Irish cream, now little white donuts. My day is getting better and better." He brought the bag of donuts and two paper towels, then he slumped into the high-back wicker chair next to the table. "When did you have time to get these?"

"My mom messaged me late and said she and Angie had picked them up in Kihei before they came up last night. My grandmother's idea."

"Ain't she sweet? You see, Ike, this morning is what I mean." He spread his arms wide. "A nice relaxing start to the day. Better than chasing Europeans, their damn gold dukats, and crazy Macedonians. Those

Czech guys are the good people, buddy, and I hate what happened to their men, but frankly, I don't care if I ever see them again. I've said it over and over, let me be in my little job in Alexandria for a couple more years, then I'm done."

I didn't want to upset him this morning but asked, "And the annulment? Will it be an ordeal?"

He had stuffed another donut in his mouth and gave me a side glance. Holding up a finger, he finished chewing, then washed it down with a gulp of coffee. "I don't think so. They'll charge Doris with something … espionage, accessory to murder … stupidity. It's been less than a week, so it won't take much to get the annulment going. We had moved none of her things into my house at least."

I gave him a pat on the shoulder. "And I'm not in a hurry for you to retire."

"We'll see. My home has tripled in value since we bought it. My nest egg would make a good down payment on a beach home near Tampa … hell, maybe even here." He winked, then put his feet up on the rail. "You know I don't like to discuss it, but my son, Edward, is up for parole in thirteen months. If he gets out, there's another reason for me to move on—I won't have to stay close to Jersey. I hate the winters in D.C., so I'd have no trouble giving that up, and I don't know what Edward will want to do."

"Whatever happens, I'm coming to visit you. You're my boss, a mentor, and I count you as a good friend."

"Scary, huh?" he asked.

"What?"

"I'm twice your age, diverse backgrounds, and I've

definitely got the better tan." He winked. "And I order you around at work, and yet, in only eight months, we can call each other friends."

My throat tightened, and my voice fluttered. "That's the best part."

A knock on the door.

Eddie grinned. "If you're through admiring me, why don't you get the door? I'm the old guy, remember?"

"Done." The front door rested thirty feet from the lanai, and my face flushed as I grabbed the handle, wary of who might have knocked. I stared through the peephole and saw a woman with dishwater blonde and gray hair and hazel-blue eyes. Pushing the handle down, I opened the door a couple of inches and spied on our guest. "If you bring intrigue, we don't want any. If you're hungry, we have a half-bag of white donuts left … but you better hurry for those."

Marconi pushed against me and strolled into the hall. "God, how do you sleep in this heat?"

I left the wooden door open, raised the utility door's screen, then followed her to the lanai. "The electricity quit during the night, and the air conditioner didn't come back on."

"What? We never lost power."

I shrugged.

Eddie stood and gave her a brief hug. "I would offer coffee, but we only have one of those little pods left. Want a donut?"

"Nah. Rita Faye made coffee and cooked bacon and cinnamon toast. She's on our lanai rubbing her feet, and Susan is still asleep."

I shook my head and smiled. "She makes great

cinnamon toast." I pulled another wicker chair from the dining area and placed it next to Eddie. "Have a seat, boss. I'm sitting here telling Eddie how great he is, and he agrees."

Eddie snorted. "What else? Ike Pierce likes a winner. But damn, I'm sore as hell today, Angie. What about you? And Ike and I agree that this morning is what a tropical vacation is supposed to be like."

"Finally, huh?" She glanced at her watch. "But in thirty-six hours, we'll be home. I found on my weather app that we should expect nineties next week in Alexandria, and humidity around fifty percent."

Eddie groaned. "Nice. I'll keep wearing my Hawaiian shorts to work."

"Commissioner Bates wouldn't like your legs."

"When's the last time you talked to him?" I asked. "Does he know of your kidnapping? He called at a weird time the other night."

"I don't know what he was thinking—something about he was counting the hours forward instead of backward. He never said why he was up in the middle of the night there. I'll message and tell him we'll talk on Tuesday morning."

Eddie leaned forward. "Are you going in on Tuesday, Angie? I can't do it. I'm off until Thursday."

"Wednesday for me," I said.

She nodded. "Wednesday, officially, but I might sneak by the office Tuesday afternoon. My temp assistant has until next Friday, then Kate is coming off childcare leave a week from tomorrow. I can't wait. It'll be good to have her back. Her son is almost three months old already."

A knock rattled the door, and my heart skipped a

beat. I hadn't locked it.

"May I come in?" Hrubý asked, letting the screen slam behind him.

"Stepan." Marconi jumped to her feet, hurried to the entryway, and gave him a long hug. "I've been wondering about you." They drifted back to the lanai, and I followed them with another chair, shoving it between the others.

Hrubý shook his head and refused to sit. "Let me stand a while." He glanced at the near-empty bag of donuts. "Ah, Lieutenant Stone … white donuts. This is your lucky day."

"It sure is. Did you make arrangements with Lieutenant Talích's family?"

"We have had … difficulties. Most of his immediate family is dead and buried in various countries. Mr. Žăk has found a contact name in Vienna." He wiped his face. "I had hoped to ship his body directly to burial near his parents, but it seems not to be an option."

"I'm so sorry, Stepan." Marconi grabbed his right hand with her left.

"Thank you. Danny Keaka contacted me this morning. He will try to push for the coroner to finish his business today. He wants to retrieve as much evidence as possible but will release the body to us before we leave."

"That's good of him," she replied.

"How are Mr. Žăk and Vitaly after last night?" I asked.

"Apparently, they drowned their sorrows, as you say, last night, giving them both hangovers." Hrubý rubbed his eyes, looking a bit as if he had partaken.

"They deserved some downtime," Marconi said. "We all do."

Hrubý nodded as someone else knocked on the door.

"Busy place," I mumbled. "Can I help you?" A teenage boy stood at the door, wearing a tank top and showing tattoo sleeves from his wrists up to his shoulders. He balanced a cardboard box lid, holding four white paper sacks with one hand—the other hand carried a drink caddy with four paper coffee cups.

He smiled. "Breakfast from Chef Malo, courtesy of Danny Keaka. These are Chef Malo's famous cheese, fruit, and pork crêpes. Mr. Keaka said to bring everything to the cement picnic table next to the old courthouse entrance. He has utensils and plates there."

Eddie rubbed his hands together. "Let's go."

"You just ate a dozen baby donuts," I said.

Eddie shrugged.

Marconi opened the door and let the young man set the box top on the round glass dining room table.

"Uh, I have two more sacks downstairs for a Rita Faye and Susan?"

"My folks," I said. "I believe at least one is awake. Downstairs, in the far corner on the right."

Hrubý pulled out his wallet and handed him a five-dollar bill. "Thank you. We will give Danny Keaka our compliments of your service."

"No problem," he replied, backing his way toward the door. "Cool, cool, cool." He turned, then vanished around the corner.

"Wow, those crêpes … the fresh pastry smell," I said. "Eddie, if you'll lock the door, I'll carry the box."

"Got it, buddy."

****

Keaka waited at the picnic table, his back to us and his head down, typing on his phone. He jumped when I dropped our food bags on the table. "Damn—oh, *aloha*, good friends."

"Hey, Danny, thanks for breakfast," I said.

Eddie wiggled Keaka's shoulder. "Thank you. It smells terrific."

Marconi rolled her eyes. "Eddie thinks he has space in his belly even after donuts."

Eddie rubbed his belly. "Growing boy needs his food, Angie."

She patted his gut and pursed her lips. "All I'm going to say is if you want to live a few years past retirement …"

Eddie waved his hands. "I got it, I got it. I'll be good when we get home."

Keaka showed us half a smile and pointed. "Have a seat, guys." He picked up his water bottle and stared past me.

Hrubý leaned against the cement table. "Today, you seem to wear your serious face, Danny Keaka. Do you have something to tell us?"

Keaka nodded. "Oh, right. Please sit down, folks, and eat. Cold crêpes aren't my favorite." He stood and helped us unload our food onto the dinner-sized paper plates he had brought from his restaurant. He handed us our plastic wear, then showed us his way of loading his crêpe. "There. It's how I like them but decorate them the way you want." He pulled a bag of macadamia nuts from his pocket. "I already had three while I helped Malo put this together." He picked another paper sack off the ground and removed small cups of pineapple juice.

We rested in the shade with the cool breeze blowing while stuffing and eating our crêpes and watching the boats in the bay.

Eddie acted as if he hadn't eaten in days. "Woo, fantastic, Danny. Hey, you look like you have more energy this morning, but Stepan is right … something's up, isn't it?"

"Yeah, I feel a lot better today. I slept well but got up early. Lots of chatter going back and forth on my phone messages and the radio scanner. The power went out for a while, and when it came back on, the scanner kicked in, and I heard a bunch of commotion on the police channels, including the U.S. Marshals."

Marconi picked her paper napkin off the ground and wiped her mouth. "Breezy today."

Keaka held up a hand. "Finish your breakfast, then we'll talk, yeah? How do you like the crêpes?"

"Malo is fantastic, as usual," Marconi said.

Hrubý nodded.

The table grew quiet except for the grackles gathered near us, squawking and waiting on our leftovers. Keaka kicked at them, scattering the bunch, but they right away crept back behind him.

Eddie rolled up his paper plate, shoved it into the empty paper bag, then slung back a gulp of juice. "Come on, Keaka, spit it out. You're going to bust wanting to get us up to speed."

Keaka erupted into his big smile. "You got me, Eddie. I have something to tell you. Unfortunately, this involves keeping you busy for the rest of today. I'm waiting on Ano."

Marconi groaned.

"Sorry, but I need you. And Stepan?"

Hrubý waved a hand. "I would rather give Mr. Žăk and Mr. Kharkov a down day."

"Up to you, but I wanted you to know the coroner in Wailuku has come in early and is examining the lieutenant's body. They should release it to you by noon."

Hrubý sighed. "A bit of good news. We can take him back with us. I will have Kharkov make the final arrangements, and I appreciate no delay."

"You're welcome. A quick conversation with the coroner and, so far, the bullet hole in his body is a similar caliber used on the dead man found in the shed next to the lava tube—they collected those two bodies this morning. The other body at the base of the hill died from traumatic fall injuries—no bullets or stab wounds. The coroner cannot establish if the fall was accidental or if someone pushed the man, as he couldn't determine any defensive wounds." Keaka fidgeted with the cigarette pack. "Oh, and both the bodies' ribs were crushed … like a vice."

"Is there more?" Eddie asked.

"Yeah, there's always more. The dead men are all European. Braddah Henry and I found a Kosovar on the little boat before it exploded, the dead man at the lava tube was Kosovar, and the man we found in the landslide was Macedonian."

"All Tasev's associates," Hrubý said.

"Apparently," Keaka answered, then shrugged. "Helluva way to treat your friends." He glanced toward the banyan tree's central trunk and waved. "Hey. Over here."

Ano stepped around the tree trunk, dropped a

cigarette butt, and stomped on it. He wore his red boots and torn jeans with a black *Rock'n'roll* t-shirt. "Morning, friends." Ano sauntered toward us, then stopped next to Keaka. "Damn, Danny, where's my breakfast? I've been flying my ass off for you."

Keaka laughed. "Dude, this is actual food. Malo wouldn't make you a weed omelet."

"You need to get him to loosen up a bit." He removed his cap, scratched his head, and glanced toward the bay. "A little cooler today, huh?"

Keaka pulled his legs from under the table, then swung toward Ano. He yanked the last cigarette from the pack, shoved it into the space in his teeth, then tossed the empty package into the round trash container. "Buddy, you know I appreciate you running everywhere. But you didn't come here to discuss the weather, did you?"

Ano nodded toward Marconi, showed her a sly smile, and turned to Keaka. "The weather's not much to talk about in Maui. I wish I had a meteorologist's job here … not much to do. But you're right, I didn't come to discuss cloud coverage. So, after I dropped off Angie and Henry's family the other night, I noticed a black helicopter sitting on the helipad on the other side of the little building over there. It looked the same as the one that whipped by me yesterday coming through the valley. And no numbers on the tail."

"How is it legal?" I asked.

"Glad you asked. I wondered the same thing, so I took the initiative and cornered the manager inside his terminal, if you can call it that. Manager … shit. They get eight or ten landings a day. All he does is stick his feet on the desk and grab a snort of whiskey out of his drawer. But, anyway, he acted dumb over the black copter and said he didn't know who it belonged to. I told him I saw it flying yesterday afternoon, so why didn't he ground it like it should've been, and why the hell didn't it have identifiers on the tail? He shrugged like a teenager caught red-handed, so I got a little rough."

Eddie grinned. "I wish I'd been there."

"Yep, it got ugly for a second until he stood. He's a short little dude, and I hovered over him. I grabbed an arm, and he choked out a little info. He admitted four men left from Wailea yesterday morning with a bunch of gear. They returned at dinner time, but only two men came back, and the gear unloaded wasn't nearly as much as they started with."

Keaka took Ano's right arm and shook his hand. "You're a good man, Ano. You'll make a detective yet."

Ano pulled away and winked. "Detective? Why the hell … I'd have to take drug tests."

Turning toward us, Keaka plucked the unlit cigarette from his teeth and pitched it into the paper sack. "All right, let's go, friends. The helipad manager … what's his name, Ano?"

"Chuck. I've known him for years, and he still doesn't like me. Imagine."

"It seems Chuck has knowledge he needs to share with us. Anyone for a quick trip?"

"I'm with you, Danny," Ano said. "My jeep is running good. Why don't you ride back with me? We can both talk to Chuck, and you can drive it to my house for me while I fly my copter home."

"I'm out," Eddie said. "They wore this old man

slick yesterday. But don't forget, wake me up later." He stood and nodded toward Ano. "Thanks for breakfast, Danny." He strolled away, heading straight to our suite.

Hrubý shook his head, then pushed his phone into a pocket. "I cannot help. Mr. Kharkov has messaged me and requested my help in arranging the shipment of the body." He turned. "Angie, please accompany me to Wailuku."

Marconi looped her arm into the crook of his and nodded. "Gladly. I'll let Susan and Rita Faye know. Maybe Eddie can check on them."

"If they're releasing his body, we should get the coroner's hard copy report today," Keaka said.

"Again, much appreciated," Hrubý replied—the whites of his eyes had turned pink. "Please contact me if you find out more. Tasev may still be on the island."

"Agreed." Keaka ran a hand through his hair. "So, braddah, you're it."

"I can't wait to meet Chuck," I said. "I want to watch Ano knock him around."

Ano grabbed my shoulder, then patted my head. "I'm a nurse, Henry, not a bouncer." He stroked his gray beard and smiled. "But I can scare people … it's easy."

Keaka stuffed our leftovers into an overflowing trash container and wiped his hands on his shorts. "All right, then, let's have a visit with Chuck."

Chapter Nineteen

"Ano, you drive like crap," Keaka said when we popped over a speed bump near a mall. He grabbed a strap hanging down from the Jeep's top. "I can't even type a message on my phone."

"Then put the damn thing down." Ano let go of the wheel and pointed out his window with his left hand. "See? Up there to my left."

"The golf course?"

"No. There's a new brewery opening on the other side of the clubhouse. It's only seven miles from my house. Life is good, man."

"We'll try it." Keaka stuffed his phone into his shirt pocket. "I owe you several brews."

"Yes, you do."

Keaka half turned toward me. "Braddah Henry? You still back there?"

"Barely," I said while rubbing my head. "The bump bruised an old wound."

Ano laughed. "Wounded pride?"

"My own battle wound," I answered. "A dark cave, untrustworthy woman, evil men."

"Sounds like a country song."

Keaka scratched his forehead and glanced at Ano. "Guys, I've got three marshals showing up at the helipad in thirty minutes. We'll take his place apart if we have to."

Ano slowed abruptly behind a police car. "Hell. It's Tristan, the newbie cop who moved here from California. If he stops you, he'll kill you with lectures. I'd rather get the ticket, and he could shut the hell up."

The police car turned, and we sped up again. I had to talk louder. "Danny, has your camp been in contact? Did Doris and Nika have great evenings?"

"Weird, but it didn't sound like it. I guess those two don't know each other, and Myung told me they were like two cats in a sack—they fought and hissed all night. Myung made them sleep next to each other on a pallet on the floor, and it sounds like Nika Campbell's not fond of roaches."

Ano howled. "Yeah, they got big ones over there." He headed left onto a curving drive ending in a cul-de-sac, then pressed the brakes hard as we approached a square, corrugated metal building with a red roof. A white helicopter, empty and unattended on the helipad, squatted next to Ano's green machine. Large orange balls ran along the electric wires overhead, highlighting the danger for pilots landing on the square. "How you wanna do this, Danny?"

"Do what?"

"I think I should let you off here so my best buddy Chuck doesn't notice my jeep, much less me. You and Henry go in first, and I'll bring up the rear."

Keaka nodded. "Good idea. I hope he's awake."

"Yeah, he needs his beauty sleep. Flash your shiny U.S. Marshals badge, and he'll open his eyes."

Keaka dug through the Jeep's glove box and found Ano's cigarettes. "I need something to calm my nerves."

Ano grimaced. "No, no, not that pack … those

287

aren't tobacco. Wait … hell … don't put it back in there, man. I don't want your spit on my stuff." He reached over and slapped the glove box shut.

Keaka grinned, stretched behind him, and patted the seat. "Come on, braddah. We'll light this later." He slid the joint into his pocket.

"I don't smoke—"

Keaka slammed his door.

I slipped out of the back and glanced at Ano, who gave me a wink.

"Danny's the best, Henry. See you in a minute."

"Okay."

Keaka had hurried ahead of me by twenty steps. I jogged to catch up, and the other side of the helipad came into view. "The black one's gone, Danny."

"I noticed, and it looks dark inside Chuck's little mansion."

The path dropped to a narrow stream, and we had to jump across muddy water flowing down to the resorts on our right. We climbed again, rounded the corner, but hesitated outside the front door.

Keaka peered inside. "Hmm. Someone's on the cot. I hope he's only asleep."

My heart skipped. "Tasev taking care of witnesses?"

"Only one way to find out." Ano came around the opposite corner as Keaka tried to turn the doorknob. "He keeps it locked? This is a state-owned helipad, and it should be open during the day. Ano, do you—"

"Don't get your knickers twisted, Danny. It's Sunday, dude." He dug in his hair near the nape of his neck, pulled something, then handed it to Keaka. "You remember my bobby pin trick?"

Keaka glanced at me. "Uh, sure, I remember, but why don't you go ahead. It'll be faster."

Ano grunted. "Yeah … whatever." He jimmied with the lock while peering through the rectangular pane to the right of the door. "Man, Chuck hasn't budged. You need to call for backup or something?" The lock released, and Ano turned the knob.

Keaka pulled his pistol and nudged me with his elbow. "You're my backup, Ano. Let me go first." He glanced through the window again, then let the door float open a third of the way. "Hello? Chuck?" He shoved the door and walked inside. "Hey, Chuck. I'm Danny Keaka." He scanned the mess, stepped back, and grabbed my sleeve. "No one else is here." He holstered his pistol. "Come on." He strode to the desk and glanced at papers strewn over it. "Find a light switch, you guys."

Ano flipped a switch, and four long fluorescent bulbs flickered on, giving a brighter view of the disorder. Someone had attached a Hawaiian flag to the wall behind the desk, and two dented file cabinets rested to our right near a yellow vinyl chair. A hula-girl calendar draped open to December 1993 hung crooked next to the yellow chair—I guessed it to be Chuck's favorite month. A coat of dust covered everything.

Keaka raised his eyebrows, pointed at me, then toward the figure on the cot. "Check him."

Waving my hand to stir the dust away, I pointed at my chest. "Me?"

"Yep. You're here to help, remember?"

"Right." I approached the unmoving body.

Keaka pulled his gun again and nodded. "Give him a shake. I'm covering you."

I bent over and noticed the face half-covered with a light blanket. "Mister? Chuck?" No movement. I touched his shoulder and leaned closer. Glancing back toward Keaka, I said, "I think he's breath—"

"What do you want?" The sleeping figure grabbed my collar with a pudgy fist. "Who are you?" He struggled to a sitting position and seized one of my wrists when I tried to back away.

Ano hustled to my side, Keaka behind with his gun pointed. "Let him go."

Chuck grimaced and released his grip. "Hey, hey, hey. Put the gun away. What the hell is going on? Who are you?" He pushed against the cot three times, struggling to his feet, then pointed at Ano. "You're back? And you brought friends."

Keaka nodded toward the desk. "Over there."

Chuck stared down the barrel of the gun. "I'm Gambino. Charles Gambino. And who are you?" He maneuvered past Ano, dumped himself into the old-style wooden office chair, and pulled himself forward. The plastic casters squealed across the stained cement floor.

"Danny Keaka. I'm affiliated with the U.S. Marshals. That's Detective Henry Pierce over there … and you know Ano."

Gambino smirked. "Ano. We've known each other for a while. Thinks he's a tough guy."

Ano leaned on the desk into Chuck's face. "I am a tough guy." Ano stood straight before claiming the yellow chair. "I'll make myself at home." He sat, crossed his legs, then grabbed the calendar, flipping through it. "I like October better than December."

Keaka rolled his eyes. "Anyway, Mr. Gambino, I

have a few questions."

"Like what?"

"Usage of the helipad. I need to know the comings and goings of the last five days."

Gambino grinned. "It's pretty informal here. Many people come and go."

"You have FAA requirements."

Gambino waved a hand in front of his face. "FAA? Do you know how many tourist chopper flights flutter around this island every day? A hundred, I bet. FAA? They couldn't care less."

Keaka showed a half-grin. "We'll see."

Gambino slumped forward, leaning his elbows on the desktop. "Look, Keaka. I don't want any trouble with the FAA, the U.S. Marshals, or any … other people." Gambino glanced to his right at one pile of papers on the desk.

"What other people?" I asked. "Ano said you told him about a black helicopter coming and going the last couple of days, carrying a few interesting characters."

Gambino nodded. "Yeah, I told him. There've been three black choppers this week. The larger one disappeared the other day … Monday or Tuesday, I think … supposedly an accident or something. Another one headed to Moloka'i early this morning with two men, and the third one's been buzzing around here off and on."

Ano dropped his cap into his lap and scratched his head. "Did any of the three birds have the identifiers painted on the tail?"

"Nope … like I told you yesterday." Gambino shoved back his chair and pulled open the right bottom desk drawer.

Keaka pointed his gun.

Gambino shook his head. "Relax, dude." He pulled out a bottle and set it on the desk. "Who needs a snort of whiskey on a Sunday morning?"

Keaka erupted. He grabbed the bottle by its neck and threw it to his left. It whizzed by my head and smashed against the wall. Glass shattered, and liquid flew over the cot and bedding. "I've already had breakfast, and you're a corrupt son-of-a-bitch, Gambino. The men operating those black copters sunk my boat, they've carried kidnappers and murderers all around the island, and one blew past Ano yesterday in the ʻĪao Valley." Keaka holstered his gun, then glanced at his watch. "There's an SUV load of marshals showing up here in fifteen minutes. I can tell them one of two things—arrest this asshole for abetting several crimes, or I can say Mr. Gambino has been cooperative. I can't guarantee the FAA won't grind your bones to dust because there must be accountability somewhere. But I am giving you a choice … for now."

"Did money exchange hands?" I asked. "If these people are who we think, your life is trashed."

Gambino drew a deep breath. He steepled his fingers, looking at Keaka, then Ano. "It's already trashed … but all right. I'll tell you whatever."

Ano smiled and nodded. "There you go, Chuckie."

"So, Mr. Gambino, Chuck … tell me as much detail as possible, yeah? Who were those men in the black helicopters?"

"Okay. There were three."

Keaka tilted his head. "Men?"

"No, black helicopters. Originally, like I told you a minute ago—nine men total. They came in last Sunday, and two of the birds rested on the pad for a day after the guys left to do whatever they were doing. Frank, my part-time mechanic, said one man talked about losing a copter over the water between here and Moloka'i. Funny … I've seen nothing on the news."

I chuckled. "We're familiar with it."

Keaka ignored me. "The men spoke English?"

"Two of them did, well, kind of. The others spoke something I never heard."

"Macedonian," I said.

Gambino squinted at me and made a face. "Macedonian? How the hell would I know that?"

I glanced at Ano. "It wasn't a question."

"Wait." He shoved a chubby palm in my face. "Frankie said something like an Albanian, Hungarian … Macedonian? Like Alexander the Great, isn't it?"

Ano leaned forward in his chair, shaking his head while staring at his feet. "Not quite the same, Chuck."

Gambino became more animated, seeming to enjoy our questions. "Okay, Macedonian." He shrugged. "Anyway, they all spoke it to each other, but only two spoke passable English … well, wait, one spoke English, but the other guy was decent. He had an accent, but he's the key guy I talked to."

Keaka rubbed the bridge of his nose with a finger. He gave me a sideways glance. "Did anyone wear a fedora?"

Gambino showed a slight smile and nodded. "One sure as hell did. His buddies chose the whole Hawaiian shirt and cargo shorts look, but the one guy always showed up in slacks, a polo-type shirt, and the stupid fedora. He had alligator shoes on and carried a raincoat when he first got here. He sweated like a pig in that outfit."

"His signature look," I said, "and his dad's."

"His dad's here, too? Sorry, I never saw an old man. He'd have to be a million years old."

Keaka shut his eyes for a moment. "No, no, Chuck, it's only a comment." He rested half his butt on the desk. "The man with the fedora you talked to is probably Karanos Tasev, a nasty man who should be in jail for murder. You are a lucky soul. If you had crossed him, well, consider yourself blessed."

Gambino rubbed his forehead. "I've figured it out … slowly. I'm glad they're gone."

"What do you mean?"

"Like I said, the two guys—"

"You said six guys?" Keaka asked.

Ano pounded a fist on the desk. "Dammit, Chuck, you first said nine men, and yesterday you said four."

"Well, when they came in last week, all three helicopters radioed to me in a hurried fuss that they had flown in from Honolulu, and their birds were running out of fuel. As they landed, I had to squeeze them in next to the white copter out there."

"Who does it belong to?" Ano asked.

"It's mine, man. A beauty, isn't she?"

Ano frowned. "And what's that smell? Mothballs? How do you stand it?"

"Keeps away the roaches," Gambino replied.

"Didn't seem to work."

Keaka sighed. "Anyway, "those men landed last Sunday. Then what?"

"Wait … I got their names." Gambino opened the drawer above his formerly hidden liquor. He pulled out a notebook, flipping through it until he stopped next to the last page. Pointing, he rotated the notebook toward Keaka. "Those are the nine names and where they signed."

"Hell, I forgot my readers," Keaka said, pushing it to me. "Here, braddah, read this."

At first, it all appeared to be scribbles. "It's hard to make out," I said. "None of the names mean anything to me—probably fake, anyway. Which name matches the guy with the fedora? And what's the last name … right there?" I pointed to it for Chuck to see. "It looks like a 'K.'"

Gambino took the notebook and spread it on the desk. "I can't remember. A huge guy scribbled the one you're looking at. Monster-sized dude. He grunted more than he talked. I'm surprised he could write. It sounded something like Koo-rick or something."

Keaka slapped his forehead. "Koorick? Kurić. What's the first name? Does it start with an 'M'?"

Nodding, Gambino pulled the notebook near his face. "Seems like it, yeah. He said Mayteg, Mataj … hell, I don't know."

Keaka pursed his lips. "Matej Kurić? Is that name familiar, Braddah Henry?"

I nodded. "Sure enough. The guy that died on the beach … your informant. He said the word 'matej,' but I never guessed it to be a person."

Keaka frowned as we heard brakes squeal. He stepped to the window. "Marshals are here." He opened the door, held up a hand, showed all fingers and thumb, and then shut the door. "Five more minutes, Chuck. So, I assume you checked their IDs?"

"No," he muttered.

"Why not?"

"They said they lost them."

"All nine men lost their IDs?" Ano asked. "Didn't it seem a little suspicious?"

"My turn," I said. "And I bet this is where the money comes in, doesn't it?"

Gambino, fidgeting with his hands, stared down at his lap. Quiet for a moment, he finally nodded. "I refused service at first without an ID, then the fedora guy pulled out a roll of hundreds, peeled off ten bills, and pitched them on my desk."

Ano leaned toward the desk from his seat. "It's called a bribe."

"I know that. I pushed the money back toward him, but he yanked a gun from a back holster I hadn't noticed. Scared me shitless. He said to take the bills and keep quiet, or I would never get to spend the money."

Ano sneered. "Hey, Danny, is it a crime to take a bribe under duress?"

Nodding, Keaka answered, "It's a tougher charge, but maybe." He opened the door, waved to the marshals, and turned toward the desk. "Chuck, I'm going to have my friends take care of you for a couple of days for your own protection, but this is a turning point in your life. You've been cooperative so far, and if you continue, we can make an arrangement. If anything you've told us comes out wrong, we'll throw the book at you. Understood?"

Gambino nodded.

"Now tell us the rest … nine men, six men, four men, two … now they've all gone … somewhere? Let's narrow this down."

"All right. But I'm holding you to it, Keaka."

Keaka stood straight and crossed his arms. "I don't

break my word. Now go on."

Chuck's hand disappeared into the drawer again, pulled out a bottle of rum, and he knocked back a slug. "So, they were down to two copters after the one crashed or whatever—six men were here after that. They came and went twice on Thursday and Friday. Yesterday one copter left early with five men—they had stuffed it with gear, too. After they left, another guy showed up I hadn't seen before—walked up, didn't see a car. I noticed him checking the second black copter, so I asked who he was—he pulled a gun and said to mind my own business. He started the engine and slid into the pilot's seat. I told him to tell me his destination, and he yelled 'Moloka'i,' then gave me the finger."

Keaka slipped outside and motioned to a marshal to roll down his window.

Ano slapped the desk with his cap. "Shit, Chuck, I certainly understand the man flipping you the finger—who wouldn't want to—but why didn't you call the police? At least once a week, I have a near collision from a dopey, inexperienced pilot flying a copter where he shouldn't be."

Gambino shook his head.

"This whole southwest side of Haleakalā is under your watch."

"I'm scared, man. Those guys seemed vicious." Gambino wiped his face.

I glanced through the door as Keaka shoved it open. "Watch out, braddah. All right, Charles Gambino, I have alerted the authorities on Moloka'i to look for a black helicopter with no markings. In a minute, you'll head out with two of the marshals out there. Another will take your place here if any of your new friends come back. Now … a copter left yesterday morning with five men and lots of gear. Earlier, you said only three men came back. The big man was one of them? Did you recognize the other? And what about the fedora guy?"

"Yeah, yeah, I saw them all several times. After they landed yesterday, I went out and talked to them for a second. Two guys seemed a little roughed up, but his big friend looked like he had been in a bar fight. Fedora guy never showed. I peeked through a passenger window, and I didn't notice any gear. The big guy shoved me aside, but not before I noticed two long pieces of cloth. They had to be rifle covers, so I backed off."

I glanced at Keaka, then Gambino. "We found two dead men yesterday in the ʹEke Crater area. One had a Macedonian passport. We were told the other was a Kosovar."

A light knock, and a male in a full U.S. Marshal uniform peered around the door. "Are you ready, sir?"

Keaka nodded toward the door. "Yes. Marshal Herrera, this is Charles Gambino. He is to be the marshals' guest for a few days. He'll be staying at the Coconut Castle near Honolulu."

Gambino pushed to a stand, then frowned. "Castle?"

"You'll like it," I said. "Food, alcohol, TV … and it's safe."

He rubbed his chin and gave half a smile. "It sounds all right. What then?"

"It's up to you," Keaka said. "We'll find out how good your information is."

Still half smiling, Gambino shuffled to the door.

Keaka grabbed his arm. "Oh, one more thing."

Gambino shook hands with Marshal Herrera. "What?"

"The guy going to Moloka'i … did you see him again? And you haven't told us where the big man and his pilot headed. Were they coming back?"

He shoved his hands into his pockets, squinting with one eye. "The Moloka'i pilot landed back here again for twenty minutes or so. I was here in my office when I heard it take off. He didn't ask for clearance or anything. I rushed outside, and it looked like two men were in that bird. And the huge guy and his pilot? Unclear. They mentioned Haleakalā, then something, something sugar."

"Sugar?" Ano asked.

"Yep. And they mentioned Kaho´olawe, too. I figured they were feeding me crap. How could they get to Kaho´olawe?"

Keaka shut his eyes. "Dammit … sugar." He backed away and nodded. "Marshal Herrera, Chuck is in your hands. Please have Marshal Lin hang here in this building and tell her to buzz me if a black copter comes back, and she should call the police, too."

"Yes, sir."

"Chuck … you'll hear from me."

Herrera opened the left rear passenger door for Gambino, then helped him into the seat.

We left Lin, then followed Ano to his helicopter. "Danny … dammit … I know what you're going to say. Kaho´olawe again? It'll be a tough nut to crack for those guys if that's where they're headed. The authorities won't know who they are."

Keaka smiled. "You picked up on it, huh?"

"Natural assumption. You would figure they would try to get those two women off Kaho´olawe and escape somewhere."

"Yep, but Tasev hasn't shown himself. My hunch is he's the one going to Moloka'i, so we've lost him again." Keaka pulled his phone and started swiping through his contacts. "But I'll call McNelly and Myung and tell them to be on the lookout."

I leaned back against Ano's helicopter. "You think they can find your camp, Danny?"

"Doubtful." Keaka finished typing, dropped the phone into his shirt pocket, then yanked his gun from its holster. He pulled a full clip from his front pockets and slid it into the weapon. "All right, men, this is for keeps, yeah?"

"Kaho´olawe it is, buddy. Let me get my stuff out of the back seat." Ano turned, but Keaka grabbed his arm.

"No, we're staying on Maui … Haleakalā."

"Haleakalā? The upcountry? The crater? Where?"

"At the base."

"It's a helluva big mountain. Could you narrow it down a little?"

"Sugar, Ano." Keaka grinned, showing the gap in his teeth. "Sugar."

Ano rolled his eyes. "Oh, shit." He flung open the pilot's door, then gave Keaka a side glance. "Are you doing this to me on purpose? You know it's haunted."

"Sugar," I said. "The guy that died on the beach said the word 'sugar,' too. I mentioned this the other day."

Keaka smiled, passed in front of the helicopter to the passenger side, and reached for the door handle. "I remember that. The poor soul gave his life and tried to tell us, and it's been slapping me in the face. Think about it. A closed sugar mill. It's an isolated spot— people spooked away by the old stories over the years. An excellent place to hide." He pointed toward me. "Jump in, braddah. We'll tell you a quick ghost story."

Chapter Twenty

Ano pulled high over Wailea, then pointed us to the north. The arid part of Maui ended abruptly next to the green summit of Haleakalā. I had ridden on brief police helicopter rides, but nothing like this. Ano's copter appeared to be from the Vietnam era and had a hard life, like its owner. Something had ripped the rear vinyl seats in the middle, yellow stuffing pushing through the cracks. The worn door seals made this ride much louder than the others I had taken, and air whipped through the cabin. At least the swirling air dissipated the choking fuel smells.

Keaka turned toward me, winked, and yelled. "Hang on. It's only ten minutes." I gave him a thumbs up.

Ano muttered something into his headset. He pointed to the floor by Keaka's feet and thumbed back to me.

Keaka leaned over, then held up two pairs of headsets. I took a pair, cupped them over my ears, and he did likewise.

"Can you hear me, Pierce?" Ano asked.

"And me?" Keaka asked.

"Yes, pretty good. It helps cut out the noise," I answered.

Ano nodded. "I've spent a lot of money and time on this engine and the other important parts that make this baby fly. It's not the Taj Mahal on the inside, but I tell you what, I would have no problem flying it to Kaua'i and back."

"It's your baby, and you know best," I said. "Kind of like the *Miss Mio* and Danny."

Keaka shook his head. "Don't make me depressed, braddah. It's something I got to get started tomorrow with the insurance company."

Ano slapped Keaka's left knee. "You think your insurance company will pay up for your boat sunk by an attack from a mysterious black helicopter?"

Keaka covered his face with both hands. "Oh, man. I hadn't thought of it. They'll call it a terrorist attack, and I won't get a dime."

I changed the subject. "So, tell me the ghost story, and where are we going?"

He rubbed the back of his neck, then used an index finger to poke Ano in his ribs. "The place is an abandoned mill in the middle of a closed sugar plantation. A few people … hint, hint … say it's haunted."

I didn't need a headset to hear Ano laugh. "Some people? A hundred old sugar workers say it is, and I say it, too. I've experienced it, I can tell you."

"Experienced what?" I asked.

Ano veered left, heading straight west. "The haunted part had always been a big joke, I thought. Most of the sugar industry died in the eighties. The environmentalists hated the smoke generated from burning sugar cane stalks and field stubble. The smoke got terrible through the area, and the Maui winds carried it toward the airport. It became a public safety issue. Anyway, the sugar industry folded, and the workers became unemployed or went to work in the pineapple fields. The companies left the old equipment, and it still sits today, rusting and falling to pieces. The biggest plant is off the highway between Kihei and Kahului."

"Is it to the east of the main road?" I asked. "I think I noticed it the other day."

"Yep, it's a mile or so off the road, but it's so big it seems closer. These days, it looks like a metal recycling center instead of a sugar mill. An industrial accident happened a week before the shutdown—some equipment collapsed, and a fire started. Others say a radical eco bunch caused it. The worst part? Fifteen workers died."

"Wow. Is that the haunted part?" I asked.

Keaka smiled. "Tell him, Ano."

Ano grew quiet for a moment and tilted the copter's nose down for a slow descent. "New Year's Eve in 1999. Two buddies and I hung out there in case the Y2K thing crashed down around us like the so-called experts predicted. I figured other people would be there, but we saw no other activity when we parked. A bunch of scavenged trucks hunkered in the main yard, but everything was so dark … I mean, pitch black. My two friends and I had been more worried about gathering our weed for the night, and we didn't bring much in supplies. We each had a sleeping bag, a sack full of junk food, and only one flashlight between us."

Keaka chuckled. "Good thinking."

"Stifle, Keaka. I suppose you ignored the whole Y2K thing."

Looking back, Keaka grinned. "Not exactly, but instead of playing poker with my family, I offered them an evening cruise on my brand-new boat, the *Miss Mio*. We docked at one a.m., and civilization seemed intact. So, I got up early the next morning to watch bowl games. Michigan, and a guy named Tom Brady, beat Alabama in the Orange Bowl."

Ano laughed. "Been awhile, huh? Anyway, my buddies and I made a nice camp near the central office. Its windows were busted, but the door was locked. We didn't try to get in since it'd be trespassing, even with the place shut down. But I still remember at eleven forty-eight. Something happened."

I leaned forward, pushing my hands hard against the headphones. "What something?"

"We heard this gigantic crash, metal on metal, squealing … like the whole damn plant came back online."

"And how much had you smoked?" Keaka asked.

"Plenty, but it didn't make the three of us hallucinate the same thing."

"What then?" I asked.

"Voices, and I mean a bunch … like a hundred men were talking. We smelled smoke, sirens started up, cursing. Spooky, man … spooky."

Keaka grabbed his shoulder. "The weed, dude. You got in each other's heads."

We veered to the right as Ano tightened us into a circle directly above acres of rusted machinery.

"We went home, and I slept on my couch that night … with all the lights on. But, anyway, at midnight at the mill, everything went quiet again. We turned our radio on, and Y2K turned out to be a big nothing, and we drove back to Kihei." He exaggerated a smile, then pointed downward. "So, where do you want to land?"

Keaka motioned to his right. "Ninety degrees to the right over past the conveyor belts."

"Got it."

"It looks used—I count five circles in the dirt," Keaka said.

"Probably alien circles," Ano said while pulling off his headset. "Hey, look. Tire tracks, too. I don't see any black helicopters, though."

"Me either. Take us down," Keaka said.

"Are you sure?" I asked.

"It's daytime, braddah. Don't be scared."

"I'm not worried about ghosts or aliens," I said. "Tasev and his guys are scarier. Aren't we setting down right in the middle of them?"

"They've probably heard us already," Ano said while fiddling with the controls. "There's no sneaking up now."

"Great."

"Hang loose, braddah," Keaka said. "We'll be a good three hundred yards from the old office. I'm guessing it's their spot, as it's the only place for protection from the elements." Keaka coughed. "Damn this dust."

"Dry season," Ano replied. He sat us down, cut the engines, and pushed his door open. Turning to look at me, he pointed. "Jump out, Henry, and pull the cord at your feet."

I did so. The dust settled around us while I flopped the back cushion forward, revealing three rifles, a backpack, and a vest.

"Remington, Model 5s. Bolt action .22. I don't like big caliber guns at my house for just the occasional mongoose or rat." He pulled on the vest and fastened the bottom snap. "Hand me the pack of ammo." He yanked the top zipper, shoved a hand into the bag, and pulled out a fistful of bullets, dropping them into the main vest pocket.

Keaka grinned, jerked his Magnum, and shoved it toward me. "Take this. I'll take a Remington."

I grabbed the pistol's handle and pointed the barrel down.

"You like irony, braddah?"

"Not especially."

"These rifles? Guess where they're made?" Keaka asked.

"Remingtons? I would have guessed the U.S., but I'm probably wrong these days."

"Partly right … the stock, anyway. They make the barrel and action in southern Serbia, not all that far from Skopje."

"No way," I said. "Is that a sign?"

"We'll see."

Ano fiddled with each door. I presumed to lock them, then he tucked the rifle under his arm. "Yeah, Danny and I have the small-caliber—we'll piss them off first, then you'll have the big .357 to do the rest." He snorted.

The wind stopped as a cloud drifted over us, all shadows disappearing. The cloud floated on, the sun emerged, and a gust of wind hurled sand in our faces.

I shrugged. "Now what? We go stomping across a quarter-mile of open space?"

Ano pointed to our right. "The office is on the other side of this mess."

Keaka laid a hand on my shoulder. "You got to trust us, braddah. We know—"

A gunshot echoed in front of us. The window burst on the copter's front passenger side, shards of glass exploding over the inside.

"Dammit." Ano grabbed my arm and pushed. "I bet this seventy-two-year-old man can outrun you. Come on, Danny. Get under the belt."

They ran, me following, ducking and weaving to the old conveyor belt area behind a collapsed, rusted section of metal. Another shot echoed, and the right rear window of Ano's green helicopter ruptured inward.

Ano dropped to the hard ground, leaned against a sheet of oxidizing tin, and cursed. "Dammit, it's going to be breezy going back."

A bullet struck again, this one ricocheting off a steel beam hanging over our heads. Keaka yelped, his left ear dripping blood at the lobe.

I bent toward him. "A nick above the lobe. There's a piece missing the size of a pencil lead."

Keaka pulled his shoulder up and bent his head over to put pressure against the wound. "Well, this is a hard way to shoot with my head tilted."

Ano leaned forward onto all fours, scooted, then sat in the dust. He grabbed his rifle, placed the barrel on a metal rod jutting from the rubbish, and fired twice.

"What are you shooting at?" I asked.

"Anything. I wanted him to know we're armed, too."

"Only one shooter?"

"Pretty sure."

"Keep doing that, but try to aim better," Keaka said.

"Okay. I've only got thirty shots or so left. Then what?"

I tried to see past Ano. "You keep the guy busy. Looks like thirty yards to the next pile of metal on our right and junk piles here and there toward the office. I'll go there first, circle back around, find the office, then try to come upon the shooter from behind."

Another shot pinged off the helicopter's tail.

Keaka checked his ear. "I think it's stopped bleeding. Come on, we need to stay put. My friends will be here from Kahului in fifteen minutes."

I grinned. "When seconds count, the cops are minutes away."

He scowled. "Be nice and sit down. We got your folks safe—"

"Time's up, Danny. Maybe I'm turning into Hrubý, but I want to finish this. They wanted to kill my mom and grandmother."

"Tasev is dangerous."

"I can be, too. Ask Tasev's dad."

"Revenge is a fool's mission." Keaka crouched while Ano shot wildly behind us.

I winked. "Ano will shoot himself if you don't keep an eye on him. Stay here."

I stood halfway when Keaka grabbed my shoulder. "All right, this is your deal, then. I'll help Ano give you cover, but you run like the damn wind. Message me when you can, and we'll try to let you know when the cavalry arrives." He kissed two fingers, pointed to the sky, then shuffled toward Ano, resting his rifle barrel on a stack of rotting wood pallets.

I patted Ano's shoulder. "Ready?"

He nodded. "Go."

Gunshot noises assaulted my ears, and I lunged to the right, running while partly bent over, holding

Keaka's gun in front of me.

I darted to the next pile of metal, but it offered no place to hide for long. An old corroding dump truck stared at me through broken headlights, its tires long ago rotted. Another cloud drifted overhead, giving a moment of relief from the sun, with an odd quietness settling around us again. The guns had stopped, and the wind died. Metal scraped against metal … then it was over. The sun peered through, the wind moaned, blowing dust in my face, and the gunshots returned. I stood straight and dashed across a hundred yards of open space.

Scurrying past two more dilapidated trucks, I noticed a square cinderblock structure. The windows were shattered, and the door hung from a top hinge, pitching with each gust. I ducked next to the nearest wall and stood next to a window opening. An engine was running, likely a generator, the noise breaking through the howling wind. My phone vibrated. I pulled it, glanced down, and noticed Keaka's message. They had seen a figure move away from the scrap heaps, then the shooting had stopped. I should expect a visitor.

I noticed one bulb shining from the ceiling, dust motes swirling near it. The light was bright enough to reveal a desk holding three manilla folders scattered in front of a sleeping old-style computer monitor. I saw no other movement, so I pointed the gun, stepped through the doorway, and scanned the room.

A broken chair hunkered in pieces at the entrance, and a rolled-up, grimy sleeping bag had been shoved against a two-drawer file cabinet. A thick blanket of dust coated the desk except for where files had been scooted along its top.

Someone had dumped three leather pouches on top of the computer monitor—each held a passport. I didn't recognize one picture, but the second showed a face, maybe familiar, with a description in Cyrillic. Could this be one of the dead men? The word Kumanovo showed at the bottom, like the one on the identification card we had found on the shattered body at ´Eke Crater. I opened the third passport and glimpsed the face, right away comprehending the reason for the comments about it. The face showed a character a kid might conjure in a nightmare … those shimmering, piercing black eyes.

Two manilla folders contained nothing. The third one held one sheet of paper with the number seven scribbled at the top. Someone had printed several names, each numbered in two groups separated by a line sketched across the page. Number one showed Miomir Kurić, number two, Matej Kurić—that name again. Number three listed something in Cyrillic with the name Shai—General Shai, I presumed. The name of Karanosz Tasev had a line struck through it. I guessed this to be the old dead Macedonian, but I didn't remember a spelling with the letter 'Z' at the end. A second Karanos Tasev was next—I assumed Tasev, Junior. The other two names I couldn't identify.

The second grouping below the line totaled seven more names, each with a cube drawn next to it. I didn't recognize any except for numbers six and seven— Stepan Hrubý and Henry Pierce. Tasev's to-do list? I folded the paper and shoved it into a back pocket.

Footsteps. I had heard nothing else over the chugging generator and whistling wind. I sat in the darkest corner and waited. Keaka's .357 grew heavy, making my hands shake. This time, there would be no discussions. I would shoot, he would be dead or injured, and the world would lose another killer. But what if Keaka or Ano showed? I couldn't be too trigger-happy. Another gale brought a blast of dust into the office, the grains assaulting my face. I covered my mouth, determined not to cough, then blinked several times to clear my vision.

My eyes refocused just as a shadowy hulk stepped through the door jamb, grunting when he stopped and showing me a curled-lip smile. His passport picture hadn't done him justice. He seemed a foot taller than me, his head almost touching the ceiling. A black mustache and goatee highlighted a long face, pockmarks covering his high cheekbones. A purple wound glowed from the bridge of his nose, highlighting glaring black pupils surrounded by the bright whites of his eyes.

He opened his mouth, then hesitated. His right arm hung to his side, his hand behind him. Licking his lips, he squinted and, in an odd accent, said, "You … you killer. My uncle dead."

The weight of Danny's gun pulled my arm—it seemed gravity had doubled its pull. Could I lift it fast enough before the man could shoot?

"How do you know me?" I asked.

"Coosin Karo…niss. He tells me."

"Karanos Tasev is your cousin?"

He clenched, then unclenched his teeth and shouted. "No. You listen! Tasev is uncle. Coosin Karo…niss is other Tasev."

I leaned against the desk with my left hand, hoping it would steady me. "And what is your name?"

He sneered. "I do not tell any. But you will die ... so." He smiled. "My name Matej ... Koo ... ric." A scowl flashed across his face. He licked his lips again. "Matej Koo ... ric."

"Do you know Miomir Kurić?"

He stood straighter and gave a big smile through yellow teeth. "My siss ... ter."

"Sister? So ... where is she?"

"She take care of Matej. She always near."

I tried to make this simple. "Your uncle attacked a friend of mine. I made him stop. Your cousin kidnapped my family, and we will stop him, too."

His complexion flushed dark red, almost purple. He pointed, dropping a pistol behind his feet. "No ... you die."

"I don't want to harm you—"

He lunged like a big cat, shoved me against the file cabinet and hugged me under my arms. Air spewed through my mouth and nose. A crushing vice grip ... the pressure ... a stabbing pain on my right side. A rib, maybe two, had cracked.

I leaned my head back, then smashed it forward against his face. He roared and released me, blood streaming from his nose as he stumbled toward the doorway. Crumpling to the floor on my knees, I still held Keaka's gun. I aimed but screamed, a shock of pain taking my breath. I pulled the trigger blindly, hitting him near his Adam's apple. He fell to his hands and knees near the desk and collapsed, rolling onto his side.

He shuddered, twisted his head back toward me, and gave a long moan like a wounded animal, blood gushing from his mouth and pooling near his head. I raised the gun. My third kill. The moaning stopped. His lips moved, then turned white. He raised his left arm, pointing the weapon he must have grabbed from the floor.

I stumbled back as his pistol erupted in a wild shot, the computer monitor shattering as I collapsed to the floor. My face throbbed as if someone had thrown a handful of pebbles at me, and my left eye hurt like a wasp sting, making me twist my head sideways to see. No movement from the hulk of a man, his chin resting on the floor, and dead black eyes staring through me.

Pulling to a stand while leaning against a wall, I noticed droplets of blood had fallen on the dusty desk's top. I shoved Keaka's gun into my waistband, then pulled my t-shirt over my head, causing a stabbing pain again under my right arm. My sleeve smeared blood over my face after it rubbed against my cheeks. Time to find my friends.

My breaths came in gasps. I stashed the passports into an empty folder and stepped over the giant man's body, his blood pool inching toward the sagging door. Now unconcerned with other shooters lurking in the shadows, the pain drove me forward. I had to take a chance and choose a straight path toward Ano's chopper. Dust swirled and coated my sweaty body as I ducked under a wrecked door propped against another jumble of rusting metal. Someone had stamped large footprints in the loose dirt, likely where Matej Kurić had positioned himself when shooting. I peered over the barrier and found a direct line of sight to Ano's helicopter, the right-side windows smashed and holes showing along the tail.

"Ano … Danny," I called out. "The shooter's

down."

Ano stepped beyond the conveyor belt, his rifle still pointed my way. "Henry? Come on out so I can see you." He stood straight, keeping his aim steady. An uneasy feeling crept down my spine.

"You come out farther."

"Step out, Henry. I need to make sure you're alone, buddy."

"Where's Danny?" A hand brushed my back, then slid down my sweaty skin.

"Right here, braddah."

I turned, leading with my left elbow, causing the Magnum to slide out of my waistband and drop to the dirt.

Keaka rubbed his gut. "Careful with my baby, man." He picked up his gun and slid it into his empty holster. He patted my cheek and pushed my head to the side. "Oh damn, man. It looks like hell. Come on." He pulled his phone and touched the screen to call 9-1-1, telling them to clear a pad.

I gasped. "Where's the cavalry?"

He glanced at me and shrugged. "Ano will take us to Kahului Medical Center."

We stepped into the open, and he waved. "It's good, Ano. He's here, alive but hurt." Escorting me by my left elbow, we shuffled to the helicopter.

Ano had bent over into the front passenger seat and pulled out an emergency kit. "Here, Danny. You'll find peroxide and bandages inside. Is there a lot of pain in the eye, Henry?" He opened the rear passenger door and groaned, seeing the shattered glass scattered across the seats.

I let go of the bloody green t-shirt.

Keaka held my hand down as he gazed at my eyeball. "It's really red, man. A little blood pool is in the white area on the left side. Nothing I can do without making it worse." He opened the kit, pulled out an oversized bandage, then handed it to me. "Try to keep it closed and this over it, but don't push too hard. Did he hit you?"

I gasped. "Guys … guys, listen. The eye hurts like hell … but he's cracked at least two of my ribs. He shot at me and hit a computer monitor. It burst everywhere, and a piece flew into my eye. And you got to know something else."

Keaka opened the peroxide, poured the liquid over a cotton ball, and dabbed my face. "Be still, braddah."

"I killed him, Danny … one shot in the throat."

"Yeah, I must have come in right after you took off. Weird looking dude."

"Matej Kurić. He told me."

"Kurić?"

"Yes. He told me Miomir is … was his sister. And get this—"

Keaka dabbed my face. "Slow down, buddy. Tell us later."

"No, listen. Tasev is his cousin, and the old Tasev is his uncle."

"You're making no sense, Henry," Ano said. "All the bad dudes are related?"

"And I've got a list in my pocket with people's names, including mine."

"Settle down and keep it for now."

I sighed. "On our first fishing trip, you asked me how many people I've killed … it's three."

"Listen to me. I don't want you to think about it.

All three men would have killed you."

"Yeah … I know."

"You'll drive yourself crazy, buddy. Let it go." Keaka pitched a third bloody cotton ball into the helicopter. "Much better. You may get by with no stitches on your pretty face."

The helicopter's blades turned, stirring another cloud of dust. "Come on, guys," Ano said. "I've brushed the glass onto the floor. Be careful, though. Sit up front with me, Henry."

I slid into the seat, then turned toward Keaka before he shut the door. "I don't want it to get easier, Danny. Killing shouldn't."

Keaka shrugged. "It's what I tried to tell you and Eddie the other day. Things happen. You can push them back into the shadows, but the memories will always be there."

We rose from the ground, and Ano pointed us north, passing over the stub of a dead palm tree's trunk. He touched my leg. "You're a fine cop, Henry. You got a good heart and a good soul. Keep your humanity."

****

Ano waved from above, headed east and back to Maui. The red dust of Kaho´olawe assaulted us—Eddie and Marconi covered their eyes and noses with the inside of their elbows.

My trip to the emergency unit had been brief, and the doctor said I had been lucky. She had rolled tape around my mid-section, confirmed at least one broken rib, and told me the glass shard's entry angle had burrowed deep into my left eye's tissue. Unfortunately, the doctor couldn't be sure if she had removed all the glass until a surgeon could look at it. The eye patch would stay for now.

We had lost Tasev again, using his cousin as a decoy at the old sugar mill. Hrubý showed tears when we told him late in the evening and insisted he would have finished the job. Keaka didn't respond, giving Eddie and me brief hugs before leaving us in our room. For now, I couldn't bring myself to tell Hrubý about the Tasevs' family tree.

Keaka had told us to meet him before dawn, and Ano would fly us to his camp so Eddie could see Doris before she found herself in the Honolulu jail. Afterward, a new air-conditioned U.S. Marshals helicopter would take us back to Lahaina.

Doris Chen exited the cement-block building, first in line. She stared at the ground, marching toward another waiting helicopter, this one with a logo I did not recognize. Doris never made eye contact with Eddie, and he stood with crossed arms as she marched past him.

Nika came next, still showing a nose bandage, and she stepped past me, offering a weak smile. She halted, triggering the snaking chains holding her to yank and pull tight against the guard's grasp. She turned back toward me. "Ike … I'm sorry about your eye. You're a good guy. This is my fate, though. My destiny, I guess." The tears running down her cheeks appeared spontaneous this time. "Help me … please."

The agent pulled Nika away, guiding her in front of him, a slight limp seeming to slow her. She tried to turn back again, but the man pushed her toward the tan helicopter, the swirling wind twisting her hair like long tentacles. Another man grabbed her by the arms, pulled her aboard, then shoved her down on the bench seat beside Doris Chen, jostling Chen's bandaged shoulder. A female agent slid the door shut, and the helicopter's blades burst into faster rotations.

We all shielded our eyes again from the whirling red dust. The helicopter veered left, picked up speed, then headed toward the Ka'iwi Channel and O'ahu.

Shading her eyes, Marconi snapped her nicotine gum and leaned into me. "Careful, Henry. She said, 'help me' while staring at you through those teary, big brown eyes. It's all an act with her … everything. Trust your instincts."

I nodded. "My instincts? Who do you think broke her nose? And, yes, I get it—it's all an act."

****

Talích's body had started its long journey home on Sunday evening. His remaining family of two cousins and an elderly aunt lived in Vienna. Kharkov told us they seemed uninterested in pursuing a burial next to his parents killed in Kosovo near the Serbian border, an area the Serbs still claimed. Instead, the aunt offered a gravesite in Vienna near Talích's uncle.

Keaka commandeered two black vans to take us to the airport before lunch on Monday. We gathered in Lahaina next to the banyan park. My mother and grandmother wanted to ride with Hrubý's men—I rode with the others, slumped into the rear seat. The pain pill dulled the aches in my eye and my ribs but had left me woozy.

It would be a quick ride from Lahaina to the airport, and everyone grew silent. I finished a coffee Keaka had given us, then asked, "So now what?"

"Home," Marconi said from the front passenger seat. "I don't want to hear any more of the Tasevs,

Kurićs, or their rotten family connections. I'm tired. We've been two-thirds of the way around the earth tracking Kurić's crimes, and I only want to be a plain detective. It's what I like."

Eddie patted her shoulder from behind. "A damn good one you are, Angie." He clenched his jaws, then groaned. "And Doris … does anyone know of a capable attorney for an annulment?"

"Look, we can only do what we can," Keaka said. He stopped hard at the last red light before the road headed north to Kahului and the airport. "I've got two years left on my legal agreement with the U.S. Marshals, but I'm going fishing as much as possible. I'm pulling for you, Eddie. At the least, we've taken away another two thousand dukats from Kurić and the expected buyers, yeah? Even better, we stopped them from trafficking a bunch of young women."

Hrubý scratched his chin stubble and glanced to our right up the slope of Haleakalā. "I will revisit America," he mumbled, then blew out his cheeks. "But in the end, we cannot forget the people caught in the web of that evil empire."

"And?" I asked.

"Prague is in a vital location, sitting in the middle of Europe, and there will always be other opportunities to thwart Kurić's plans … and Tasev's. Greed never ends—we cannot give up."

"I don't think getting Tasev concerns greed," I said.

Hrubý's neck and bald spot flashed bright red.

"Ouch." Keaka chuckled.

Marconi whipped her head toward me, a scorching glare coming my way.

"Tasev is a murderer," I said, "and he must be stopped. But, then what?"

Hrubý played with his bag's zippers, never looking at me. "What do you mean?"

I leaned forward, my head hanging between Eddie and Hrubý. "There'll be others … won't there? Tasev told us himself. Will the organization cease its activities because of his death?"

Hrubý shook his head. "Correct, Henry Pierce, but do not forget about yourself. You have now killed both a Tasev and a Kurić. They will hunt you like game."

"Your name is on the list, too," I said.

"No surprise."

"So, capture Tasev, kill him, whatever. Miomir Kurić remains the key."

Hrubý straightened in his seat and stared ahead. Marconi turned away.

Eddie patted something in his pocket, then winked at me. "This airport locker key may be 'the key.' We'll find out where it leads us. We won't be bored, Ike, so hang on tight."

I offered nothing while gazing out the window with my unbandaged eye. I'd hung on tight for the last eight months, almost getting my family and me killed. Now, I risked losing half my sight, and the whole Kurić empire would be targeting me. There must be other ways to make a living.

A word about the author...

Mark retired in 2017 after thirty-three years working in higher education finance and started writing again.

The Wild Rose Press released *Peculiar Activities* on October 6, 2021, the first book in the Detective Henry Ike Pierce series. This manuscript won first place in the mystery category of the 2019 Oklahoma Writers Federation annual contest.

The second in the series, *Shadowed Souls*, is a 2022 release.

The U.K. publication, *Painted Words*, published his flash fiction piece, "Alone in Warsaw," in its Autumn 2019 edition.

Mark grew up in Duncan, Oklahoma, then attended the University of Oklahoma, earning bachelor's and master's degrees in political science and public administration. He and his wife have three grown children. They celebrated their fortieth anniversary in November 2021.

Mystery/suspense/international intrigue novels are his favorite reads, and he's found an unusual niche with medieval murder mysteries. His favorite music includes Elvis, Chicago, Earth, Wind & Fire, and Boz Scaggs (among many others).

mejbooksllc.com

CPSIA information can be obtained
at www.ICGtesting.com
Printed in the USA
BVHW030614221022
650053BV00014B/567

9 781509 244065